A Low Country

Morgan Shank

SHANKBOOKS

Copyright © 2023 Morgan Shank

All rights reserved.

ISBN: 979-8-9877846-1-7

For the Writer's Guild, and more specifically, such esteemed members as Mr. Wendell Shank, Mr. David Martin, and Mr. Josh Holsapple.

Without you, none of this would've been possible.

ACKNOWLEDGMENTS

This book grew from a lifelong obsession with the American West. I took multiple road trips through Nevada, Utah, Arizona, New Mexico…and I ultimately convinced my family to join me. The inspiration for A Low Country's scenes, characters, and story ultimately came from these trips and from the extended getaway with my family.

During this trip, they suffered my early risings for photography, endured my nonstop commentary on desert beauty, and followed every step of the itinerary I planned. Our southwestern adventure helped create this book and inspired its trilogy. Therefore, I believe my family is at least halfway responsible for the entire project.

Specifically, I thank my brother, my sister, my mother, and my father.

You helped inspire this book, and I am forever grateful. Perhaps this could be my gift back to you after your accompaniment and support in all my failed projects until this point. This is my tribute to our trip, a homage to getting caught in a sandstorm, running out of Gatorade in a desert, and enjoying a sunset above Dead Horse Point State Park.

Most importantly, it's a tribute to family, to the blessing of a stable home, and it's a promise to myself that one day, I'll try to raise a family that halfway measures up to what you've accomplished.

I love you all, and I sincerely thank you for taking the journey with me. Now, I invite you to one more.

Welcome to Low Country.

Chapter One

WHEN SHARLA HEARD THE DISTANT CHEERING, SHE THREW her bottle out the window and tromped downstairs. She burst through the door and waded into the sun, blinking at the light and deciding she wasn't drunk enough. She stiffened at the immediate press of bodies, the instant clamor of voices. She yearned to go back, but then she remembered she'd already thrown her bottle away, so going back would only leave her in bed with a desk for company.

She gritted her teeth, clenched her fists, and struggled deeper into the mob, finding herself in a current that swept toward the town square. First one step, then another.

She'd only meant to stay in Opek a few days; a few days to drink and drown memories of her blood money. She'd finally traveled to the desert and buried the rest, refusing her imagination any possibilities. Best to dump the coins in Low Country and never return.

Yes, Low Country: the stretch of land that encompassed the Owl's groin, where none but bandits, Claws, or the destitute wandered. The Owl—the watchful symbol of Benania—always roused itself when High Country suffered invasion. But now, probably because of the newer and more exciting opportunities to the north, the Owl's attention lapsed from Low Country. Therefore, Low Country had crumbled to pieces. No, worse than pieces. Nothing but blood and dust and tumbleweed.

To pretend otherwise was foolishness, so Sharla should've known better than to join the festival.

At least the townsfolk were smiling. Faces as weathered as old leather and as lined as dry parchment broke into grins of missing teeth. Pleasant greetings, exclamations and shouts; the sounds of people who'd temporarily forgotten they lived in abandoned, forsaken countryside. People determined to celebrate midsummer harvest, a ludicrous remnant of a forgotten Lodian religion.

Stop, Sharla thought. Enough cynicism. It didn't matter when or why the celebration happened. What mattered was that for once, people were happy—a precious sentiment in both Low Country and Opek. Although Opek remained in High Country, its isolation combined with its proximity to the lowlands historically earned it the same treatment as its dustier neighbors.

Cheers roused the crowd and people jumped around Sharla. She heard shouts of joy and cries of celebration, as though the town had accomplished something legendary.

A moment later, the bodies shifted enough for Sharla to see the reason: the horse dance. A display in the town square, now cleared of spectators, where the town's best horses tossed dusty manes, reared triumphantly, and kicked at the crowd as they shared the excitement. Sand and dust streaked their hides, coating them shades of brown and tan: they'd been at this awhile.

It was a display of finesse, of versatility. Riders exchanged horses, leaping onto unfamiliar mounts and guiding them through the circle, encouraging them to rear, to kick, to prance, to dazzle. These cowboys were the best on the mesa, and now they showcased their hard-earned skills.

Sharla shouldn't have joined the spectacle. She should've stayed in the crowd. But Renn was there, wrestling a black stallion and laughing as he did.

His horse was purely for show, well fed and watered by someone with rare coin. It was a gift offered for the celebration, one that only enhanced Renn's visage. Green eyes flashed under long, blond hair. They heightened a strong jawline and confident, handsome features. His coat gripped his lean build, a sturdy frame well-adjusted to the elements.

Chapter One

A cowboy who drifted with the herds, seasons, and opportunities, he circled through Low Country ever year. He'd told Sharla this all while she'd struggled to hold his gaze, to keep from admiring how the sunlight glowed through his hair, how it accentuated his tanned skin. How it burnished him as though he were copper or gold, as though he were one of the ancestors descended to change her life. He'd told her all this while they'd looked out over the mesa, the world at their fingertips, and she'd wondered about all the places he'd gone, all the towns he'd seen. She'd questioned how he could return unscathed, with unwavering enthusiasm and charisma. Nothing about him felt real…and perhaps that was why she kept coming back.

A man completed his turn and threw his reins to the crowd, clambering from the horse while he laughed and shook his head. She intercepted the reins before conscious thought, climbing into the saddle before reality struck. She joined the dance, balancing with her legs and hunching her shoulders as she allowed a ridiculous grin. It felt like a horse race, a competition. *No, it's just a dance.*

She'd slipped, revealed too much of herself for the world to see. This recluse who'd wandered into Opek, she was excellent with horses. Indeed, she was one of the best. She'd surely received training, the product of talented teachers with expertise no one in Low Country could find. She was no ordinary woman, but someone with a proud heritage; someone to watch for, to remember.

Her unease came and left, banished by Renn's expression. He smiled, winked. She followed him around the perimeter, riding beside him as their horses pranced and bucked. He hadn't known of her skill with horses—a detail ripped from her past, revealed to the world. Another piece of herself she'd sworn to forget, to bury with the money, to leave in the south.

But Renn always exposed every inch of her, and he left her yearning to shed more.

He spoke to her as they moved, his words lost to the crowd. The spectators ate everything up, lapping as hungrily as dogs. They'd discovered a drama here, a coupling unfamiliar to the horse dance where two strangers matched each other's skill and their horses relished the attention. Sand and dust kicked from hooves, billowed into a haze, and gritted across Sharla's lips, scratching her head and tangling her hair. She squinted, but it only enflamed Renn's profile. She shook her head to clear the dust, but that only tilted his face, swirled it into multiples. Perhaps she was more drunk than she'd thought?

It was only the two of them now. The other horses had drifted into the crowd, tugged away—by former owners? By townsfolk eager to stretch the moment?

Renn kicked his mount, urging it to rear again. He was enjoying this, relishing it. Every bit the performer, the vision that had changed her world. She followed with grace, with poise, as his ever-present shadow, his watchful companion, the lighter steed to complement his darker one. As though they were two edges of the same coin, balanced elements that interwove. Moving around each other, grinning at each other, calling to each other. Guiding their horses around and around, kicking more dust and more sand, moving faster and faster until the townsfolk blurred, smeared, became nonexistent. Only the circle of sand between them, shrinking as they leaned from their mounts, drew toward each other.

Sand coated Sharla's skin, filmed her lips and tongue, and fuzzed her vision. It made Renn difficult to see, almost difficult to hear. No, that was the wind; it had picked up, whipping across the circle to buffet the horses' manes and shake her in the saddle. Gusts blew her hair across her face, blocking her vision. She leaned away from Renn, struggling to sit upright, to calm her horse, to comb her hair away. Her horse didn't listen. He continued prancing, almost bucking, and now his snorts, his shrieks, carried a shrill note. A scared one.

Something had changed. She frowned and struggled to calm her horse, to listen to the howling wind and chattering spectators. The wind gusted so badly she couldn't brush her hair away fast enough. She hunched and cupped hands around her eyes, peered at the heaving bodies. They moved away, toward the streets and empty buildings, as though fleeing a nameless assailant.

Chapter One

Sand bit with the wind, stinging her skin and smiting her eyes. She tried to shield her gaze and saw the world had muddied, thickened, coagulated into dirty smears and streaks of blowing sand. A sandstorm, so soon, so unexpected? A chill crept up her spine, and she scanned the emptying streets. This couldn't be natural.

Down the street, the entire false front of the Boar's Head Inn—where she'd spent the last several days—groaned and tore loose. Planks flew, pelting townsfolk and spinning into alleyways. With an almighty roar, part of the roof wrenched away, leaping heavenward to join the increasing gale. It now howled hard enough to wrench Sharla backward. Her coat flapped like a sail; her clothes tangled like rope. She nearly toppled from the saddle and struggled to dismount, to step onto safer territory.

Screams and shouts of panic. Chaos disintegrated the festival. Townsfolk struggled for the safety of buildings, stumbled into each other, and were lost in the confusion. Those who fell molded the streaking sand, mounds of earth now surrendered to the elements. An older woman here, a crying toddler there. Stranded in the sandstorm, stricken by the gloom. Shapes that blotted, disappeared. Incredible and indescribable, the sand came from all directions, painting the world brown and rendering it formless, indistinct, the barely remembered details of a nightmare.

Sharla stumbled and temporarily forgot to cover her eyes. She lost the reins of the horse and it bolted into the blur. Somewhere nearby, she heard Renn calling, and she struggled toward him.

A new sound, shrill and intense. A scream from somewhere beside her. A different sound followed: a wet squelch as though fruit had ruptured. She recognized that sound. Stiffening, she turned.

Shapes as unclear as the rest, flailing and wrestling in the daze. One jerked and fell. The other ran forward, accompanied by new horses that darted alongside. A smaller, leaner, more compact breed. Native to the desert, possessing a skill and agility she'd only heard whispers of. The horses moved down the street, running townsfolk down. More horses, more people on foot. Glimpses of dark skin, the pale features of ram skulls atop heads. They were horned like devils, as colorless as death. Sharla saw bows and arrows, spears and crude axes that all possessed the same bleached coloration, as though made of bone.

No, they *were* made of bone. Sharla knew it in the same instant she recognized the newcomers for who they were: Claws of the Savage Land.

Terror, stark and unexpected, struck her like a fist to the gut. She doubled over and fell to her hands and knees, shuddering for breath. Low Country hadn't experienced a raid from the south in all her years. Claws were used in stories to frighten children, or to sober over-eager crowds at taverns.

The sand stung like a horde of biting insects, spreading fire across her skin. She cowered and shivered. The Claws probably already thought her dead, had probably moved past her because they didn't see her as a threat. But then the familiar anger came back, the brooding current she'd barely suppressed through drink and heavy sleep, through traveling all those miles as though she could outrun the past and bury it with the blood money. The anger that enflamed her chest like a hot coal, that stoked her energy every morning and kept her moving through the darkest nights.

She wouldn't go down like this. Not without a fight.

Horses flew past like wraiths, gone in an instant. Barely imagined, figments of dreams. They moved deeper into town, lost to the elements while more followed. A never-ending torrent of Claws, funneling into Opek like ants from an anthill.

She considered this as she crawled forward—recognized that maybe she should just play dead. Wouldn't it be smarter to wait out the storm, to save retaliation for a day when her chances were better? But no, laying low was what she'd already tried for four years; cowering under the bed while her father beat her mother and her limbs thumped the floorboards. Sharla never lifted a finger, and had it made her feel better? On the contrary, it turned her into something darker. Something she'd never found peace with.

No. Far better to let the monster out.

Chapter One

Ahead of her, a Claw crept toward a nearby house. He squatted low to the ground—she knew it to be a "he" because of the broadness in the shoulders, the musclebound arms and legs—and moved with a bone axe and a hide-shield. Shrieks inside the house gave away its occupants, and he mounted the porch and approached the door.

Sharla grabbed the shattered remains of a plank that'd probably blown from the Boar's Head. She hoisted it like a mallet, as though it were its own bone axe, and she ran to the Claw. She cracked the plank across his ram skull with a sharp report. His head wrenched sideways, and the skull fell askew. He collapsed across the porch and Sharla bent with him, fumbling for his axe even as she heard howling behind her.

Another Claw, coming fast.

His footsteps sounded across the floorboards before she'd retrieved the weapon and she threw herself forward, rolling across the porch in a filthy mess of clothes and hair. His axe smashed beside her face, spat splinters into her eyes, ground through wood as she retaliated with her own stroke. Bone axes still did the trick—Claws apparently sharpened their arsenal—because her newfound weapon tore his left shin in a messy spray.

He shrieked and staggered forward, a weight that crushed her to the porch. He grappled with her, sought her eyes with his fingers while she struggled to pull the axe from underneath him. He grabbed a fistful of her hair and smacked her head against the floorboards. Her world bounced once, twice, before her axe bit his neck. The angle was all wrong—he was above her and taller than her—so the blow tore a hole but failed to decapitate. He wheezed sickening fumes across her face, sagged against her and rolled sideways.

She followed with a better strike, decapitating him. She flinched, fell from the body, and scooted away. She sat and stared for a moment, fighting for breath and inhaling sand.

Shouting. She turned and spotted another rider. This one certainly appeared to be a man, tall and broad, with a skull unlike the rest. Sharla assumed it to be from a dhorak, one of the winged serpents of the south. The jawbone loomed from his face like a javelin, a pale scepter jagged with teeth. Dark eye sockets were surrounded by red and gold paint, and a headdress of feathers was draped across his shoulders.

She swallowed and staggered to her feet, fighting for balance. His arm whipped forward and she ducked back by reflex, flailing as a spear dashed the floorboards before her. She toppled off the porch with the shaft, rolling in the dirt as his horse moved forward.

He pulled a knife, drew his arm back for a throw—and smashed sideways as another shape plowed into him. Sharla heard Renn's wordless bellow and caught a glimpse of his hair as the riders toppled toward the house. Renn's horse drove the Claw's through the door and they disappeared inside. Hooves thundered, shouts and screams erupting, but before Sharla could raise her head, something slapped about her waist. A hoop of rope coiled tight and wrenched her backward.

They'd lassoed her as though she were a cow, a fumbling pony.

She shrieked from the pain and humiliation and scrambled for the line above her head, trying to cut it with the axe. More ropes slapped about her arms. Hands grabbed her left wrist, prying the axe from her grasp. Claws hooted as though catching her was a bit of sport. They were taking her rather than killing her like the rest of the townsfolk? Capturing her as a trophy, a piece of war loot?

The Claw behind her stopped long enough for those beside her to wrestle the weapon free, but that brought them too close. She kicked from the side of the porch with both legs, kneeing the first Claw in the side. He jerked and staggered into the one closer to her waist.

She rolled into them, pressed her attack. The axe ripped into the nearest Claw as the other grabbed for her. She twisted to meet him and found his hands stopping her arm, but his neck was suddenly close enough to…chew? Warmth across her gums, copper in her mouth. He jerked, shrieked, detached with a tearing of skin. He released the axe and she slammed it into his chest, wrenching through whatever hide armoring he wore like it was flimsy paper.

Chapter One

The rope yanked across her waist again, wrenching her backward. The axe fell behind her. She forced herself into another roll to meet the Claw. The rope's tension collapsed as she leaped upright and charged.

Her captor drew his own axe and stepped forward. Too close to dodge him, she merely angled away, jumping beside him, and the axe struck at the rope she'd tangled herself in. It bit through and missed her skin, a narrow dodge that left her whooping in celebration, adrenaline.

She lunged at him, pressing the rope into his face and tangling it with the horns of his ram skull as they fell. His axe tumbled into the road as the breath whooshed from his chest, she atop him, elbows at his throat. The skull fell from his head—the sole weapon available—and she heaved it like a club. Mashed it into his face, heaved it upright, and brought it down again. A third time, and then a fourth.

Now she'd lost count, consumed by the need to live. Meaty smacks and shuddering breaths. The ram skull slicked with his blood. She dropped it and gasped for breath.

Renn. He was still in the building with the other Claw, whom she could only assume to be their chieftain.

She rolled, made it to her hands and knees. She squinted into the sand and saw enough to curdle her stomach: the Claw exited the house with Renn's body draped over the saddle. Dead? No—why would the Claw bother to take him? Renn was a trophy of a cowardly raid on an unsuspecting, innocent town.

No.

Sharla crawled forward, shaking her head as though pleading with the chieftain, but he drew a horn to his mouth—what appeared to be a curled ram's horn—and blew three long, sonorous notes. Then he turned and fled into the haze.

"No!" Sharla screamed.

Her voice cracked and she scrambled to her feet, tripped over the rope, and went down again. She struggled to free herself but heard thundering hooves and felt their vibrations in the ground. She turned and saw the other Claws fleeing with the chieftain, many of them with other bodies draped over their saddles. Some hung limp while others struggled, screaming and writhing in rope bindings.

The horses galloped around her while the remaining Claws ran on foot. Sharla barely saw an incoming axe before she threw herself to the ground and covered her head with her arms. The Claw hooted as he passed her, the wind of his strike passing over her head, and then he'd gone with the rest.

The final Claws disappeared, and the sand lifted. The wind lessened, slowed, dispersed. The elements settled and the haze withdrew. Evening light glared across empty streets and ruined buildings, with doors wrenched askew, shutters blown inward, and roofs hanging at crooked angles. It looked as though the town were abandoned, forsaken by the ancestors.

Sharla sat in the middle of it, surrounded by corpses and staring at the horizon, the land of the Claws who'd just taken the only man she'd loved.

CHAPTER TWO

BODIES DRAPED OVER PORCHES, FILLED DOORWAYS, AND crowded the street. Some people stumbled toward their deceased loved ones, kneeling and crying. Others turned in circles as though looking for any hint of the sandstorm.

Everyone was speechless, dumbfounded by the senselessness of it all. There'd been no provocation, no warning or meaning. The Claws hadn't slain the whole town, and they'd barely taken possessions.

Nothing more than a warning; a message. A declaration to the ancestors, to Benania, the Owl, and everyone else: *We're here.*

Sharla still held one of the bone axes. She eventually found another one, and she wandered the streets like someone who'd just fought through hell. She wore filthy, torn, bloodstained clothes with her hair strewn everywhere, its blonde color soiled a dirty brown.

She reached the edge of Opek and stared over the mesa, at the footrails that led toward the desert. In the distance, the blot of the sandstorm moved further south as it covered the escaping Claws.

If they came from the Savage Land, it meant they'd traveled far enough to pass the southern towns. Perhaps these were already overcome? Or perhaps they'd experienced similar raids, been taught similar lessons? But why?

Sharla screamed with frustration. She screamed until her voice cracked, and she tried again. She repeated the effort until the strength left her body and she collapsed. She lay on her back, sprawled with the bone axes at her sides, and stared at the pale sky.

They'd acted as only Claws could: pillaging and looting for the sport of it, the thrill of it, ransacking Low Country while the Owl looked the other way, just as it always did. Opek hadn't seen Watchmen in years, and she knew the rest of Low Country endured a similar plight. In times when the king abandoned his people, when all laws were tossed to the wind and buried with the forgotten innocents in a remorseless desert, who would ever know about Opek?

Who would ever know about Renn?

Finally, *finally*, the familiar anger returned. Temporarily satiated by her prior vengeance, it roared to life. It boiled in her chest and filled her mouth with the taste of blood. No, that was already there—residue from the Claw she'd slain.

She spat and stood, wiping her mouth with the back of her hand. She hadn't slain nearly enough of them, not after what they'd done to Opek. Not after they'd taken Renn.

Her plan was simple, the only one that made sense. She'd return to her money, retrieve enough of it to hire a suitable band of toughs, ride into the Savage Land, and free Renn. Nothing else would suffice.

She'd met him the day after she buried the money. Neither of them could explain how they knew. It was there, unspoken and undeniable: the longing they recognized in each other's gazes, the energy in each other's limbs. They'd sparked each other, set each other alight. She'd told him her hopes and he'd done the same. How did someone retreat from that step? How did they kill that promise? She'd never waded so deep with anyone; he'd upended her world.

She'd recognized him as the foundation on which to start over…and then he'd been taken. The promise of her new life, stolen along with everything else. But she wouldn't let it happen, not this time. She would fight for their lives. She *had* to.

She marched into town, passing townsfolk who cried or stared. She ignored them and none spoke to her, for they'd never known her. For all

Chapter Two

they knew, the Claws had come to Opek because of her, seeing as she held their weapons and wore their blood.

Perhaps they *had* come to Opek because of her. Perhaps all this happened because of her family's sins. Perhaps the ancestors still hounded her for taking the gold instead of burying it sooner. Thinking about *that* only boiled the anger to such a degree that she found it difficult to think or see straight, so she determined to avoid thoughts of her past altogether. She could atone later.

She strode into the Boar's Head Inn and marched to her room. She retrieved her canteen, her saddlebags, her clothes. She only possessed a handful of belongings, but those were all she'd needed. Best not to keep much when you moved from town to town; it only made you more tempting to thieves or bandits.

She made to leave, but lingered in the doorway. She stared back at the bed and the memories it provoked—the warmth of Renn's limbs and the gentle, heartfelt laugh that rumbled from his chest. For an agonizing moment, she yearned for something other than the anger, something that reminded her of their good times. A memory to carry her through the dark days and cold nights to come.

But she'd never been one to remember the good, however badly she wanted to.

She swallowed and left the room. She entered the stables and retrieved her horse. She'd named it "Nun" after she'd been gifted it by a Lodian nun outside a monastery near Keth. She was a brown horse that usually contrasted with Sharla's blond hair, but today, their colors looked all too similar.

Sharla didn't speak with the stablehand or the owner, for no one was around. Everyone still wandered the streets in a daze. As she exited the stables, she saw a few Lodian monks from the monastery down the street. Hunched, robed figures who mopped their sweating faces with their sleeves, they hovered about corpses and grieving individuals like timid pups who sought a few scraps. Feeding off Opek's agony, its mourning, and placating themselves by offering the same empty blessings and liturgies they always gave. She spat at the one closest and kicked Nun into a gallop.

She rode through Opek to reach the same footrail she'd earlier examined. She descended without a backward glance, guiding Nun through the precarious switchbacks, flinching as scree tumbled downslope. The Claws were amazing riders if they'd traversed this so quickly. The sandstorm—though it may've concealed their approach—would've made their route more difficult.

Long before she reached the desert flat, her neck and shoulders ached from the effort of peering over the edge, of guiding Nun around the corners as carefully as she could. The footrail was one of the few along the mesa, one of the only routes into Opek for miles. Unsurprisingly, the town was sparsely populated and rarely visited unless the visitors came from the west…and no one ever came from the north. No, never from High Country.

Pinyon pine scuttled the rocks and scree in scattered patches. The rest of the forest bunched behind Sharla to the east, leaving only a few trees to populate the desert flat. The expanse spread below her in a rippling mirage, a length of heat that swam like an ocean. The pines offered pathetic attempts at shade while sagebrush glowed in the evening light, enjoying water she'd never find. Occasional sand dunes rolled like low hills, broken by sandstone outcroppings or bluffs. The sunset bloomed red across the mesa face and turned the scree and talus orange.

Most of Low Country was sandstone, old rock that still bore etchings from when the Claws prevailed. This was before the Owl drove them away to claim the land for itself, thereby provoking raids like the one Opek had just experienced. Couldn't the Claws forget the past? Or maybe the past wouldn't leave them alone?

Sharla grimaced at the thought and hunched lower in her saddle. She knew a little about the latter sentiment.

By the time she reached the flat, the sun kissed the western horizon. This far south, her perspective offered a clear view of the sunset, unobstructed by the mesas or buttes that crowded the tablelands in channels and patterns. She stared down a valley toward the sun, a straight that beckoned with promise and beauty. The clouds turned gold, vermillion, and red, while to the east the horizon already blushed pink and purple. The sky stretched over her in a magnificent canvas, an expansive display as though the ancestors worked a show purely for her.

If only the ancestors had been so kind a few hours before.

She spurred Nun forward and watched the sagebrush glow silver, golden. Watched as it darkened with the setting sun, bruising and brooding in clumps of shadow. When a distant butte finally obstructed the sun, she entered a realm of dreams, of fiery heavens and ripening sands.

Magical, or so she'd thought in her younger days. Now, it only stirred thoughts of isolation. An alien landscape surrounded her. No, it surrounded all Low Country. It *was* Low Country. Generations would come and pass, but this desert would never be claimed; not by the Owl, not by the Claws, not by anyone. It would consume their blood and wait for the next.

The sands mellowed toward pink, a dark purple. The sagebrush appeared to wilt in the shadows while the pines turned into foreign, bristling shapes. The heavens lapsed; the clouds receded into wispy streaks, then nothing.

Stars emerged, full constellations she'd never learned. Barely visible before the moon rose, a full display that darkened its surroundings. The landscape silvered under its ethereal glow, casting strange, twisting shadows. Dunes shifted and wavered, stretching farther or closer—but that was probably just dehydration. She forced herself to drink warm water from her canteen, grimacing as the draught curdled her stomach.

She made it a little farther before she finally conceded to her exhaustion and approached a small bluff, an outcropping that hid her from the breeze. She tied Nun to the gnarled branches of a desert juniper and curled herself into a ball, using her clothes and saddlebags as a makeshift bedroll.

The next day, she found signs of the Claws' passage. Scraps of torn garments here, a bloodstained rag over there. Once, she nearly rode over a crumpled body on the other side of a dune. A woman with willowy features and blood-crusted hair. Some of the townsfolk had apparently struggled to the point of death. But Sharla never saw Renn.

She focused on that thought and continued forward, clenching her jaw and hunching as the desert heat rose with the sun. She already felt herself weakening under the ceaseless fire, as though every heartbeat were a hammer blow. She felt the dehydration spinning her thoughts, weakening her limbs, and she knew she couldn't drink enough water to replenish herself. Better to keep moving toward the midday shelter she'd discovered on her first trek through the flat, the journey she'd sworn never to repeat. Not even a week later and she'd already broken her promise. Not even a week later and everything had already gone to hell.

At times, she thought she heard people talking and jerked her head around to find the sounds merely came from gnats around her ears. She felt her lips drying and cracking with every breath, as though they'd eventually peel off and blow away like scrolls. Every blink itched and every breath stirred sand clumped over her teeth from yesterday's storm.

When she reached the stream at the midday shelter, she finally cleansed her mouth. She dirtied the water by splashing her face and gargling her throat. She struggled through the first mouthfuls while Nun drank her fill, and she curled beside the horse after tying her to another juniper. She sought rest under the drooping branches, and she prayed all afternoon for *one* more breeze.

Toward evening, she mounted Nun for their final approach.

When she was a few miles out, she heard a cry, thin and weak. She frowned and kept moving, dismissing the noise as that of the gnats. When the unmistakable wail of a woman sounded again, she couldn't ignore it.

Turning Nun, she crept closer to a dune and peered over its edge to see a wagon slumped in the sagebrush. A wheel appeared to have shattered. The wagon's contents were already strewn over the brush. The Claws might've toppled the wagon, but bandits had arrived to pick through the offerings. Sharla couldn't see the contents from this distance,

Chapter Two

but she saw enough flashing to recognize gold. Or gems. Merchants, then? Traveling the flat alone, without a caravan or escort? Idiotic. Unforgivable.

Sharla scowled at their stupidity, and she watched a man drag the struggling woman toward a rock outcropping, his hand already fumbling with his breeches while the other gripped her shoulder. She squealed and thrashed while staring at a body toward the front of the wagon, someone who might've been her husband. Other men were busy hauling handfuls of spilled loot toward their horses. Three in total, but Sharla lingered too long, because an instant before she ducked her head out of sight, one of the men glanced in her direction.

She swore and crouched beside Nun, listening for any signs of approach. Occupied by their loot, the bandits didn't move toward her. She heard them muttering, speaking with each other. Then she heard tearing clothes, and the woman's squeals elevated. Sharla led her horse down the dune, mounted, and rode further south, struggling to ignore the woman's cries. Nothing could be done for her, not when Sharla was even younger and smaller than she.

The familiar bluff slid into view: a crescent shape of sandstone. Juniper and pine crawled about it, festering amid the sagebrush like sentinels to guard her buried hoard. She brushed through the vegetation, led Nun into the sandy soil, and realized that she hadn't returned with a shovel. She had to use her axes; it couldn't be helped.

She tied Nun to a juniper and set to work, turning the axe head to catch the sand in as broad a scoop as she could. She continued the motion, hauling sand until she panted for breath. She continued as the sun sank, as the shadows stretched, as the colors glowed gold, then orange, then blood-red. Continued until her axe finally struck the corner of one of the boxes she'd buried; a piece of the collection she'd spread her blood money through. She dropped the axe and grasped the box, heaving it upright and clearing it of sand.

Her horse snorted, whinnied in warning.

She jerked up, spotting someone in the brush. A scruffy face as lined as a weathered pigskin—one of the men she'd seen at the wagon. She clenched her jaw and stood, dropping the box before he could see. She saw the other man at the far side of the brush, creeping around a juniper with a battle axe poised and ready. Real steel this time, Benanian-made and far superior to the bone armament that still hung from Nun.

She leaped from the pit and ran to her horse, hoping the men hadn't seen her axe or the box. The man in the brush stood and waved a dagger with an ugly smile. She stopped beside Nun, raised her hands.

"Please," she whimpered.

"Anything you want," he said, edging around the brush and stepping toward her. "Anything and more. I'll show you the time of your life."

She inhaled, waited for the man to her right to step closer. "At least it'll be better than Opek."

When the man took another step, she pulled the miniature crossbow from her saddlebags—one of the only possessions she'd allowed herself to take from home—and raised it toward the man with the battle axe. He stood no more than ten paces away, easy pickings at such short range. Her precaution of traveling with a loaded crossbow finally paid off: the bolt hissed across the distance and caught the man in the throat. He blinked, coughed blood, and sagged to one knee. The move stunned the second man into inaction; only for a moment, but enough for Sharla to step around Nun and flay his throat with the bone axe. He dropped with a wet gurgle, thrashing and kicking as blood sprayed the sagebrush.

Nun reared and kicked as she moved past the writhing bandit and up the bluff. There'd been three bandits at the wagon, and sure enough, she spotted the last one several strides away. He sat atop his horse and leaned forward with his own axe, but after seeing her grim, bloodstained expression, he considered his options with a furrowed brow. After a moment, he turned his horse and rode west, toward Mela and Tigon Land.

The direction Sharla needed to travel.

She watched him go with a frown, recognizing he'd surely bring news of her to the rest of his fellows, wherever they were. Then again, he probably didn't have many men to back him up, seeing as these

Chapter Two

appeared to be an isolated, desperate bunch. He could tell the Watchmen, but everyone knew their reign had slackened long ago. Besides, with such chaos as Claw raids befalling Low Country, who would pay any heed to the description of a crazy woman with bone axes?

Well, now she had steel ones. Sharla collected the new axes and knives from the fallen bandits and packed all of them with Nun. She searched the men's purses for coin to add to her own, gathering a hefty stash to use in Mela.

Mounting Nun, she kicked her toward the west. She hunched forward, clenched her jaw, and squinted into the burning horizon.

"I'm coming, Renn," she muttered. "Don't die on me. Not when we've just started to know each other."

Chapter Three

MILES TO THE SOUTH, DORMUN REDSKULL SLOWED THE PACE of his raiding party on the second day after the attack. Most of the captives ailed: heads lolling, limbs flopping, faces blank with exhaustion and dehydration. They watched canteens exchange hands and licked their lips as drops of water, gleaming like diamonds, fell to the brush. Some of them continued to flail, kick, and shout. Others accepted their fate with grim silence, a resignation that spread through their ranks until all of them lay still.

Dormun considered this with equal parts satisfaction and disgust: satisfaction that his raid had been a success, and disgust when he saw how fragile the northerners really were. To think the tribes had lived in fear of them for so long.

To think he'd originally encouraged this stance.

He waved his hand and halted his horse. His riders circled as they found room to dismount and lower their prisoners to the ground.

This far south, the homeland lay only a few hills beyond. The northerners probably wouldn't recognize the border—they'd ignored *any* borders for the entirety of Dormun's life—but the tribes had learned their land and could ride it by heart. They knew *all* their land, even the vast hills and canyons now invaded by the northerners, the pests who spread like locusts to strip the land bare and slaughter its inhabitants. After hearing the tales, Dormun had ordered peace for a time, convinced the northerners had finally claimed as much as they desired.

Chapter Three

Convinced that Kine Tarroful told the truth.

"They always lie," he muttered.

He turned to the blond-haired man on the horse behind him, bound and gagged after his initial attack had marked him as a threat to be reckoned with. After Dormun survived their initial skirmish and knocked him out, the man had said nothing. Intelligent, alert, calculating, and brave, he was someone to watch. Someone who never resisted when Dormun dismounted, led his horse beside a nearby creek, and pulled him off of it.

The man tumbled to the ground. He stared at Dormun with those green eyes, watching and thinking.

"Redskull."

Dormun blinked at the improper address, but then recognized the voice. He stiffened and turned to the man beside him, one whose cloak wore the dust and dirt of their desert travel. The cloak rippled, tracing the outline of dhorak scale armor underneath. Killing a dhorak: a feat Dormun would never have believed if he hadn't seen it for his own eyes. How the man accomplished *anything* he did, Dormun couldn't imagine. Perhaps it was better not to try—to allow some mysteries to stay hidden, protected by the spirits until the Final Ascent.

What Dormun *couldn't* ignore were the man's features, now concealed by his hood. Dormun had only seen the face once. He remembered the discoloration across the man's features, birthmarks with no explanation or premise. He remembered the man's angular, hardened nose, drawn eyes, and teeth Dormun could never see—teeth that clicked deep in the man's throat.

The man was one of the monsters from the east, the dark land across the waters. He was from a country no tribe dealt with. Dormun had heard of wars with that country, conflicts the tribes had barely survived. The elders said the dark men threatened the Final Ascent by bringing shadows to cover the world, but none of their kind had been seen in as long as Dormun lived.

But Dormun had prayed, and the spirits had provided one of the men to assist him; he couldn't refuse their blessings; not when they offered such results.

"Shaman," Dormun answered.

The hood turned northward. "None follow us."

"They will."

"You've baited them."

"Yes." Dormun nodded, folding his arms across his chest. "Kine will come."

"Kine?"

Dormun tilted his head and struggled to remember which term Kine had used. "A…Watchman. The northerners say they're Watchmen, but they never see us."

"We would've been visible for miles." The hood turned to Dormun. "Don't overestimate yourself."

Dormun frowned. "You know nothing."

"I know the Owl, and it's not to be trifled with." The hood inhaled. "At least, not unless you know what you're doing."

"Do you?"

"I know how to make an impression. And we obviously have. But Opek's survivors might speak of demons and Armageddon rather than Claws."

Tribal elders would probably think the same thing, but had they ever helped Dormun? Not now, and not in all the years he'd warned of the spreading northerners. The elders left the problem to him, and he'd solve it without their help, without their empty prayers or blessings.

"*Claws*." Dormun lifted his dhorak skull to spit at the shaman's feet. "You speak like the northerners."

"Old habits. I apologize." The shaman paused. "You're certain they'll see this as an attack by your tribe?"

"Kine will."

"He's some sort of captain?"

Dormun frowned at the strange term. "He leads them. He will come."

Chapter Three

The shaman folded his arms across his chest to mirror Dormun's pose, and Dormun struggled to ignore the notion that even though the man was thinner and leaner, he still projected an air of power and command. "It's to be a battle, then," the shaman said.

"Kine will die."

"And then?"

"We take our land."

The hood turned to Dormun. "Low Country?"

"All of it. It belongs to our ancestors. We wait there for Final Ascent."

"That sounds…expensive."

Dormun couldn't suppress his involuntary shudder, the chill that pricked his spine. The shaman's assistance exacted a toll, even if the nature of his dealings remained vague, nameless. Some of the tribal land along the eastern coastline that faced the shaman's territory had fallen under shadow. A thick, impenetrable cloud had blackened the sky as though a dark animal hide rolled from the heavens. It weighed the trees down, crushed the brush, set every animal fleeing and every tribesman praying. Could it be the shadow the elders warned about?

What none of them understood was that Dormun had brought this shadow to their heartland, that he'd willingly allowed the blight through his cooperation with the shaman…and even he didn't know what the darkness concealed.

Perhaps he *did* risk the Final Ascent. But taking back the tribal land was worth any price. How could he offer the spirits any less? If he, the leader of the only tribe that still fought to reclaim the homeland, didn't stand for his people now, how could he call himself a true chieftain?

He cleared his throat, turning to the shaman. "You take more land?"

"Such was the nature of our agreement."

Dormun licked his lips. He stepped closer, lowering his voice to hide the words from his raiding party. "And…more tribesmen?"

"Only a few." The shaman shrugged. "I'm a generous man, Redskull. I don't require much."

"Your favorites."

"I consider it only fair, given the magnitude of what you've asked me to do." The shaman waved his hand toward the north. "Wage war on Low Country? No one else would try that."

"Take the dying," Dormun said. "The sick."

"I never asked for anything else."

Dormun frowned at a sudden thought, and he looked at the captives. "Why not them?"

The shaman followed Dormun's gaze. "You can ensure their safety?"

"They're alive."

"They must make it to the coast," the shaman insisted. "They must reach the land you've given me."

"They will," Dormun answered, relieved. Even if he didn't understand the nature of the shaman's doings, he could still spare a few more of his tribe.

"You might want to take better care of them, then. Give them water and food."

"Yes." Dormun nodded. "They'll live."

The shaman watched him for a long moment. Again, Dormun struggled not to flinch, not to shudder, to ignore the prickling, numbing sensation of dread whenever the shaman lingered—as though the man could see Dormun's soul, to the secrets only the spirits knew.

But wouldn't the shaman also speak with the spirits? Even if he didn't hail from one of the tribes, wouldn't it be the spirits who gave him such powers? Different spirits, maybe. Or at least, spirits Dormun had never known—not when they brought such darkness.

He clenched his jaw and turned from the shaman, breaking eye contact to stare at the blond-haired man beside his horse. "They'll live," Dormun repeated. "Help us kill Kine."

From his peripheral, Dormun saw the shaman, nod, clap his hands. "It's settled. Let the Watchmen come."

Chapter Four

COLONEL KINE TARROFUL SQUINTED AT THE FIGURES assembled at the far end of the road. Framed by Keth's outskirts, they looked small and frail, shimmering in the desert heat and wavering in height. There were only a few of them, but he suspected more to be in the surrounding buildings, watching their leaders and biding their time. Perhaps they waited to see which side would come out on top: the outlaws or the Watchmen. Or perhaps they'd sided with the outlaws, but now waited to see if they would survive the Watchmen's attack, and as soon as Kine demonstrated his iron fist, they'd return to the Watchmen with familiar cries of allegiance, gratitude, and celebration.

Oh, the tired game they all played.

Kine exhaled and rubbed his dry eyes. He shouldn't have stayed up so late the night before, but the pleasure house was full and the wine was robust. Imported from the Lhorian Isles and Liadinia besides, it was one of the many benefits he'd brought Low Country: peace and wealth, safety and rest. Alliances between bandits and Watchmen, truces on all sides. Despite the strongest borders enjoyed by Low Country in years, no one ever recognized the age for what it was. No one ever relished their newfound comforts. Instead, they rejected Kine's efforts; they tore themselves down.

No, they tore Low Country down. They claimed to want something different, but the only difference they'd find would be the same war that originally consumed Low Country, the turmoil that persisted until the

Claws had been removed, the bandits dealt with, and the borders resolved. No one understood the details because no one wanted the gritty truth. Aye, Kine had borne the weight of that responsibility for forty years, and he'd largely been left to carry it alone.

"So ungrateful," he muttered.

"Colonel?"

Kine turned to the man beside him, Lieutenant Colonel Gashar Begg of the Gold Battalion. A fancy name for a sprinkling of gold trim, the type of filigreed capes all officers bore. Gashar's was white, but already colored brown by sand and dust, while Kine's own was the burning yellow of breaking dawn. Each of them wore the Owl across their back, its piercing eyes capped by the Watchman's helm. Beneath this, they bore steel plating, with the breastplate, gauntlets, and greaves bearing the same Watchman insignia. At least with appearances, the Owl spared no expense. If only the same could be said for the Owl's regard of its own country.

That wasn't quite true, though. The Owl catered to High Country, keeping its nobles and merchants well fed. It proved itself nothing more than a snake in owl feathers, following the trail of money rather than the trail of dead innocents who littered its Low Country. Instead, the Owl had left that task to Kine, had tasked the Third Regiment with protecting Low Country before pulling the rest of its forces farther north.

"You're thinking again, Colonel," Gashar said.

"A habit easily succumbed to, Lieutenant Colonel."

Gashar nodded toward the figures at the far end of the street. "Not thinking about those men?"

"Should I be?" Kine scratched his beard. "That only makes everything harder."

Gashar echoed his exhale. "You think they'll surrender?"

"No. They've spoken with the bandits."

"You think Senit knows?"

"I don't know." Kine frowned at the notion. "I sincerely hope he doesn't. If he's encouraged this, well…that's only another thing to worry about."

Chapter Four

"Nobody needs that," Gashar agreed.

Kine eyed him for a moment, uncertain whether the man meant the comment as sarcasm. Twenty years younger, with sandy blond hair and a beard to contrast Kine's graying features, Gashar had adjusted to the Watchmen's policies readily enough, handling himself as Kine would. Indeed, Gashar had accepted more than most, had supported Kine even when Kine's negotiations became less and less with other Watchmen and the king, more and more with bandits and outlaws from the mines.

A necessary sacrifice to hold the peace, but few beyond Keth understood this. Indeed, Kine had stopped trying to keep track of the Watchmen throughout the rest of Low Country, for they only reported when necessity and custom demanded, and even then they provided few details. No matter. The rest of Kine's network had proven far more capable, reliable, and prompt than the Watchmen ever had.

Gashar caught his look and shrugged. "I was enjoying myself, Colonel. I think most of the town was. For the first time in a while, things were going well."

"Aye." Kine considered this, nodded, and spurred his horse forward. "Then let's settle this quickly."

The vanguard of Gashar's battalion followed the two officers. The rest were encamped along the Shapan River, patrolling its length from the Great Canyon to the mesas that marked the beginning of High Country.

The other battalions of Kine's regiment—Silver, Steel, and Ebony—patrolled the southwestern, southern, and southeastern portions of Low Country. In truth, the Shapan River was the only border exclusively managed by Watchmen, whereas the other borders were maintained by the rest of Kine's network.

A less knowledgeable man might've described this network to consist of "drug cartels," but this represented a gross overgeneralization. Kine knew the truth ran deeper, bloodier, and longer than anyone cared to know. It had taken many demonstrations, negotiations, and truces struck over corpses and burned ranches for him to broker a pact between the other cartels, those who presently managed the lands "policed" by Watchmen.

The Watchmen reassured the populace while the cartels repelled the true dangers, and nowhere but Opek and the northeastern portion of Low Country remained exempt—largely because this was the only portion of Low Country with no reward to offset the risk of smuggling drugs. Containing nothing but the pine forest of eastern High Country, this stretch of the border was only inhabited by Opek's populace, and Kine knew how little they desired his product. Too influenced by Lodian monks, set in tradition. They didn't understand fairy ichor or gargev powder, didn't want anything but ranching and religion. Aye, theirs was a dying breed; but then, most of Low Country was. They just refused to accept it yet.

Well, all of them but a few.

Kine frowned at the men at the end of the street. He fingered the helm he cradled under his left arm while his right hand gripped the reins. Keth's residents had evacuated the roads long ago, retreating behind locked doors and shuttered windows. Kine felt their stares nonetheless. He felt their tension as though it were a storm cloud that ripened the glaring sky, as though all Keth held its breath.

A wind whistled through the buildings, blowing tumbleweed over porches and stirring Kine's hair over his eyes. The townsfolk said nothing, waiting for him to make the first move. Ancestors above, they were dragging this out.

"Citizens of Keth!" Kine shouted. "You know who I am: Colonel Kine Tarroful of the Third Regiment. My Watchmen have brought you a new age. You have food, drink, and safety. But you spit in our faces and choose to rebel. Why provoke the Watchmen? Why provoke the Owl?"

The two forces had drawn within a block of each other, close enough for Kine to hear the graveled voice of the man who responded. When seen up close, none of the townsfolk looked particularly impressive: they were slight men and a few women in ragged clothing with dirt-streaked skin and dusty faces. All of them looked to be ranchers, with a scattered

Chapter Four

assortment of swords, spears, and shields, many of which looked so rusty as to be worthless.

"You say you bring food, drink, and safety?" the leader—a man apparently as old as Kine—called back. "What about the bodies in our inns, the addicts who use fairy ichor until their minds melt? What about those who use so much gargev powder their heart stops and their bodies rot until someone finds them after smelling it? Keth stinks of its dead, and the rest of Low Country is no different. You call yourself one of the Watchmen, but if these are your Watchmen, you've brought Low Country nothing but ruin. You've ruined your title and soiled the Owl's honor."

Kine snorted—he couldn't help himself. The audacity of the man. The *lunacy* of the man, spouting what he thought to be truth, apparently having read a book or two that convinced him of the way things ought to be.

"They grow more arrogant every time," he muttered.

"I'm sure he considers himself righteous," Gashar answered.

"Aye. A regular monk, this one." Kine cleared his throat. "Before our day, Low Country stank of the dead because bandits and Claws raided its towns. Your ranches burned and your families were slaughtered. When was the last time you saw a bandit or a Claw?"

Kine waited while the townsfolk shuffled from foot to foot, nervously eying their leader until he cleared his throat and answered.

"We just spoke with the bandits south of here, and they told us they're just as unhappy with your action."

"So, the bandits encouraged you toward mutiny." Kine shook his head. "Funny that they're not here when you need them. Makes you wonder, doesn't it? Isn't it interesting that the bandits always promise, yet they never deliver?"

A few of the townsfolk muttered to each other, edged from their leader. They had obviously considered this, but their leader's apparent charisma or sway had convinced them to pick up weapons they would've left to rust. Another worthless fellow, propping himself up on the hopes and nostalgia of his weary countrymen, a man who looked to happier days that would never return, at least not while the Owl focused its attention elsewhere.

Kine cleared his throat and raised his voice. "The bandits will say anything to convince you toward rebellion. They'd rather have you deal with me so I can spare them the trouble. It only makes for a silly game, because I assure you changing leadership accomplishes nothing—not unless you convince the king himself to ride here.

"And so, I'll say this once: lay down your weapons, abandon this rebellion, and everything goes back to the way it was. Peacefully surrender, and no arrests will be made. No harm will come to anyone, and no families will be broken. We each return to our loved ones, and we continue as if nothing happened. All will be forgiven, and I will collect no debts."

"Aye," the leader answered. He even managed to sound disgusted. "And we all know how valuable debts are to Colonel Tarroful."

"Your answer, sir?"

The leader hesitated, looked from side to side for support. Nobody met his gaze, and most people kept backing away. Indeed, in the time he'd been speaking, the gap between him and the townsfolk had widened. He stood several paces apart, propping himself with his spear as though it held him upright. He wavered, frowned.

A scuffling drew Kine's attention to the left, a noise that drew murmurs from the men behind him. From an alleyway between two buildings, an apparition stumbled into the street. No, a horse and rider streaked with so much dust and sand as to appear cloaked. At first, he assumed the hunched rider to be dead; they looked boneless and lifeless, draped across the horse as though a corpse. But then they tried to push themselves upright, falling from the horse and collapsing into the street.

Perfect. Another addict to spoil Kine's justice, to vindicate the leader's claims. Kine turned, but a cry drew his attention back to the rider. They lurched upright and staggered forward, shaking as though their legs could barely sustain them. This close, he saw the rider to be a woman, with a torn coat, hair in disarray, and eyes staring through everything.

Chapter Four

"—aws...cla..." she muttered.

Kine heard creaking saddles and snorting horses as the men behind him turned to intercept. He raised his hand to stifle their movements, drawn by the desperation in the woman's face. "Woman," he said. "What's the matter?"

She inhaled with a shudder and locked gazes with him, her eyes burning with a sudden fervor. "Claws," she gasped. "Claws in Opek."

Something curdled Kine's stomach: the familiar weight of inevitability. As if from a distance, he felt the world drawing to a cliff, a precipice that would irrevocably change everything. "You rode from Opek?"

"Yes." She swayed. "Only stopped long enough for water and food."

It was then that her horse collapsed, falling to its side with a meaty thump. As though the sound robbed the strength from her, the woman sank to her knees and crawled on all fours. "Opek is raided...Claws took captives."

Before he knew what he was doing, Kine had dismounted and knelt beside the woman with his helm abandoned to the dusty street, the rebellious townsfolk entirely forgotten. "Who?" he breathed. "Which Claw did this?"

The woman sputtered for breath, hair covering her face. "They wore...skulls. Ram skulls. Their leader had something...else. Something red."

"A dhorak skull." Kine sat, stunned. His mind had emptied, and his chest had stilled. The world had muted, all sensation dispersing like sand across the ocean. An unbearable cold pressed down on him like a sliding glacier.

"Dormun Redskull," he whispered.

Now, the cold reached his head, his heart, until everything became ice—a crackling rage that thickened his breath and tingled his fingers.

They'd had an understanding. They'd agreed to leave each other alone, to never set foot across each other's borders. He'd respected Dormun enough to keep his own end of the bargain, but look how the man repaid him. He was no better than the townsfolk who spat at Kine's back.

No, Dormun was no man. He was just a creature, an animal.

A Claw.

Kine mounted his horse. He spurred it forward without putting on his helm, without comforting the woman. His Watchmen shouted, but they fell behind him, drifting through the street like dreams that fled the dawn. Everything paled in comparison to the fury that coursed through Kine's chest, now warming everything until his blood boiled, until his breath steamed. Until he could've channeled magic and flattened the town, until all former weariness had dispersed. The last forty years had melted away and he'd become a teenager again, determined to change Low Country. Ancestors above, he'd once been so certain of everything.

At least back then, Dormun Redskull had been a friend.

The townsfolk were turning to run, but he couldn't see them anymore. He only saw Redskull's Claws, fleeing after they'd slaughtered his innocents. Someone threw a spear and it crackled across the legs of his horse. The horse squealed and pranced sideways. Kine dismounted and examined it, saw that it had probably only been bruised. He turned and followed the mob, the dispersing townsfolk. They fled through alleyways and banged on doors for admittance; they pleaded with those inside. Kine Tarroful was prone to be erratic, they knew. If he didn't get his way, it was far better to lock your doors, to wait until his drunken outcries subsided.

But it wasn't the drink this time. It was something instinctual—just like a Claw.

Someone came at Kine with a battle axe, an angry youth who thought himself as determined as Kine. Kine stepped inside the strike—moving with years of practice that offset his age—and he passed his sword through the youth's side. The adolescent sputtered and went down, writhing and kicking red tracks in the street. Behind him, a man thrust his spear. Kine pivoted around the weapon and hacked the man's face. Blood spattered Kine's armor and his yellow cape, dotting it with rubies that shone in the midday sun.

Chapter Four

Shouts from Watchmen behind him and screams of townsfolk ahead of him. Thundering hoofbeats from everywhere and nowhere, passing around Kine as he strode deeper into the press. Ahead of him, the leader had dropped his spear and stumbled over someone's body. He'd apparently twisted an ankle in the process. Now, he dragged himself away and snatched harried glances at Kine.

"Mercy," he spluttered. "Ancestors above, mercy."

"Mercy," Kine said. "Once, I thought I could teach this country about mercy."

The man's eyes bulged as Kine's blade darted through his chest, in and out, as quick as a serpent.

"But this country never wanted to listen." Kine exhaled and looked around the street. It wasn't how he'd wished this to end, but with the mention of Dormun Redskull, everything had changed. Kine had lost himself again, drowning in those memories of when he'd first returned to the raided township, found the broken body of his wife across the porch.

"Your orders, Colonel?"

Kine turned to Gashar, who watched him from atop his horse. When he'd first met Kine, Gashar hadn't known what to make of his brand of justice, honed and refined in the king's absence. But by now, Gashar managed to look collected, even calm as he watched the street.

"Gather your battalion," Kine answered. "Leave only enough men to keep the peace. We're riding to the Great Canyon."

Gashar frowned. "The Great Canyon?"

"We're riding to meet Senit."

Gashar nudged his horse a step closer, dipped his head to bury the words between the men. "You think that's wise?"

"It's our only choice now." Kine wiped his blade on the leader's shirt and sheathed the weapon. "Dormun Redskull was stupid enough to ask for a war. Now, he'll get one."

Chapter Five

SOMETIME IN THE NIGHT, RENN FOUND SHARLA. HE'D ESCAPED the Claws, traveled on foot, and found her in the middle of the tablelands, her makeshift camp hidden in a grove of cottonwoods beside a stream.

Renn approached under the moonlight, his features strong and proud, unblemished even after capture and captivity. His eyes glinted with a sharp, deadly gaze that penetrated her heart, melted it. She sank into his embrace, gripped his shoulders and drew him tight, smiled and felt her eyes moistening with tears of joy, almost—

She stiffened, drawing back from the saddlebag she'd clutched to her chest. She blinked herself awake and stared at the full moon, which lit the surrounding clouds with its ethereal glow. It burnished the buttes and drew shadows across the desert flat, hard claws that blotted undergrowth and darkened the horizon. Nun lay beside her, the only sign of life. The night was still but for the distant wail of a coyote, pleading from somewhere in the distance.

Only a dream. A dream of Renn's presence, his life.

She hugged herself, staring toward the western horizon as the moon drifted toward it. She listened to the coyote, heard its cousins echo from across the tablelands: mournful sounds that resonated, strengthened. There was no Renn tonight, but there were others to keep her company. Others to hold solace with, to sit with until dawn.

She didn't catch another wink of sleep, and when the sun's pale glow crept from the east, she forced her stiffened joints into motion. The

Chapter Five

night's chill had left her shivering through the final hour, and she eagerly stretched, squatted, relished the warm blood rushing to her numbed legs.

Renn's absence weighed on her like a boulder on her heart, tugging her southward. Longing for him burned in her chest, filled her with fire until she could barely think or breathe for fear of suffocating on the smoke, the funeral pyre of their hopes and dreams.

A funeral pyre?

"You idiot," she said. She felt her hands trembling and wiped them on her legs, spitting into the dust. "You bloody idiot."

There'd never been hopes or dreams. There'd only been a few days; a time of peace and stability, the first she'd known. Still, it had never been more than that. Best to keep things in perspective, or she would fall to pieces before she ever made it past Mela.

She glanced at her reflection in the pool nearby. Blond hair—now dusty and scraggly—hung over smooth, strong cheekbones of what could've been a regal face. Gifts from her family—ancestors burn them all—that would certainly draw every eye in Mela. That was before one saw her eyes, a sapphire blue that shone through her dirty complexion, hardened by pain and toughened by battle. They communicated a woman who knew how to handle herself, a woman who'd certainly draw all the wrong types and encourage the rest.

"We'll get him back," she told her reflection. She decided that was stupid, so she turned and spoke to Nun instead, who eyed her with a solemn expression. "We'll get him back," she repeated. "No use getting scared about it."

Despite everything, her heart still ached. "Ancestors above." She shook her head, exhaled, and started gathering her saddlebags. "So heartsick over someone you don't even know. If you know what's best for you, you'll leave him behind. Keep riding like you're supposed to."

So why did she persist?

She thought about that after she mounted Nun. Perhaps she persisted because he was the only person she'd met—the only person she'd allowed herself to know—since she'd left home four years prior.

He was a beautiful, loyal, trusting confidant who'd been taken after trying to save her from death. She'd allowed herself to imagine a future with him and it had felt like...home.

Sharla frowned. The answer wasn't good enough, and she knew it. Entirely sentimental, and too optimistic for an uncivilized land like Low Country. One didn't succeed with their head in the clouds. She only had to look at the example of her mother for that.

A simple ranching town fed by streams that ran though the northern tablelands, Mela was the only settlement to inhabit the desert flat for miles. Hemmed in by buttes and fingers of the surrounding mesas, the landscape dropped from the town's southern edge to herald the descent toward Tigon Land.

"Tigon" was an older word of the Common language, roughly translated to "canyon." Tigon Land merely referred to the "canyonland," a dark labyrinth of brooding passages that ate through the earth for as far as the eye could see. The superstitious stayed away, the folk with common sense knew better than to approach a likely hideout for bandits, and everyone else simply didn't trust the landscape. It was too confusing, unsettling, terrifying.

She examined Mela as she drew closer, searching for any sign of a recent raid. Mela looked untouched, shimmering in the desert heat. Pinewood buildings here, much like everywhere else in Low Country, and the resultant yellows cheered her spirit, a welcome improvement from the muddled browns and reds of the landscape.

She fingered her battleaxes as she approached, wondering where to start. The escaped bandit had surely arrived ahead of her, and encountering the rest of his crew was probably inevitable. Nevertheless, she didn't have other options.

She'd been to Mela once, years prior, and she knew of only one inn to approach: the Poached Bison. Never mind the fact that bison had never been seen around Low Country's southern reaches, but only northward toward Keth and High Country. It seemed ranchers were the sentimental sort.

Chapter Five

She passed a few ranches on her way in, or at least what passed for ranches in these parts. The rocky countryside made fences too much trouble, and open grazing was the usual practice. Cows dotted the terrain, animals that surely wandered the southern precipice with alarming consistency. How many did the ranchers lose every year?

She positioned the axes to wear them where people could see: hanging from her belt aside either leg. She drew the bone ones clear enough for people to spy their bleached heads, to communicate the danger to anyone who considered anything. A woman with axes was interesting enough, but someone who carried the weaponry of Claws?

As she hoped, the arsenal appeared to discourage those who examined her. Townsfolk shifted their gazes, pursed their lips, turned elsewhere. The slouched figures at porches or in alleyways—whom she assumed to be bandits or outlaws—eyed her with narrowed gazes. A few individuals were draped across rocking chairs with slackened expressions and empty looks, those presently enjoying the highs of fairy ichor or the numbed totality of gargev powder. Some of them drooled down their chins, flies buzzing about their gaping mouths.

A sorry sight, but with no Watchmen to oversee things, it wasn't surprising. Indeed, she hadn't seen any Watchmen since leaving Opek. It was as if their ilk had simply...up and left. They'd probably grown weary of their charade and stripped themselves of armor, traveled elsewhere to live in peace. Good riddance to all of them.

Now, she saw men moving around her. A few women, too, but all of them belonged to the group she'd originally identified as those likeliest to be bandits or outlaws. They shifted around her as though she swam upstream, walking behind or before her. Tracking her movements, watching her progress.

It appeared the escaped bandit had already told the rest of his crew about her, and that they'd already recognized her presence. But that was surely impossible, because his crew couldn't be *this* big? Mela moved as though the entire town reacted to her presence, and without Watchmen, she suddenly realized she might've overlooked significant details.

Perhaps there'd been a rebellion? Perhaps the town had recently overthrown the Watchmen? Perhaps the local drug cartel had simply demonstrated its strength, had overwhelmed the rest of Mela to deny anyone who might edge into its territory.

No going back now. She'd already made an impression, for better or worse.

She ambled toward the Poached Bison, careful to appear as though she moved in no hurry, careful to make no threatening moves. She entered the stables, looked at the broad mustangs which inhabited it, and quickly perceived there was no room for Nun. A glance behind assured her she should *not* leave Nun anywhere in the street, not with her saddlebags begging to be rifled through. Surely there was a stable hand to watch the horses?

Or…not. She saw nobody anywhere. She swallowed and finally led Nun to the back of the stables, dismounted, and tied her off on a center pole. Easy pickings for anyone who entered the stables, but Nun couldn't fit anywhere else. Ancestors above, Sharla had probably entered the stables reserved for the drug cartel anyways. No wonder they were full—purposed that way to keep anyone else out—and the sheer audacity of her entrance probably amounted to a declaration of war.

"Just focus, Sharla," she muttered. "Focus on what you can control."

She looked her horse over, determining what to take and what to leave. Wearing too open an arsenal begged for conflict when she just wanted to talk. Better to intrigue someone? To leave her coat open, shirt hanging low? No—then they wouldn't take her seriously. Best to walk slow and confident, with her battleaxes hidden under her coat. She'd leave the bone ones with her horse on the off chance someone who decided to loot her would see them and worry about a curse from a shaman.

"I'll be back, girl." She patted Nun's nose, temporarily delighted to find she wasn't trembling. She inhaled, turned, and strode toward the Poached Bison without a backward glance.

She walked through the front door, perhaps a bit *too* confidently or dramatically. It clattered against the wall and drew every gaze in the

Chapter Five

room. A sea of eyes watched her, hazed by pipe smoke or glazed from drugs. Nevertheless, most of them were alert, conscious, and picked over her physique as though she were a naked prostitute. So much for entering unnoticed.

She edged a path through the crowded room, stepped around tables and chairs. They haphazardly filled the common room, with scattered bowls and tankards throughout. Stains blotted every surface and streaked the bar, where the barkeep looked her over while scrubbing a mug with a dirty rag. He was short and broad; she couldn't tell whether his frame was owed to muscle or fat, but his face was piggish enough she decided not to look too carefully. His hairline failed to conceal a few scars, dashes of white across skin darkened by years of sunlight. Could this be the local emperor himself, the head of Mela's cartel?

Sharla avoided eye contact and headed toward the far corner of the room. She hesitated, deciding a drink would make her look normal. She inhaled, turned, approached the bar.

"Your cheapest ale," she said.

The barkeep raised his eyebrow and grinned. "Cheapest? Not sure you want it."

"You think I'm a noblewoman?" Sharla placed her hands on the bar and leaned across in what she hoped would be seen as a gesture of confidence. Too late, she recognized the motion tugged her coat over her legs and revealed the battleaxes. She froze, mentally cursing herself.

"No," he said. "You're something else."

Sharla swallowed, managed a weak smile. "Yes. And I asked for your cheapest ale."

The barkeep nodded, set the rag down, and turned to the glassware behind him. "Of course, milady. I'm assuming you want a clean mug as well?"

"It wouldn't hurt."

Everyone was listening, and conversation slowly filtered from the back of the room. At first thinking this a ridiculous notion, Sharla recognized that she was the only woman in the room—at least, the only woman who appeared somewhat *clean*, whereas all the others looked like overdosed prostitutes…and probably were. Dirty clothes, tangled hair, dazed expressions.

The barkeep set a mug before her—obviously stained—and poured some ale. He grinned at her all the while, nodded when he pulled the bottle away. "A gold piece."

Sharla stared, temporarily forgetting to hold her composure. "You're serious."

His grin slid away like oil on water. "Deadly."

She clenched her jaw and fished through her coat for a gold piece—struggling not to clink it against other coins—and slipped it across the bar.

"My thanks, milady."

She avoided eye contact and took the mug, moving toward the corner she'd originally intended on. She settled herself against the wall, where she could keep an eye on the room and watch for any men who might've followed her from outside.

Things were off to a shaky start. She grimaced as she raised the mug to her lips, relishing the bite of her first swallow. At least no one had attacked her or seemed to have recognized her.

Then again, they were probably slitting Nun's throat.

She choked at the awful thought, spluttering into her glass. More attention drawn to her, and none of it any friendlier than before. She lowered the mug and wiped her lips with the back of her hand, looking at the tabletop while she waited for the stares to subside.

"You shouldn't have asked for that."

She blinked and raised her gaze to the man who'd spoken, a slouched profile beside the window on the other side of the table, warded in shadows beyond the rays of sunlight filtering through the dirty glass. "I'm sorry?"

"His cheapest ale. You challenged him, and he tested you for it."

"Some test."

"Some order."

"What?"

Chapter Five

The man shook his head. "You're obviously better off than any woman in here, so asking for that only singled you out."

"Who's interested?"

"Everyone." Now his tone sounded amused, as if he could barely keep from laughing. "You know where you are, don't you?"

"Mela."

"Half-true."

He finally leaned into the sunlight to reveal a dark complexion, a skin tone that must've hailed from the Savage Land or farther south. His olive-colored skin contrasted with his black beard and hair, both of which were streaked with red. Dark brown eyes, as eager as the barkeep's, yet more appraising and calculating; eyes that missed nothing. A faded brown hat with a low cap and a wide brim accompanied the riding coat and clothes he wore, which were colored by the same browns of desert travel.

"You're in Senkha's territory," the man said.

Senkha must've been the leader of this cartel. Sharla swallowed and considered. "I suppose you're Senkha?"

The man leaned into the shadows, assuming what was apparently a comfortable position. "No. But I know him."

"You're part of his cartel."

"No. But I respect him."

"You enjoy his empire?"

"I enjoy that he keeps Watchmen out of Mela. Or rather, that he scared them out and killed those who wouldn't leave."

It was basically what Sharla guessed had happened. She fingered her mug and pondered how to proceed. "Why don't you like Watchmen?"

"You like Watchmen?"

"No."

"Why not?"

She hesitated again, and then asked herself why she bothered. The truth would come sooner or later. It was the whole reason she'd ridden here, and this fellow seemed as good a candidate as any with whom to start headhunting.

"Because I'm from Opek, and we never see Watchmen. We didn't even see them when Claws rode in and destroyed half the village. Took our people."

"How long ago was this?"

"Two days."

"You rode straight here?"

"No." Sharla shifted in her seat. "I followed them."

"Why?"

"They…took someone."

A pause.

"And you were trying to get them back?" the man asked.

"Yes."

"And now?"

Sharla leaned forward. "I'm looking for help."

"To bring them back?"

"To kill the Claws and bring *everyone* back."

"Most would call that suicide."

"And you?"

After a time, the man drew himself into the light again. He folded his arms on the table and eyed her with that appraising look.

"You're looking for someone to help you track down the Claws and fight them, risking everyone's lives for the sake of the person you lost?" he asked.

"He's worth it to me."

The man stared at her for another moment. Said nothing. Sharla felt her heartbeat through the mug, through the seat, throbbing until she felt certain everyone could see her mounting indecision, her desperation.

"How long have you known him?" the man finally asked.

"Long enough." Sharla frowned. "What's it to you?"

"You were the one who said something."

"Because you asked."

"I didn't ask about him."

"You asked why I wanted him."

Chapter Five

The man thought for a moment. Looked to the common room as if he'd lost interest with her. "I suppose I did."

"Will you help me or not?"

The briefest smile touched his face. "What, you're headhunting? Came here to look for a few toughs to follow you into battle?"

"Yes."

"Are you looking for help or are you *hiring* help?"

"You're asking because of the gold piece?"

He shook his head. "Lady, you walked into a trap. Luther, the barkeep and owner of this fine establishment, tested you and found you wanting. You're not who you pretend to be. Not when you hand out gold like it's copper. I'm guessing you have more on you."

He leaned toward her with an intensity that made her flinch. "I could call my friends and we'd beat the coin from you. Take it from your horse. Leave you with the rest of the whores and let Mela have its fill of you."

Her grin felt sickly now, and she felt sweat trickle down her neck. "You don't have friends."

"You calling me a liar?"

Sharla swallowed. She was bluffing now, and she'd never played this sort of game. "If you had friends, they would sit with us."

"We're not the sort who hug."

"You stab instead?"

"We watch strangers."

Sharla felt her stomach plummet, and she remembered all the men who'd watched her outside. "Those aren't your friends. They're Senkha's."

"Are they?" The man leaned back and began picking his fingernails. "A history lesson then, seeing as you're apparently new to both Mela and Low Country."

"I don't have time for this."

"You have all the time in the world." He locked gazes with her again. "Because if you leave without my permission, my men will gut you at the door."

Coldness crept through her stomach and built up her spine, which felt like an icicle that spiked her to the chair. "You don't have any men."

"Try to leave and find out."

"But Senkha…"

"Yes. Senkha." The man leaned forward, clasped his hands together. "One of the infamous twins, the brother of Senit, who runs a drug cartel on Low Country's western front. You know what Low Country was, before the cartels?"

"A hellhole."

"Precisely. You know who changed it?"

"Senkha?"

"Someone who calls himself Kine Tarroful."

Sharla frowned and sipped more ale. "I've heard of him."

"He had the idea to stop the violence, the raids from the Savage Land, the fights along the border. But not by stopping the drug trade. He'd enforce it instead, and he'd order the rest of his Watchmen to do the same." The man shook his head. "Mind you, he's no captain or anything. He commands a single regiment, but it's the only one the Owl sent down here. Apparently, the Owl doesn't care for its own people, and Kine took the hint. He arranged for the Watchmen to enforce the drug trade, to allow crime, to form cartels. Cartels that keep truces with each other, that govern their territories, police the drug trade, punish those who resist, and enforce Low Country's borders better than the Owl cared to. Sounds like a good idea, right?"

"Sure."

The man snorted. "Maybe. In truth, Kine overstepped. Created a viper's nest. Because now the borders aren't just enforced: they're stuck in permanent war. Keeping peace by holding daggers to each other's throats? That doesn't sound stable."

"You're a philosopher?"

"I read the times. I understand that Watchmen and cartels have never held peace; they've kept each other at bay. They're rabid dogs, and no one knows who holds the leashes. Kine thinks he does, but everyone's afraid to find out, to risk starting a war. Senkha was foolish enough to

Chapter Five

drive the Watchmen from Mela, and when he did, it left a house of cards waiting to fall."

Sharla shifted on her seat. "Seems like a bold statement."

"Boldness only looks like boldness to people afraid to take a risk." The man hesitated. "I'm one of those toughs you described. I took a risk, and now Mela is mine even though Senkha thinks it's his."

Sharla stared at him, certain everyone in the inn must've heard him speak. "You're insane."

"No. My name's Arlon. Pleased to meet you."

He offered a hand for her to shake, and she stared at it.

"No?" He drew back. "Some would consider that offensive."

"Are you trying to get us killed?"

"No, *you* are. You're trying to hire people to hunt Claws. Then you asked me to prove I was tough. I did."

"You expect me to take you at your word?"

"No, I can do better." He waved his hand at someone across the room, beckoning them over. "I can start a revolution. Kill some of Senkha's men and encourage the rest to take over."

"I don't want to hire you."

He grinned again, a full grin with all his teeth. "Too late. I've seen your face, lady. I know who you are. I also know you're chasing love. I know you feel the ache of loss. I know it keeps you awake at night, that it never lets you settle, that you toss and turn with the knowledge that he's out there, waiting for you." He inclined his head, eyed her with a significant gaze. "Or at least…I know you tell yourself this. Sound familiar?"

"Go to hell."

"Let's both go. Sound fun?"

Sharla stiffened as a heavyset man approached the table. He possessed the same broadness as Luther, but with several additional feet of height.

"Arlon?" the man asked in a low, gravelly voice that contrasted with Arlon's smooth one.

"Jyrak. Round up the rest of the crew." Arlon gestured to Sharla. "This young lady has hired us for a job."

"A job." Jyrak eyed her. Brown hair and a grizzled beard carpeted a face of strong cheekbones, a hard jawline, and weathered skin. "She got the coin?"

"Plenty of it." Arlon eyed her. "And she wants to make a daring escape."

"'Daring?'"

"I didn't—" Sharla began, but Arlon interrupted her.

"What's your name? You never said."

She scowled at him. "Sharla."

"Sharla." Arlon nodded. "It's a pretty name."

"I'm leaving."

"All in good time, my dear." Arlon turned to Jyrak, raised his eyebrow. "Things are about to get exciting. Keep your hands ready."

"His what?" Sharla asked.

Jyrak seemed to understand. He nodded, held Arlon's gaze for a moment, and moved toward the exit. Arlon stood and stretched.

"What are you doing?" Sharla demanded.

"Giving it a minute."

Sharla decided they'd concluded their conversation. She pushed her mug aside and stood.

"I'd wait," Arlon said.

"I'm not doing anything for you."

"So rude. You asked for my services, but I suppose you younger ladies all think you're owed something with flash and sparkle. As though everyone's a mage offering you the time of your lives. This isn't flash or sparkle…but it might be the time of your life."

Arlon reached into his coat, withdrew a loaded miniature crossbow, and shot Luther in the face.

Chapter Six

LUTHER ROCKED AGAINST THE GLASSWARE BEHIND HIM, knocking bottles to the floor and spraying himself with alcohol. For a moment, he stared at Arlon past the bolt between his eyes, as though stunned at the man's rudeness. Then, he toppled across the bar, dead.

Deafening silence, as though a gust of wind had swept the common room and hushed every conversation. Sharla's breath squeezed in her throat, and she stared at Arlon in shock. He met her gaze and grinned.

Chaos erupted everywhere. Shouts, screams, chairs toppling and glassware falling. Bodies scrambling in every direction, a mindless current that buffeted Sharla and pressed her against the table.

"This side, if you please." Arlon beckoned her with the crossbow.

She felt herself moving around the table as though suffused in molasses.

"Ashes and demons, don't forget that." He waved the crossbow at her bottle.

She stared at him, and when she saw he wasn't joking, grabbed the bottle and hurled it at him. He caught it, had the audacity to nod a thanks to her, and set it on the windowsill behind him. He tucked the crossbow into his coat, gripped the tabletop, and heaved upward, crashing it onto its side even as Sharla flinched from the unmistakable thwacking of loosed crossbows. Bolts shuddered against the other side of the table. She sank against the wall, fumbling for her own crossbow, and then decided to grab her battleaxes instead.

"How do we know which ones are Senkha's?" she asked.

"Whichever ones are trying to kill us."

It was near impossible to hear anything over the din. Raucous voices and yelling, some of it slurred and drunken. Footsteps padded closer to the table, several bodies that hurried to meet the two. Arlon took a long draught from the bottle, sighed in appreciation, and rounded the makeshift barrier. He met the first man with a bottle to the face, smashing glass and spraying fragments across the countertop. The man staggered as Arlon reached with his other hand to draw a stiletto blade from a sheath under his coat. He ducked a swinging axe and thrust the blade through the man's ribcage, continuing forward as the body toppled sideways. Three more men bowled him into the bar, and they wrestled over the wood.

Sharla stepped forward and raised her own axes. The men hadn't been watching her, and she caught the first in the back of the head, spraying blood across Arlon's face. He grimaced, and the other men yelped in alarm.

"Sorry," she said.

A roar as men from beside her recognized the new assailant. Two came at her, steel flashing through shafts of sunlight, and she scrambled to escape. Rolled over the bar and across Luther's corpse. She clawed at the shelves to pull herself upright. Everywhere was broken glass slicked with blood.

Steel flashed and she jerked away, colliding with the shelves. Men clambered onto the bar, reaching for her, and she gashed one arm, leaving herself exposed for the man to grab her coat with his other hand. She dropped her axes, twisted from her coat, and shrugged it off in time to see the next blade swiping at her chest. Yanking her coat to intercept, she caught the blade in the garment and wrenched it sideways to twist the second man forward, close enough for…a punch? She tried it, an experimental sock to the face. Too high; she crunched his nose, jammed her wrist, and sent him shrieking backward.

Blood spurted as he toppled from the bar and she cursed herself, shaking her wrist and unfolding her coat. She examined the rent

Chapter Six

garment, staring through the hole in time to spot the first man picking up her lost axe. She moved close, grabbed him by the hair, and dragged his face into the shattered glassware along the bar. She heard a ripping, tearing noise, and she pulled him through the debris until he stopped moving, sliding from her grasp in a motionless heap.

Arlon had shoved the remains of his bottle into a man's neck, kicking his legs from underneath him before grabbing a nearby stool and clubbing another man in the head. "You okay?" he called to her, grabbing his blade as more bodies shouldered through the mob.

"He ruined my coat."

"You can borrow mine."

"Not a chance!" she snapped, shrugging her old coat back on. "This was…"

Renn's. She blinked as she remembered. Yes. It was the coat Renn had lent her.

"Sharla!"

She ducked an incoming bottle and snatched her battleaxes as the glass exploded above her. She stood and saw Arlon defending himself against two other men while half the common room moved toward them.

"Senkha has a lot of men…"

"Can't leave through the front anymore," Arlon answered. He lunged and struck, sending both men backing away. "We go up."

He ran for the stairs without waiting for her to respond. She scrambled after him, hopping around bodies as best she could, slipping on the blood-slicked floor. The men stood several heads taller than her, and their extra height lent them a longer stride. They rushed alongside her to the stairs, overtaking her to cut off her escape.

"Arlon!"

She turned to see other men hurdling the bar behind them, running for her. She whirled at a snarling, growling noise: Arlon leaped back toward the men with a flashing blade and a dark expression. His hat had fallen somewhere and left his hair to fly free. Blood splattered it and turned it redder, matting it over his face as he downed one man and dismembered the other.

She hurried up the stairs. His footsteps thumped alongside hers; roaring announced the men behind him. They pounded to the inn's second floor, running past bedrooms. One door opened in their face; Arlon pushed it from their way and knocked the room's occupant flat. They charged toward the window at the far end, a beckoning square of sunlight that glowed through the corridor. The shouts from behind them echoed through the enclosed space, a combined howl that rattled Sharla's bones.

Arlon hurtled into the window, smashed through it in a spray of glass. He hit the rooftop and rolled, scrambling to catch himself before falling over the edge. Sharla held her breath as she joined him. Wind whipped across the building, blew her hair over her face, and disrupted her balance. She crouched low and followed Arlon along the eaves. They circled the building as men spilled out behind them, crowding the space like termites. She spared a glance behind to see them too close for comfort, several raising crossbows. She threw herself forward and tackled Arlon as bolts hissed over them, whistling in her ears and thumping against shingles. She rolled with Arlon toward the far end of the roof, where they almost toppled into the street.

"My thanks." He stood and offered his hand. She accepted it and rose with him, briefly assessing herself to note she'd lost an axe. She turned to see it tumbling over the edge, where more men reloaded their crossbows.

"Ashes and demons," she muttered. "This is insane."

"You really like that word."

"What else do you call this?" she answered, following him to the other side of the inn.

"Exciting."

He jumped from the roof to land on the stables below them, a height of several feet. Sharla paused and considered. Not terrible, given they were only jumping from the second floor.

He looked up and frowned. "Now wait a moment—"

Chapter Six

When she landed, their combined weight took them through the roof and onto the straw-covered floor in a rush of boards, splinters, and dust. A confusion of shrieking horses and thrashing bodies greeted them. The spooked animals bucked, reared, and kicked at their stall doors.

Sharla groaned, rolling over to find Arlon already upright, offering another hand to pull her up. How did he recover so fast?

"It would've been better to wait," he said with a grin.

"You jumped off a rooftop," she hissed, ignoring his hand and standing. "Don't lecture me on the details."

"Well." He looked through the hole to the men on the roof. "Looks like you helped us after all."

She followed his gaze to see the men weren't willing to jump after them—not when Sharla had torn a hole through the stables and created a longer fall. Instead, they shouted at each other, turned, and clamored for the window they'd emerged from. The rest had cocked their crossbows and raised the weapons. Sharla and Arlon dove apart from each other as more bolts thumped around them. Sharla landed near Nun and jumped upright to place a hand on her nose and speak to her.

"You good on a horse?" Arlon called from the far side of the stables.

"How else would I have gotten here?" she snapped, untying Nun and hauling herself onto her.

She turned to see Arlon emerging from the stables on a mustang, sleek and black, as beautifully dark as the man's hair and eyes. Arlon and beast combined in an impressive spectacle, a shadow that rolled through the stables in an unstoppable tide.

"Riding isn't the same as escaping," he said over his shoulder. He moved to the door and examined the street. "We're preparing to escape a town."

"And the rest of your crew?"

"They'll be near the water tower." He jerked his head and kicked his horse into the street. "This way."

She followed him and squinted against the sudden colors and light. Shouting drew her attention to the inn, where bodies crashed into the street from every direction. Some ran away, while others pressed toward her and Arlon. Several raised crossbows, and she kicked Nun after Arlon, ducking low as wind whipped her face. The panic from the inn spread through the street around them: townsfolk turned and ran, ducking into alleyways or tumbling through doors. Rocking chairs toppled and people stumbled from their porches, leaving the addicts in a disoriented heap. A dog yelped and pranced away. Children shouted and pointed.

Everyone was running, moving. Sharla kept her eyes on Arlon, her sole foundation, the only sensible figure in the chaos. He turned into a side street, crossing toward the water tower that bulged over the surroundings like a runny egg yolk. It looked to be a leaning, pitiful thing, undoubtedly erected by the same fools who'd policed Mela ever since the Watchmen left.

She followed Arlon through an alleyway that pressed uncomfortably close to Nun's flanks. She bit her lip and hunched lower, anchoring herself to the sight of Arlon's horse and praying they'd exit unscathed. Crates crowded the far end; she urged Nun to jump them in a clumsy move that sent nearby children scampering and yelping. She emerged below the water tower in a town square with covered wagons and townsfolk who stared, hearing the distant chaos.

"Arlon!"

Sharla turned at the familiar voice: Jyrak rode his own horse alongside several others: a lean woman with black tresses that wound down her tanned neck, a slighter man with a shaved scalp and shifting eyes, and a darker man who stared at everything with a brooding gaze.

"Ancestors above," Jyrak muttered, frowning at Arlon. He looked past Arlon to Sharla, and then the alleyway beyond. "When you said 'daring,' I didn't think you meant 'idiotic.'"

"She wanted me to prove myself," Arlon explained.

"Not like this!" Sharla answered.

A roar drew their attention behind them, where a Claw ran the length of a porch beside the alleyway. A brawny man with dark, weathered skin that contrasted against the lighter pelt of a desert wolf draped over his shoulders, he instantly conjured memories of sandstorms, shadows, and ropes around Sharla's limbs. She stiffened. "A Claw!"

"Ovis," Arlon said. "He's with us."

Ovis roared as he swung a bone battle axe—one that appeared identical to those Sharla rode with—and he caught the first man from the alleyway in the chest. The man jerked and his momentum carried Ovis into the corner support of the porch. Ovis blinked, apparently disoriented and somehow maintaining possession of his axe while the man toppled from his saddle, collapsing across the crates that blocked the alleyway. His body prevented clear exit for the horses behind him and caused a spectacle: riders collided with each other and bowled horses over, thundering through crates and sending the contents flying. The stampede floundered on itself and spilled into the street, a mess of breaking bones, trampled bodies, and flailing limbs.

"A regular showman," Jyrak muttered from behind them. "Thinks he's the bard of this crew."

Other riders thundered from the other side of the building, and they rushed toward Arlon's crew. Jyrak swore and rode past Arlon and Sharla. "Fool doesn't even have his horse."

"With us, someone usually needs saving," Arlon explained to Sharla before he kicked his own horse forward.

She followed, uncertain what else to do. She pulled her crossbow out and cocked it, attempting to guide Nun with her knees. Riders galloped up the street while Jyrak rode toward Ovis, shouting all the while. Ovis blinked at his incoming rescuer, turned, and vaulted off the porch to collide with the first rider. They collapsed across the saddle and sent the horse rearing, kicking a second rider in the head. His hat fluttered above a spray of blood while his stray crossbow bolt struck another rider in the knee and sent him squealing.

"Blood and ashes," Sharla breathed.

"Don't expect any grace with this crew," Arlon said.

Indeed, Ovis fought like a wild animal, clawing at the rider with his free hand while swinging the bone axe at anyone who drew close. Jyrak reached his side and ducked behind an iron-bound shield, yelling at

Ovis while shrinking from crossbow bolts that rattled against the armament. Bodies crowded everywhere, a mindless tide to consume Arlon's crew.

"Jyrak!" Arlon shouted. "Your hands!"

Jyrak cursed—a phrase that apparently involved Arlon's mother—before he waved his free hand. A fireball exploded behind the riders on the street, a searing blaze of orange and red that sent men and horses shrieking, rendering them as flickering shadows and leaping shapes. It was as bright and spectacular as though the sun itself had landed in Mela, a bonfire that warmed Sharla's skin. She gaped and put her hand before her eyes, the crossbow slackening in her grasp.

"You have a mage," she muttered.

"A runemaster," Arlon said. "The best kind."

Jyrak's results would've led Sharla to agree: the entire wave of riders halted their attack, milling in confusion and terror, yelling to each other while others rolled on the ground, flapping at burning clothes. Horses and men screeched with seared skin, bubbled legs and faces. Sharla flinched and looked toward Ovis, who'd wrestled the other rider off his horse and claimed the mount. He rode to meet the crew with Jyrak, and the two made a formidable pair. They were both hardy men, but Ovis possessed a darker skin tone. His face was free of facial hair but heavily scarred, as though he shaved his face with his axes. He wore tribal paint in white streaks across his cheeks and nose. Bone claws pierced his earlobes, and his stare made Sharla flinch. Again, she saw the carnage at Opek, the howling sandstorm, the skulled figures.

"Ekonan," he said, eyes bright and intense.

Sharla realized he'd spoken to her, that he stared at the bone axes on her horse. She shook her head, met his stare and sought a proper explanation. "Um…I stole these."

He blinked and howled something in the Claw language.

"Not now," Jyrak answered, shaking his head at the Claw. He waved toward the west. "We have to get out of here."

"A daring escape," Arlon agreed. He turned and kicked his horse forward. Sharla followed, sparing a glance backward to see the riders

Chapter Six

renewing their charge, combining with the recovered mob from the alleyway to form a surge of bodies that stretched across the street. So many hardened, snarling faces sent Sharla's gut into somersaults. She swallowed and turned toward the rest of Arlon's crew, holding the crossbow as though it were an offering. What could a single crossbow do against the mob? What could *any* of them do against that army?

Well…

"Jyrak!" she shouted. "Can't you make another fireball?"

"Can't use it all at once," the mage shouted over his shoulder.

"He has limited stores of magic," Arlon explained. "All runeborn do. They're born with the magic in their blood; they cut themselves and write runebooks with it. They record a lifetime of magic in those books, and they stretch out their usage to ensure the books last."

Sharla gaped at the information. She'd never understood how mages did what they did—after all, there were only so many of them in Low Country—and the runeborn practices sounded barbaric. "But…you called him a runemaster?"

Arlon's answer was lost to shouting from ahead: another wave of riders approached from the other side of the street, crowding the west side of town. Arlon's crew circled on their mounts, hemmed in on both sides.

"Some escape!" Sharla snapped. "You shouldn't have pissed off Senkha's crew."

"He has more men than I realized," Arlon admitted.

"Of course he does! The entire south is his!"

Arlon kicked his horse northward, heading for an alleyway on the far side of the street, the only accessible exit. His crew surged after him, hurtling into the narrow space. Sharla heard a terrific groaning behind her and a screeching of splintering wood, before she risked a glance backward to see the water tower rupturing, toppling. A surge of water sprayed forward, crashing through the street in a geyser that churned dirt, dust, and sand into a muddy wash that engulfed the mob behind them. Jyrak rode at the crew's rear, slumping in his saddle and dropping an upraised hand. He'd apparently denied his own lecture to cast again.

"You okay?" Sharla asked.

Jyrak's eyes rolled to hers, and he nodded. She turned and followed the rest of the crew through the alleyway, found herself pressed behind the dark-skinned man. He rode close to the slighter man before him, hunched over his saddle, poised as though he'd ridden for a lifetime.

Sunlight flashed as they entered another street, turning to redouble their charge for the west side of town. No riders here yet, but chaos surged around the crew like flies to a corpse. Men, women, and children heard the shouts and screams behind Arlon's company and ran from their passage in every direction. Sudden, raucous voices drew Sharla's attention behind her: a few of the fastest riders were still hounding Jyrak. The exhausted wizard blinked, apparently struggling to retain focus, and the riders closed around him like nipping dogs.

Sharla shouted at him, allowed herself to slow and ride closer. She raised her crossbow—now loaded—and loosed it into a man's gaping mouth. He jerked back, jaw clamping like a bear trap, and toppled from the saddle. She tucked the crossbow away and drew one of the bone axes. She raised it and shrieked, spitting and allowing drool to string from her mouth. The remaining riders eyed her, flinched, and backed off. Jyrak blinked at them, locked gazes with her and frowned. She wiped spit from her mouth and shrugged.

"It was worth a try," she said.

He grunted. Behind him, the riders eyed each other and redoubled their charge. Sharla watched their approach and grimaced.

"You, uh…you certain you can't use more magic?"

"Didn't have enough water runes," he gasped.

"What?"

"No more water runes in the book. I didn't realize I was so low."

She turned and drew her steel battle axe this time. The leader drew closer, raised a crossbow, aimed it at such a range that to miss would require more skill than landing the shot—and feathers sprouted from his face. A long shaft—the length of an arrow—wove about as he jerked and toppled. Sharla turned to see the black-haired woman riding just ahead of her, guiding her horse with her knees exactly as Sharla had attempted

Chapter Six

to, pulling another arrow from a shoulder quiver and drawing it in smooth, graceful motion. Sharla watched the display, the ease with which the woman rode, and she felt herself frowning.

"That's disgusting," she muttered.

"It's not fair," Jyrak agreed.

The woman loosed another arrow to strike the bandit on Jyrak's other side. It caught him in the neck and punched through to hang sideways as blood sprayed and he gurgled for breath. He twisted from the saddle with flailing legs, as though he were trying to climb heavenward. Then, he disappeared alongside the rest, who were now close enough for Sharla to swing her axe.

The man parried with some kind of blade—a scimitar?—before retaliating with another swipe. Sharla barely ducked it, felt the weapon's passage over her neck before she jerked upright and swung again. They traded blows while bouncing atop their horses, a ridiculous balance between death and life while other riders fell to the woman's arrows. A chop at Sharla's leg caused her to jerk, to bat his blade away in a desperate cut that sent her reeling, windmilling her arm for balance and tugging Nun's reins sideways. Nun scrambled, toppling toward the rider to bounce against his horse.

She fell into the man's embrace, every sweaty inch of him, and found his breath clouding her face, his spit blinding her eyes. She yelped and chopped—too close to miss—underneath the reach of his blade, ripping through flesh. Blood washed down the weapon, across her arm, into her face. It filled her mouth until everything tasted coppery, until the world reddened. She struggled to push off, to reorient herself atop Nun, flailing and chopping until his weight sagged across hers and nearly pushed them into the street.

Then, his weight shifted, rolled, and he fell behind her. Jyrak offered his hand, pulling her upright, and they rode beside each other, refocusing their attention on the rest of the crew. The woman rode just ahead of them, eyeing the bloody spectacle Sharla had become.

Sharla frowned at her, uncertain what else to do. The woman held the same, appraising gaze that Arlon had rewarded Sharla with, and after a moment, she shrugged and turned back to the road.

"I suppose Keryn approves of you now," Jyrak said.

"Fantastic," Sharla muttered. "I wanted nothing else."

They exited Mela, riding for the tablelands, galloping through sagebrush and around pinyon pine until they entered the flat between Low Country's southern mesas. Sharla risked a glance backward to see Senkha's men had grown. A dark horde followed Arlon's crew, growing larger as they raced westward.

"You have a plan?" she shouted to Arlon, who rode at the head of the group. He apparently didn't hear her, or perhaps he just ignored her.

"This might be the first time he hasn't had a plan," Jyrak muttered.

"That's encouraging," Sharla answered.

"I think it might be. For him at least."

"You lot make no sense."

"You just haven't warmed up to us yet."

"Don't count on it."

They galloped across Low Country's wilderness, and the rest of Arlon's crew were silent all the while. Keryn's expression appeared locked in a permanent sneer. Ovis grinned like a madman, while Jyrak wore a grimace.

Of course, looking at Jyrak brought Sharla's attention to the other riders. They were like a black wave that swallowed the desert, inching closer to Arlon's crew. Close enough for the first crossbow bolts, for Sharla's answering bolt, and Keryn's steady arrows. Tiny armaments tossed across the desert like toys, the initial scrapping before the horde grew close enough to consume Arlon's company. Sharla cocked her crossbow, watching an enemy bolt hiss past her head as though it were thrown in slow motion. The riders were close enough to see all over again, to examine every line of their weathered, sneering faces. They possessed broken, gaping teeth yellowed by pipe smoke and lank, greasy hair that streamed in the wind.

Chapter Six

She muttered a prayer to the ancestors and looked to Jyrak for support, for any sign that he held another spell up his sleeve. But he looked past her, his eyes widening.

"Oh," he said. "That's new."

She turned to see another herd—but not cows. These were larger, with bulbous profiles that towered higher than cows, a browner color, and larger, furrier snouts. Sharla gaped.

"Bison," she muttered. "There actually *are* bison in the south."

Arlon rode for the herd. Jyrak drew himself upright and frowned, brow furrowing as he concentrated.

Sharla felt a shift in the air, a prickling of goosebumps across her skin as an unseen element moved. A sheet of blue-white flame erupted before the herd in a roaring curtain, a shimmering blaze that sent them reeling, turning, galloping. Jyrak had perfectly timed his casting with Arlon's approach—they'd apparently done similar maneuvers before— and the bison herd galloped straight for the crew.

Sharla watched as they thundered directly behind her and Jyrak to crash into the bandits. Some of the largest, heaviest animals known to Freytilians, the bison bowled horses over as though they were toys and flipped mounts and riders into the fray. The bandits were swallowed by this newer, broader wave, trampled in the carnage, and purged from the desert. Only a few bison toppled alongside while the rest of the mass surged onward, relentless and unstoppable.

A few riders still followed, those who'd ridden at the rear. They stared at the disaster ahead of them and considered. Then, they turned and rode for Mela, fleeing the wilderness to return to civilization and safety.

Sharla watched them go, alternating her gaze between the riders and the departing bison, awesomely large and majestic, stampeding toward the new territories they'd been driven to.

"Ancestors above," she said. "I can't believe I'm seeing *bison*."

"Aye." Despite his obvious exhaustion, Jyrak managed a tiny grin. "And now the Poached Bison might poach a few."

"Luther's dead. Who runs the inn now?"

"Oh." Jyrak frowned and turned west. "Not sure. That would make the poaching more difficult." He thought for a moment. "You killed him?"

"No. Arlon did."

Jyrak blinked. "I guess that explains our hasty exit."

"It does?"

"Luther was one of Senkha's top informants. Knew everything there was to know in Mela, heard all the gossip."

"Ah." Sharla frowned. "It doesn't seem like Senkha has many men left."

"Basically none." Jyrak exhaled. "I'm afraid Arlon may've started a war. At the very least, Mela will probably fall apart. A new cartel will pass through, sort things out. The cycle continues."

"Nothing new there," Sharla said. "After all, it's Low Country's legacy."

Chapter Seven

Arlon slowed the group's pace after the last bandits departed. Nun shuddered between Sharla's legs, heaving for breath. She'd already pushed Nun hard the prior several days, and the horse had barely enjoyed a respite before Arlon decided to antagonize an entire town. The rest of the crew's horses appeared to be in similar shape, and all of them floundered as the day crept on.

Even so, it wasn't until the sun sank over the far tablelands, streaking the surrounding mesas in shades of blood red and burning orange, before Arlon stopped his horse alongside a butte—this one shaped like a tower, as though it were part of the remains of a collapsed fortress. Angular spires jutted from its top to claw heavenward, columns of rock that appeared ready to collapse at any moment. Sharla stared at their heights and swallowed as a sudden rush of vertigo nearly toppled her from the saddle.

When was the last time she'd eaten, the last time she'd drank?

She barely managed to dismount before she slumped, catching herself with the reins and yanking Nun. "Sorry," she muttered, patting Nun's nose. "Sorry girl."

"You okay?" Jyrak asked from beside her. She turned to watch him dismount; he barely looked steadier than she.

"I've been riding for days," she explained. "Only stayed in Mela long enough for a drink."

"A drink and a conversation with our man, Arlon." Keryn spat the words and stomped toward Arlon. The woman had left her bow with her horse, which she'd tied to a desert juniper near the butte, but Sharla saw the flash of blades at her belt. She watched Keryn approach Arlon, worried the woman meant violence. Then she wondered why she bothered. She owed Arlon nothing. The man had nearly killed all of them.

Keryn planted herself before Arlon and put her hands on her hips. "What was that?" she demanded. "What happened back there?"

"I proved our services to the lady, Sharla."

"Sharla." Keryn followed his gaze to Sharla while the rest of Arlon's crew watched, silent. "You wanted to impress her?"

"We needed to prove ourselves," Arlon repeated. "She hired us for a job."

All eyes turned to Sharla. She forced herself not to cower from their gazes, holding Nun's reins with a white-knuckled grip as though it were a lifeline to keep her steady.

No one spoke. Ovis grinned, the slight man frowned, and the dark man pursed his lips.

Finally, the dark man spat, frowned at her. "You have the coin?"

"I do."

"Prove it," Ovis said.

Sharla hesitated, already knowing she didn't have enough to convince them of her trustworthiness. She might've ridden to Mela with the intent to hire a crew, but she hadn't expected to find so many people so fast. But now, with everyone watching, there was no backing out. She reached into her coat, drew a gold piece, and held it high enough for the dying sunlight to burnish its surface. It glowed like something molten, catching the crews' gazes,

"Is that it?" Keryn finally asked.

Sharla frowned, pocketing the coin. "I have more."

"Where?"

"Behind us."

"East?"

Chapter Seven

Sharla nodded. "Past Mela."

Keryn and the darker man spat. Ovis frowned. Jyrak sighed as though overwhelmed by the futility of it all, unpacked a bedroll from his horse, and laid it on the desert sand. Arlon blinked as if he was confused.

"You knew this?" Keryn asked him.

"We didn't cover the details, no."

"Only enough of them for you to dive head over heels for her. Was it her pretty eyes? Her glowing hair?"

Arlon scowled at Keryn. "She needed help."

"Help from our crew?" Keryn snorted and glared at Sharla. "Help with what?"

Despite herself, Sharla found her gaze wandering to Ovis. "I need to hunt Claws. Skulled ones."

Jyrak coughed. Keryn's eyes widened.

Ovis blinked, leaned backward. "Ekonan," he said, his eyes drifting to the bone axes on Nun.

"I'm out." The slight man shook his head. "I'm not here to chase Claws."

"Don't figure that's what we're about," Jyrak agreed.

Keryn shook her head, a ponderous, slow motion. She stared at Sharla like she was a disgusting, pathetic creature they'd found on the roadside.

"What *are* we about?" Arlon asked.

That stilled everyone, allowing silence to reclaim the desert.

"We're not about hunting Claws," the slighter man answered.

"Why not?" Arlon asked. "We've done everything else. We've ruled the south, owned Low Country. We've held Mela and influenced Laken. We've even owned parts of the east, anywhere Senkha was afraid to mess with. We've done everything there is to do: robbing, assassination, tracking. It was a good run."

"A *great* run," the slight man said, turning to glare at Arlon. "There was nobody else. Not even Senkha. Why change that?" He balled his hands into fists. "Why did you start everything over? You blew our cover, everything we've built toward. For what?" He thrust his shaking finger at Sharla. "For her?"

"An Ekonan," Ovis said.

"Stop saying that," Sharla said. "I don't know what it means."

"It's old tribal speak," Keryn said. She sounded tired, as though she'd recognized how exhausted she was. She moved from Arlon to stand by her horse, unpacking her own bedroll. It seemed she'd resigned herself to their fate. "Roughly translated, I guess it means *desert person*." Keryn locked gazes with Sharla. "He thinks you're a Claw."

"I'm not—" Sharla turned to the bone axes. "Just because I have these?"

"You got bored?" the slight man asked Arlon. "You decided you'd had enough of Low Country and you wanted to get even with Claws?"

"Senkha's regime was falling," Arlon said. "Dying. Only a matter of time before we had to leave."

"You don't know that."

Arlon locked gazes with the man. "I know it."

"Ambition," the dark-skinned man said, looking southward. "It makes a man restless."

"I'm not ambitious for the Savage Land." Arlon shook his head. "I want to help her get her people back."

"Her what?"

"Her people." Arlon nodded to Sharla, as though encouraging her to explain more. "She's from Opek. The Claws raided Opek, took a bunch of their people, and she's trying to get them back."

Keryn's gaze turned from Arlon to Sharla, as though the topic reignited her interest. "Opek," she said slowly. "No cartel rules Opek."

"No," Arlon agreed.

"So why bother?"

"Claws travel north, ride that deep into Low Country, right under our noses, and you don't bother with that?"

"No," Keryn hissed. "That's tribal war, not another cartel or a couple Watchmen. That's what Low Country left behind. Wars that Senkha and Senit and all the rest wanted to get rid of."

Chapter Seven

"You know it doesn't stop there," Arlon said. "This is only the beginning."

"It doesn't matter! It's not our fight. That's for the Owl to handle."

"You think the Owl will?"

"It's the Owl's sovereign territory!"

"Not the Owl's." All eyes turned to Ovis, who shook his head. "Not the Owl's," the Claw repeated. "It belongs to tribes. Given to them before small men came. Given to *us*."

"Oh, so you're a tribesman again." Keryn snorted at him. "You switch between the two pretty easily, don't you?"

Ovis leaped to his feet. Sharla blinked; she'd barely seen him move, nor had she seen him draw his bone axes. "Always a tribesman," he growled. "Always."

The slighter and darker men shifted from the confrontation while Jyrak shook his head. "Girls, please settle down," he muttered.

Ovis bared his teeth, pointed a battle axe at Keryn. "She's a girl." His gaze drifted to Sharla. "Claw. You call me that?"

Sharla shook her head, uncertain what to say. "I don't—"

"It doesn't matter what she calls you," Keryn said. "It doesn't matter what you call yourself. It matters that we're talking about fighting Claws, and we can't do that."

"The Owl will respond to invasion," Arlon said. "But it won't be until after Low Country's raided or destroyed. How many lives are lost before that happens?"

"What's it to you?" Keryn asked. "Regimes change. Cartels die, others form. We make money the same as before."

Arlon held her gaze for a long moment. "I reckon I've made enough money off burning, looting, and killing. I thought we could try something else. Something that might honor us in the Owl's eyes, maybe get us land or titles."

"Land. Titles." Ovis snickered, pulling a flask from his coat and taking a long draught. "What the small men like."

"Not me." Arlon cast his gaze around the group. "But I thought it might encourage a few of you."

"Don't cast your sins on us, Arlon," Keryn said quietly. "Don't drag us all down."

Arlon flinched. His gaze turned to hers, slow and steady. "I wouldn't—"

"You *always* philosophize," Keryn said. "I warned you about it the first time we met. It's dangerous. Makes a man think too much. Makes him soft, and I warned you what would happen should things ever go south."

Her movement was subtle, but Sharla was a veteran, having witnessed countless hours of sparring and training. She saw Keryn's weight shift, her legs bend, her hand creep to knives at her belt. Combat position.

Arlon noticed the same thing. He stared at Keryn for a long moment, his face impassive. He finally blinked, as though wearied by the conversation, and drew his stiletto. "Let's get on with it, then."

Ovis stared at them. The slight and dark men backed away while Jyrak yawned. Sharla watched each member of the crew, incredulous when none of them raised a finger in response.

"That's impossible," she finally said.

Arlon and Keryn paused, turned to face her.

"What?" Arlon asked.

"It's impossible for you to have the influence you claim," Sharla said. "There's only six of you, and we saw how many of Senkha's men chased us. How could you accomplish so much?"

The slightest grin tugged Arlon's expression. "Senkha thought we were his. He thought he'd all the south bought and paid for. Never doubted our loyalty. He was a friend."

"And now?"

Arlon watched her a long moment—or rather, stared through Sharla, as though viewing something on a distant horizon. "Senkha's of a bygone era," he finally said. "He's paranoid and weak. He hasn't controlled the south in a long time." He blinked, refocused his gaze, and stared at Keryn as though he'd forgotten where he was. "He'll fall with the rest of the south."

Chapter Seven

"Because of what you did," Keryn hissed.

"Because of the Claws," Arlon answered.

"But you're six people," Sharla repeated.

"We worked in his ranks," Arlon said. "Informed him, but we also informed each other. We knew his empire wouldn't last forever. It couldn't. I told you before: Senkha's biggest mistake was driving the Watchmen out. It unbalanced the region, left him weaker. We simply found the cracks and widened them."

Arlon gestured to the dark-skinned man. "Hesher, the best tracker this side of the Savage Land." He pointed to the leaner, shorter man. "Nithan, the man you'll never see unless he wants you to. The Watchmen have posted bounties for at least five different people who are all him. He's a locksmith, wears a good costume, and can slip through a crowded room without anyone seeing him."

Sharla eyed the man in disbelief. "Magic?"

"I'm good at what I do," Nithan said. Not even arrogantly. A simple statement of confidence.

Sharla pursed her lips, uncertain.

"No, our mage is Jyrak, whom you've already met." Arlon gestured to the burly man beside Sharla. "A runemaster, one of the few in Low Country. He can give us an escape, an ambush, or simple intimidation."

"Among other things," Jyrak mumbled. He appeared to be drifting toward sleep, apparently drained by his former casting.

"Keryn," Arlon said, nodding to the woman who still held her knives. "Our archer. Assassin. Best there is with a bow, can hit someone from blocks away. The best in Low Country."

"All of you are the best, eh?" Sharla surveyed the crew. "The best at what you do?" Her gaze settled on Ovis. "And…you?"

"Ah." Arlon looked at the Claw and thought for a moment. "Honestly, I just thought a fighter would be helpful."

"The best," Ovis said with a grin.

"And you?" Sharla asked, locking gazes with Arlon.

Keryn snorted, fingered her knives.

"I brought us together," Arlon said. "The leader."

"Yes," Sharla said, watching Keryn. "Because everyone follows your orders."

"He talks nice," Keryn growled. "Thinks he has a silver tongue."

"I think a lot. Planned Senkha's downfall before it happened." Arlon met Keryn's stare. "Among other things."

"Yes, you plotted the takeover of Low Country," Keryn hissed. "It worked. Then you threw it all away. Wrecked everything we had. Now, you want to take over the Savage Land? Try the next biggest thing? It won't work."

"We're not taking anything over. We're just helping her get her people back."

"For money?"

"For money," Arlon agreed. "If that's what you want."

"She can't pay nearly enough for that." Keryn turned her sneer to Sharla, shook her head. "You can't fund a war."

Sharla hesitated, uncertain how many of her cards to play. Then again, when else would she reveal them? "Actually, I can."

Keryn's eyes narrowed. "Prove it."

"This isn't enough?" Sharla patted her coat, the purses within. Allowed them to hear the clinking gold before she patted a few saddlebags on her horse: still more gold.

Everyone watched her now, except for Jyrak, who appeared to be asleep. Ovis licked his lips. Nithan and Hesher frowned.

Keryn blinked in obvious surprise. "More than I expected," she admitted. "But enough for a war?"

"The rest is behind us," Sharla said.

"You've said that."

"Consider what I have as a down payment toward the rest. A down payment for your services with the promise of a full payment once we complete the job."

"The job," Keryn repeated. "Where we cross into the Savage Land, find your captured Opekians, fight off the Claws, and bring them back, all without somehow getting ourselves slaughtered?"

"Exactly."

Chapter Seven

"You need more gold." Keryn shook her head. "You need chests of gold."

"I have them. But would anything convince you?"

Keryn frowned, eyed Sharla up and down before she spoke again. "And how do you happen to have chests of gold?"

Sharla hesitated. Her situation would get even more precarious if everyone knew the truth of her past; the truth of the stakes they faced. Wanted by both Claws and Watchmen? Not a great combination. But then again, they'd have to know sooner or later, right?

No. Not now. She couldn't tell them everything, not yet.

"Would you believe I'm the daughter of a noblewoman in High Country, someone who ran away?" she asked.

Nithan raised his eyebrows. "You'd have to be the princess of Benania."

Sharla laughed before she could stop herself. "No. Here in Low Country, you have no idea what wealth truly is. The amount of gold in High Country would shock you."

"So shock me," Keryn said. She stepped toward Sharla with her hands on her knives. "Tell us the truth: you're either runaway nobility or a disgraced Watchman. Child out of wedlock, perhaps?"

Sharla tensed herself and drew her battle axe, lowered herself into a fighting stance. "I guess you'll have to take the job and find out."

Keryn sneered at her, opening her mouth to say something. Then she stopped, blinked, and eyed Sharla again, as though seeing her for the first time. She turned to Arlon and back to Sharla, considering.

"No need," she finally said. "I just wanted to call Arlon's bluff. See what he was really after."

Sharla frowned, looking to Arlon for an answer. Beyond him, the sun had finally set. The sky darkened with purple bruising, mottling shadows across the buttes and mesas as the moon rose. Its light shone across Arlon's face and glinted in his eyes to confuse their emotions.

"The chests," Keryn said. "I suppose you buried them in the desert?"

"I did."

Keryn watched her for a long moment. "Well, I suppose a pretty thing like yourself wouldn't risk lying about that, not after all the trouble you went through to hire us." She regarded the battle axe, the bone armaments tucked with Sharla's saddlebags. "And you're bold enough. Bold enough to gamble, but maybe also to tell the truth."

The woman exhaled, turning to glare at Arlon. "And seeing as I just watched our latest empire crumble to the ground…" She turned back to Sharla, regarding her with a serious expression. "I need to cash out of here and leave. Find someone who'll appreciate my skills instead of throwing them away."

She pursed her lips and inclined her head. "You say you have gold? I'll stay. But only for this job." She turned to glare at Arlon. "Then I'm gone. And this time, you'll never see me again."

Chapter Eight

THE GREAT CANYON OPENED THE HORIZON, A SIGHT THAT always shocked Kine. Carved by the Shapan River during the age of dragons, the massive canyon yawned over a mile deep and ten miles wide.

The closer one rode, the more history they saw—the land's past now exposed for everyone to see. Layers of sandstone, limestone, and shale burned various colors in the midday sun: reds, pinks, various browns, and several blacks were visible before the haze and distance muddled the rest with the unending desert. In the canyon's depths, the river's whitewater sparkled. Kine suspected there were countless alcoves and tributaries which never received sunlight, or if they did, only for an hour or two a day.

Then again, the place they headed to *never* saw sunlight.

Kine frowned and tore his gaze from the canyon. Always, he let himself ruin the moment.

"You're thinking again," Gashar observed.

"I wish I wouldn't." Kine exhaled, turned to the ranks behind him as though they could offer him comfort. "I've managed to stay away from here for almost a decade."

Gashar watched him for a long moment. "You did your best, Colonel. The Claws attacking...Opek raided...none of that's your fault."

The memories burned in Kine's head, so bright and fierce they churned his gut. Gashar was too young. He didn't know the truth. He didn't know how long the Claws had coexisted with Low Country's border, how long Kine and Dormun had been…friends. Just like the "friend" Kine prepared to visit, down among the canyon's cliffs.

Kine shook his head and forced a smile. "No," he lied. "You're right. It's not my fault."

"You'd do better by planning how you're going to answer the Claws."

"Retaliate." Kine waved his hand at the Watchmen.

"Would you ever attack Senit's stronghold?"

"Not sure." Kine turned and spurred his horse forward. "I've never needed to find out."

One might've thought it stupid for only himself and Gashar to proceed: the highest-ranking men of the present Watchmen, exposing themselves to the enemy. Then again, Kine knew bringing the rest of his forces would give the wrong impression. Senit probably *would* interpret it as an attack, and he'd respond in force. Kine knew he couldn't take Senit's stronghold, not unless he had several mages and some chance weather. No, the only way to meet with Senit was on his terms, in his territory.

If you want to use a snake, you have to find it. If you want to find a snake in the desert…I reckon you start stomping around.

Gashar had never been here, so Kine led the way. Neither mount was prepared for the descent: a narrow footrail that utilized switchbacks and sheer ledges to discourage anyone from entering. Kine had seen many of its kind along the canyon—presumably leftover from when Claws inhabited the region—but most of the trails all led to emptiness; nothing but a drop to the river. The key was in learning and remembering which trails led somewhere worthwhile, be it a spring, an oasis, a hunting retreat, or otherwise.

Of course, using *any* footrail would put a target on one's head for all Senit's men. Kine knew they were watching Gashar and himself, even now. Senit controlled Low Country's western border. He knew every path through the canyon. It was obviously his business to do so, for he

Chapter Eight

kept Laken and the surrounding settlements well-supplied with fairy ichor and gargev powder.

Still, when Kine originally made the truce with Senit, he hadn't expected the man to become so...secretive. Kine knew nothing of how the bandits communicated or sent aid to each other along the canyon's length. He only knew they had eyes and ears everywhere, and that Senit would already know Watchmen were on his doorstep. Kine prayed Senit would stay his hand until he learned who the Watchmen were, and that Kine Tarroful himself had ridden to see him.

But ten years was a long time. Things could've changed.

We've spoken since then, Kine told himself.

Yes, but you've never dropped by his house uninvited.

If "house" was how you could describe it. In truth, Senit had placed his headquarters in the old ruins of Claws. The tribe that left the ruins had been cliff dwellers, scattering their buildings through the canyon in pockets or folds in the canyon wall. Formed of dirt bricks fashioned with straw, mud, and plaster, these buildings always struck Kine as eerily silent, haunted by regret. They lay in shadow for much of the day, forgotten by the world and buried by time.

Senit's village was larger than most, complete with streets that cut through the canyon wall in switchbacks. To enter the village, one first had to squeeze through a cluster of desert junipers and maintain their footing through a slope of scree, where every step sent pebbles bouncing to the talus slop far, *far* below. That drop would've been enough to deter anyone else; only those with prior knowledge of Senit's village continued.

Especially when the path took riders across a bare stretch of rock with fins in the sandstone wall above, dark pockets that surely hid bandits. Kine glanced upward to test that hunch, was rewarded for his efforts when he caught a glimpse of cloth, pulled away and swallowed by darkness.

Gashar followed his gaze, and his throat bobbed as he swallowed. "We're being watched?"

"Ever since we started."

"They haven't shot us yet."

"Don't give them any ideas."

"No." Gashar craned his neck to look down the slope. "I'm just taking things slow. Enjoying the view."

"Don't get carried away or you'll upset your stomach."

"A bit late for that."

"Don't puke. I want to keep some dignity for Senit."

"Puking." A grin fluttered across Gashar's face; he *did* look green. "A pleasant thought."

"So many of them today. Oh look, we're here."

Kine ducked under an overhang of desert rock nettle and paused to take in the view. Senit had apparently moved a whole village into his ruins, for people walked the streets; not just bandits either, but women with baskets and wagons. Children scampered through alleyways or sat in the sun. Carved into the canyon wall, only a sliver of the village presently caught daylight while the rest enjoyed shade. It was mostly inhabited by adults, many of whom peered at the two Watchmen. Smoke drifted from buildings around them and hugged the underside of the village alcove with a pleasant aroma of cooking meat, warming bread, and tantalizing spices. The buildings were all crude, following the same square shapes and squat profiles, colored no differently than the other times Kine had been here—yet everything had changed with the addition of an ordinary populace. So drastic was the shift that Kine wondered whether he'd remembered the correct village.

"I think…" A glance behind him quenched any doubt: bandits stood behind Gashar. Silent and dressed in blackened rags, nothing was visible of their faces but for their eyes. Their bare arms and legs were muscled, tanned, and they walked lightly, assuming fighting stances.

"I think we're in the right place," Kine finished.

Gashar followed Kine's gaze, saw the bandits, and nearly fell from his saddle, fumbling for his sword.

"Don't," Kine warned.

Gashar stopped, turned to watch him.

Chapter Eight

"Don't give them any ideas, remember?" Kine tried a smile but felt that it probably looked more like a grimace. He didn't like these odds at all.

After a moment, Gashar nodded. Kine turned and moved into the village, following the route by memory. The buildings rose around them, stretching up the canyon face. There must've been at least five or six different levels, impressive when viewed all at once. Ride closer and you realized how simple the dwellings were: most only possessed a single room. The windows allowed glimpses of simple furnishings: straw beds, wooden shelving to hold clothes, tables formed by chunked sandstone. Some buildings contained families who eyed Kine with curious expressions, noting his Watchmen regalia with bewilderment. Could it be they'd never seen a Watchman before, or they simply didn't know what Watchmen were doing here?

Kine struggled to suppress the last thought as they approached Senit's residence. This didn't appear to have changed, because men moved forward as Kine approached. Senit had chosen a residence at the far side of the village, probably desiring a vantage point to see anyone who entered his stronghold. The view of the canyon certainly helped—the building almost sat on the precipice that dropped to the Shapan River—but Kine didn't figure Senit as someone who enjoyed many views. No, he simply wanted to watch his empire, everything he'd built...or stolen from the Claws, depending on who you asked.

The men said nothing, merely extended their hands and waited. Kine dismounted, giving away his reins. He unfastened his sword sheath and handed it over. He withdrew his crossbow, his knives, his shield. He briefly considered keeping the blade in his boot, but then decided if Senit's men patted him down, he didn't want to start things on the wrong foot with concealed weaponry. He pulled the knife from his ankle sheath and passed it over.

"Please take care of my horse," he murmured. "She's a good one."

The men stared at him, said nothing.

Kine waited for Gashar to finish. When no one moved, he took a cautious step forward. Another. The men shifted to allow him entrance, only pressing behind them when Gashar followed Kine's lead. They walked into a room as simple as the rest, hazed with pipe smoke that scratched Kine's nose. He coughed, rubbed his eyes, and when he drew his hand away, he beheld Senit at the far side of the room.

In the several years since he'd last seen the man, Senit had changed in all the same ways as Kine: grayer hair, deeper lines across the face. Brown eyes that pricked with an intense light—that hadn't changed. A smile as smooth and slow as a serpent coiling to strike—that hadn't changed, either. And when the man stood, as lean and dark-skinned as a desert fox, Kine paused, uncertain what to expect.

"Kine Tarroful." Senit's voice was rich and deep, like a good ale that numbs the heart and clouds the mind.

"Senit…Blackhair," Kine answered. It wasn't his last name, but Kine had never learned Senit's last name, and he figured "Blackhair" was something Senit made up. Even though most of his hair had grayed, Senit's smile grew at Kine's address.

"It's been a long time," Senit said. "Too long."

"Funny. I thought you might've said it hasn't been long enough."

"Truly?" Senit stepped forward, and Kine flinched despite himself. "Is that what you think?"

"Not sure yet. I suppose it depends on what happens next."

The men stared at each other. A trickle of sweat ran down Kine's neck, merged with a larger river at his spine.

Senit offered his hand, with nothing in it. "I greet you," Senit said. "As a man should."

Kine clasped his hand and shook it. A strong grip—another thing Senit hadn't lost. Though Kine possessed a wider, stockier frame, he'd never cared for the idea of wrestling with this man.

"As a man should," Kine repeated. "But not as a friend?"

"Would you like us to be friends?"

"I'd prefer it to the alternative."

"Need there be only one?" Senit finally released Kine and exhaled, drew the pipe from his mouth and waved it for emphasis. "That's the

Chapter Eight

thing about you, Kine. You're always thinking in black and white. Good or bad. Friends or enemies. Can't there be a middle ground?"

"Not sure that benefits us."

"Apparently. You have your land, pushed toward High Country and Keth. I have mine: the entire canyon, land that's enjoyed no Watchmen for years." Senit watched him for a long moment. "If there was a middle ground, it would've saved you the trouble of coming here."

Kine swallowed, attempting a grin. "We did good, didn't we?"

"We were the best," Senit said. "I've never had problems with you, Kine. We never fought over land or prices, stolen product, or injured men. No, that's only with my brother to the south, and thank the ancestors I don't deal with Marast at the east."

He considered Kine. Shook his head. "Your men shouldn't be here, Kine. I should have them all killed."

"What's stopping you?" Kine asked, genuinely wondering whether Senit was bluffing.

"This is the first time you've had the guts to speak with me, in my village, for...blood and ashes, has it been almost nine years?"

"Over a decade."

"A decade." Senit inhaled from his pipe, puffed a smoke ring to encompass Kine's head. "That's a long time, Kine."

"I didn't need to see you before."

"And now?"

"I need your help."

Silence filled the room. The moments slid past as heavily as dropping boulders, and the river of sweat reached Kine's legs.

Senit finally exhaled, returned to his seat behind the table. "I don't help you. You don't help me. We're past that, remember? The other cartels catch word of us riding together, we'll have another civil war."

"It's all of the cartels."

"I'm sorry?"

"I'm riding to all of the cartels. Things have made it...necessary."

Senit's face had gone smooth, calm, but his brown eyes caught the light and flared through the room like embers. "No."

"Senit—"

"Round us up just to have us killed, eh? We cut each other's throats while you ride away, king of Low Country."

"No—"

Senit turned to one of the men behind Kine, waving his hand at Gashar. "Kill him."

Before Kine could blink, two men had hauled Gashar across the room, pressed him over a stone bench with his head toward the floor. A third man drew Kine's blade, brought it over Gashar's head, and swung down.

"Wait," Senit said.

The man paused, raised his gaze to watch Senit. The blade hung over Gashar's neck, but to his credit, Gashar never made a sound. Nor, for that matter, did Kine, which appeared to interest Senit.

The man watched Kine with pursed lips. "Not even a word of protest."

Kine said nothing.

Senit stepped closer. "He means nothing to you?"

"Kill him, kill me. It doesn't matter. We've brought nothing to harm you; we already handed over our weapons. I left my men above the canyon. If we wanted to trick you or attack you, we wouldn't be having this conversation."

"Conversation." Senit turned and walked to the window to gaze across the canyon. "You're begging me, Kine."

"I figured it could happen."

"You knew it would happen." Senit shook his head. "Because nothing makes me draw a sword with you."

"The fate of Low Country should. Especially if you enjoy everything you have here."

Senit turned to Kine with a raised eyebrow. "Oh. The shock and horror."

"There are Claws, Senit. Many of them. They marched right past Marast and raided Opek, took captives with them after they raided the

Chapter Eight

town. They took them across the border and they're holding them somewhere."

"You know this?"

"I was told by a woman who'd ridden from there. She hadn't stopped for days."

"She's probably dead now."

"Probably."

"Just like everyone else who was taken from Opek."

Kine swallowed. "Probably."

"It doesn't concern me, Kine, nor should it concern you. Sometimes, the Claws get rowdy. We even see a few of them here."

Kine felt himself stiffening, hardening. A fire bloomed in his gut, a familiar rage that begged to spark as mightily as in Keth. "These weren't ordinary Claws."

"A Claw is never ordinary. They're bloodthirsty and heartless, like animals." Senit turned back to the canyon. "It's why we call them Claws."

"This one is called Dormun Redskull, and his raid is a declaration of war."

Senit tilted his head, considering. "Dormun Redskull. You knew him."

The conversation stoked Kine's anger, building it higher and higher. He could barely speak through its heat, could barely keep his concentration from the memories pressing his skull. "I did."

Senit turned to Kine. "He's the one you tried to make a truce with, isn't he? You tried to make peace with the Claws just like the cartels...but Claws don't think the same way, do they?"

"No."

Senit nodded, as though they'd agreed on the most important issue. Then, he turned back to the window. "I know where this goes, Kine. We ride into the Savage Land, cross borders we've held for decades, and it turns into a war that never stops."

"They started this war. They crossed our border right under Marast's nose, and they won't stop with Opek. Time to leave your hideout and open your eyes." The men around Kine shifted at his tone and his rising voice, but Kine found himself powerless to hold back. Indeed, he'd held himself back too long, and look where it had gotten Low Country: Dormun riding through as though he owned the land.

Senit turned to Kine, and Kine felt the men around him press closer. He forced himself to stand his ground, bitterly aware his only ally in the room lay across the table with a blade at his neck.

"You created this, Kine." Senit gestured with his pipe, wearing an empty smile. "You spoke with me, Senkha, Marast. You started the cartels, helped them claim their borders. You've made Low Country what it is…and you insult me for it?"

Kine stepped forward, heedless of the men shuffling around them, at the cold light in Senit's gaze. "You said I made Low Country what it is," Kine snarled. "You were right. Do you know why?"

"I think you'd like to tell me."

"Dormun," Kine snapped. "Dormun Redskull used to be friends with me. We made a truce, just like you said. We lived together on the border, back when Low Country's borders were softer, before we drove the Claws out. He talked with me like a friend while his men rode behind my back and cut down my people. He used my friendship and stabbed me in the back. He treated me like a fool for *years* before I understood what was happening."

Kine shook his head, furious now. "We lost good men and women, Senit. Entire villages like this one, towns that aren't on maps anymore. So much bloodshed, unanswered. It only continues if we don't stop Dormun."

"What made him stop the first time?"

Kine paused. Hesitated.

"What made him stop, Kine?"

"He killed my wife." The words left a void in Kine's chest, as though speaking them resurrected her and left him an ashen husk. At first mistaking this for emptiness, he soon felt the cold anger underneath, where it froze harder than the raging fire, more impervious than the black hatred. "His men killed my wife, and when I spoke to him again, I

Chapter Eight

gave an ultimatum: if he ever returned to Low Country, I would destroy his land and everything he knew. Kill his tribe. Wipe it from the map, like he did to Low Country.

"And then I created the cartels. Made truces, negotiated plots of land. All to hold Low Country together, to stop Dormun from ever repeating what he did."

Kine trailed into silence, uncertain what more to add. If Senit couldn't understand the stakes now, he never would.

The man watched Kine, his prior smile gone like smoke in the wind. He puffed his pipe and considered for a moment.

"My thanks for the history lesson, Kine," he finally said. "But I disagree with you."

"How?" Kine whispered.

"Claws can't take Low Country by themselves. Not when you have Senkha, Marast, and I to answer their raids. You're riding against Dormun for revenge, but you should have finished him rather than let him get away. You mistook your enemy for a friend, offered mercy when you should've given justice, and now you ask the rest of us to pay for your mistakes."

Senit shook his head, turned, and walked back to the window. "I won't ride for you, Kine. Not for revenge. Not for your regrets. Do things better this time, but do them yourself."

Was that really all it was? Did Kine ride for revenge? The thoughts tangled in his head, became nonsensical. All he knew was the cold anger, the ache for completion, fulfillment, restoration. Justice done, once and for all. His hands trembled from the need; he could barely stand straight for want of Dormun's head on a pike. All for his lost wife? For the good of Low Country?

Yes, he told himself. *For all that and more.* Senit was a fool not to see it, a fool to underestimate Dormun and the rest of his Claws.

"You can have Keth."

Senit turned to face Kine, brow furrowed. "Keth," he said. "You'd just…walk away?"

"Do this with me and your territory doubles." Kine shook his head. "It triples, because you'll command the border across the north, all the way to Opek. You'll have access to Dukatt and everything else."

Senit tilted his head, pursed his lips. "You won't walk away."

"I will."

"You *can't*. Low Country's in your blood."

"I'm a Watchman," Kine said. "Now, not even that. Not when king and country turn on me. And the country *is* turning." He exhaled, aware he'd progressed too far to avoid mentioning the insurrection. "A group of ranchers rebelled in Keth before I rode to meet you. It hasn't been the first time, and I know they've been speaking with your bandits. You probably didn't even know about it; hasn't been the first time ranchers looked for sympathizers. It seems your bandits promised aid before leaving the ranchers to die." Kine clenched his jaw. "Maybe Low Country doesn't want Watchmen anymore, doesn't need them. Maybe it's better to return everything to the way it was."

"You won't walk away."

Kine paused again. Would he? He didn't know. Couldn't tell, because visions of Dormun's face blotted everything, scrambled his conscious thought. All he knew was that Dormun needed to die, and by his hands.

"I'll sail for Kathagon once we finish. Ancestors above, what do you want me to say?"

Senit puffed his pipe, considered. He let Kine tremble for a moment more, clearly enjoying the power dynamic, before he finally nodded. "I reckon you've said enough. After we're done with the Claws…you'll walk away."

"I will."

"King and country, so easily thrown away."

"They already did it to me."

Senit grinned, looked at Gashar. "Think he agrees with you?"

Kine forced himself to look at Gashar, but the younger man made no eye contact. "He knew we operated on borrowed time."

"The Watchmen are dying," Senit said. "This make you sad, boy?"

Chapter Eight

Gashar said nothing, staring at the floor while sweat rolled down his face.

Kine watched Senit grin. "Let's just kill Dormun," he finally said. "We'll figure everything out on the road."

Chapter Nine

Sharla couldn't sleep. She didn't toss or turn, merely lying on the cold ground under the distant stars, the harsh moonlight, while snores rumbled around her.

She finally sat up, left her bedroll behind, and strode into the sagebrush. She glanced back to the rest of the crew and saw Keryn sitting beside her horse, keeping watch. The woman briefly looked her way before turning eastward.

Sharla turned and picked her way through the brush, around the butte's perimeter, uncertain where she walked, uncertain what she thought. Everything had numbed now, a reality that might've frustrated her if she'd been in her right mind. She had what she wanted, didn't she? A crew, assembled and ready to ride, freshly hired to do battle with Claws. They'd been easier to find than she thought they'd be, and everyone had agreed to travel with her. They had a wizard, an archer, a warrior, and many other skills between them. So why did she feel so empty?

"I wouldn't recommend walking much farther."

She halted at Arlon's voice and saw his shape in the shadows under the butte. She frowned at him and crept closer. "Why's that?"

"I saw a rattlesnake that way."

"You didn't kill it?"

"He didn't bother me."

Chapter Nine

Sharla moved beside him and caught a whiff of brandy, heard sloshing liquid. Longing gripped her; it urged her to return to her saddlebags and find her leftover ale. "Are you drunk?"

"Not enough."

"Not at all." He still spoke as smoothly as before, with no slurring. She sat beside him as he considered the bottle.

He downed the rest, finished with a sigh, licked his lips, and dropped the empty bottle beside them. Sharla stared at it, equal parts disappointed he hadn't offered her some and that she hadn't fetched the rest from her saddlebags. Now that she'd sat, it all seemed so far away.

"You still need more," she said.

"I do."

"I can get some."

"You have more?"

She hesitated. "Probably not enough."

"We'll have to find more in Laken."

"Lots more."

"And we'll find more friends?" he asked.

"Something like that."

He nodded and stared at the sinking moon, the shadows that crept over the tablelands like fingers that grasped for the butte. "Your man won't let you sleep, will he?"

"You have someone that won't let you sleep?"

"Many of them."

"Senkha one of them?"

Arlon fell quiet for so long she feared he might've fallen asleep. She turned to find him awake, apparently as sober as ever, staring at the horizon while the moonlight colored his eyes a cold silver. "He's always one of them," Arlon finally whispered.

"You two must've been close."

"The closest."

"And then he started...dying?"

"Weakening. He's grown paranoid. Holds an empire he's desperate to keep. Watches all his borders, distrusts all his men, fears Claws to the south and Senit and Marast and Kine and everyone else. Only a matter of time before he distrusted me, too. Hell, he probably already distrusted me."

Arlon shrugged. "I *was* taking over his empire. But I learned from the best. Find any opening, any weakness, and exploit it. Be merciless. Ruthless. Just like he was. Grab the whole world and crush it." He shook his head. "Look where it got us."

"It's easier to throw his town into chaos? Watch his empire burn?"

"Easier to remember him as he was. Leave before I watch him fall."

"Run away from it." Sharla nodded to herself, biting her lip. She knew a little something about that.

"I never thought of myself as a runner, but maybe I am." Arlon winced. "Maybe I'm just scared."

Sharla nodded again. She knew a little something about that, too.

Arlon shook his head and stood. "Ancestors above, I need brandy." He watched her for a moment. "You gonna share some?"

You didn't share any of yours. It's what she wanted to say, but instead, she found herself answering, "Take it. You look like you want it more than I do."

Arlon considered this for a moment. He walked past her and left her to shiver in the cool night, thinking of Renn, her longing, and her inability to sleep. Thinking of Arlon telling her that she probably only *thought* she loved Renn as badly as she did.

* * *

THEY SAW LAKEN BY MIDDAY, APPROACHING IT WITH cautious gazes both behind and ahead, always looking for more of Senkha's men. Beside them, the mesas crumbled into talus slopes— pitted, broken land that further deteriorated. It spilled from the mesa Laken inhabited to Tigon Land below. The canyons snuck through the landscape in cruel streaks, a maze that twisted in such confusion as to leave isolated fragments of rock in lone pillars, sentinels over the brooding darkness. Stretches of a few canyons were illuminated, revealing innocent patches of rock and sand, but the rest remained under shadow.

Chapter Nine

Sharla turned to Jyrak, who rode beside her. "Runemasters live in those canyons, don't they?"

He turned to her. "Some of us do."

"So the canyons aren't haunted?"

"There's magic there." He shrugged. "But no demons or ghosts, at least not that I've found."

"You runemasters live there because the Watchmen don't go there?"

"Us runemasters." He snorted and shook his head. "You're looking at the only one of us, to my knowledge."

Sharla frowned at him. "Only you?"

"Stories and legends help cover the truth, keep people away from the canyons for fear they'll run into a bunch of us." He swigged water from his canteen. "Runeborn mages are born with aether in their blood. It travels through generations, gifts certain bloodlines with magic. The Tower—the school for runeborn mages—tracks all that, records the genealogies in its library.

"What matters is runeborn mages are the ones who use the magic. They bleed themselves while others sustain their life until they finish writing their books with the library of runes they'll draw on for the rest of their lives. Runemasters are made when multiple runeborn come together, make a pact to combine magic. They bleed themselves together, mix their blood, use the combined blood to write runes. The resulting library is stronger than the individual runeborn would've been on their own."

Sharla frowned. "So...only one of you becomes a runemaster?"

"Only me."

"And the rest of your friends?"

"They're still down there."

"Down there?" Sharla turned to the canyons with a surge of nausea. "Why do they stay there?"

"Why do you make a runemaster?" Jyrak frowned at the horizon for a moment, contemplating. "To be Low Country's most fearsome mercenary. A mage for hire no one can match. Someone to reward with all the biggest jobs that offer the best coin. All the better to situate the rest of your family, to set everyone up for life."

He turned to Sharla. "I'm friends with this crew, but my true family is in those canyons. My bloodkin. Those who've agreed to share blood, to name me their runemaster. I get the coin for all of us, the coin to stash away until the jobs are done and we sail to Liadinia and enjoy our retirement."

"When does that happen?"

"After this, I reckon. Seems that we've basically just destroyed Low Country—or at least brought another war to it."

"You have enough coin to leave?"

"Depends on how much you're offering."

Sharla turned away, uncomfortable with the idea she already developed sentiment for members of a crew who might not live past the coming battle. "And…when you run out of runes?"

"What?"

"I'm assuming you eventually use all your runes." She turned back to him. "In Mela, you said you didn't realize you had so few water runes left. With how tired you were after…it all seemed related."

Jyrak grinned, but it appeared to be a sad, weary expression. "Every runeborn has a limited lifespan, it's true. A limited supply of runes, of magic, but when that magic runs out…it feels like we've died."

He grabbed his canteen and drank more water. "It's called *Snapping*. A mage snaps from their source of aether when they burn through their runes. When I drew on water runes, I didn't realize I used my reserves. I touched önin, the opposite of aether; the lack of life whereas aether is life's presence. And it was…awful." He shuddered, his gaze looking through the horizon to something worse. "A life in önin's grip is what every mage looks forward to in the end. Best to finish the job and leave Low Country before that happens."

"Oh." Sharla blinked and stared at Laken. "I'm sorry."

"For what?"

"For your Snapping."

Chapter Nine

"It's nothing to apologize for. It happens to all of us, even you. Those who don't wield magic still lose touch with aether, one day. Only the ancestors know when."

"And then we all enter önin? It's a lie what Lodians or Hytans or anyone else believes? There's no Earth King or anything like that? We just…pass into nothing?"

"Scholars in the Tower say they know the truth." Jyrak shrugged. "But from what I've heard of them, no one wants to talk to them anyway."

"They lie," Ovis grunted.

Sharla shuddered, turning to the man on her other side. Despite his immense bulk, the Claw always managed to sneak up on her.

Jyrak snorted. "For once, you and I might agree on something."

"The spirits," Ovis said. "We follow them to Third World when we die."

"And just like that, the agreement ends," Jyrak muttered.

"The Third World?" Sharla asked. "That's a Claw belief?"

"Small people don't understand."

"Small people? You keep saying that."

"All of you." Ovis nodded to her, pointed to the rest of the crew. "Small people."

"He's not very small," Sharla answered, pointing at Jyrak.

"A small man," Ovis insisted, shaking his head. "Not just the body, but the mind."

"Nobody's perfect," Jyrak answered.

"My people are right," Ovis declared. "The small men cursed themselves. They stay cursed until we have our land."

"You and your kin will take it back?" Sharla asked.

Ovis nodded. "It will come."

Sharla grimaced at the thought, the notion that Low Country was forever destined to be a burial ground for people of both sides. Claws and Low Countrymen would war back and forth, never securing a foothold until the dragons returned and the world drowned in fire.

"Maybe there will be peace one day," she said. "Peace between Claws and the small men."

Ovis muttered under his breath, what Sharla guessed to be a curse in his native tongue. "Peace."

"It's not impossible," she said. "We've done things with borders and Watchmen for as long as we remember but...maybe it won't always be that way." She locked gazes with Ovis. "One day."

Ovis watched her for a long moment. "But not today."

"No," she agreed. "Not today."

He nodded, turned, and spat into the sand.

"Why help us hunt your own people?" Sharla asked.

"Not my people." Ovis shook his head. "A different tribe. A crazy one. You said they were skulled. Ram skulls?"

"Actually, yes."

"The Skull Tribe." Ovis shook his head. "Madmen, madwomen. Led by the worst: Dormun Redskull."

Redskull; the man who'd nearly killed Sharla, who'd rode off with Renn over his saddle. Sharla swallowed at the memory, remembered the gold and red paint across the dhorak skull. It had to be the same man. She'd come face to face with their leader, their chieftain…and now Dormun had Renn.

"I saw him," she said quietly.

"You did?" Ovis asked.

"Barely. They attacked us in a sandstorm, a sandstorm that came from nowhere and disappeared as soon as they left." Sharla shivered at the memories. "They probably had a mage."

"An entire storm came and went with them?" Jyrak asked.

"A sandstorm so bad, you could barely see the other side of the street," Sharla said. "It was chaos."

"Probably the best word you could've chosen." Jyrak shook his head. "Sounds like they have a chaos mage."

"A chaos mage?"

"A mage powerful enough to control a chaos structure, be it a pyramid or square. A combination of runes too unstable to be held by

Chapter Nine

anyone for very long, not unless they're tremendously strong." Jyrak shrugged. "We call those people chaos mages, but they're extremely rare. They're nobody Claws should have access to."

"What's that mean?"

Jyrak considered for a moment, his gaze flitting from her to Ovis. "I don't know. The tribe we're hunting might be getting help from someone."

"Who would help a Claw tribe?"

Jyrak shook his head, brow furrowed. "The tribe must've paid them, obviously."

"Tribes don't carry our gold."

"No." Jyrak shook his head. "Not coin. Something else."

"What would that be?"

"Chaos mages are like runemasters. They practice arts forbidden by Tower regulation, so they sell themselves to the highest bidder. Whomever this chaos mage works with might be just as powerful, and I don't know why they would be interested in the Savage Land. Doesn't make sense."

"Chaos mages," Nithan groaned from ahead of them. "This keeps getting better."

Sharla blinked, suddenly recognizing that the crew had been silent, listening to her speak with the two men.

Keryn shook her head. "We have no idea what we're getting into."

"Don't think anyone does," Jyrak answered.

"We turn back?" Nithan suggested.

"And go where?" Arlon asked. "We already torched Senkha's town, ruined his border. The rest of the cartels will fight this out, so if we went anywhere, we'd have to leave Low Country."

"How convenient of you to have sorted this all out," Keryn said. "You wanted to start over, so you burned our bridges and gave us no options."

"Low Country is collapsing," Arlon insisted. "It was only a matter of time."

"You're impossible."

"I'm alive. We're all alive. We'll see this through, set ourselves up for the next chapter. Find new pickings somewhere else, another country."

"*You* will, maybe." Keryn shook her head. "I told you that after this, I'm out."

"Right behind you," Nithan answered.

Silence settled over the crew, restless and uneasy.

"We'll gather more riders and leave this place," Sharla finally said. "Travel to the Savage Land and finish things."

"Any idea how to find these *riders*?" Keryn asked.

"I found you lot in an inn." Sharla shrugged. "I reckon we try the same thing in Laken. Walk into the rowdiest inn, look for trouble."

Jyrak snorted. "Shouldn't be difficult. We just push a Claw into the room."

"I'm the best fighter." Ovis grinned wider. "The best."

"We don't have to empty the whole town," Sharla insisted. "We only need to find a few men and convince them to join us."

"Convince?" Keryn scoffed. "You have no idea what you're doing here, do you?"

Sharla hesitated. Conceded and shook her head. "I just know we need men."

"And we try not to make a mess of things this time," Nithan said. "Sounds good to me."

"Everything sounds good to you," Keryn answered. "So long as you stay behind and let everyone else do the work."

"I'm no fighter," Nithan said, gesturing to himself. "Does this look like a warrrior to you?"

Sharla had to admit Nithan had a point. Compared to the lean, fearsome builds of Keryn and Arlon, the brawny frames of Ovis and Jyrak, and the darker appearance of Hesher's obviously foreign identity, Nithan didn't have much going for him. Merely a scrawny man in worn clothes.

"You can keep a lookout," she suggested. "Stab anyone who gets out of hand."

"Right," Nithan muttered. "Because all I'm good for is stabbing people."

"It's what she hired us for," Hesher said. The man sounded amused.

"She hired us to hunt Claws. I reckon that's what you and I will do, and everyone else fights them. That's not our job." Nithan shook his head and scowled at Hesher. "We don't fight. We stay out of the way."

"You might, maybe," Hesher answered. "I reckon I'm ready to kill some Claws."

"The skulled ones," Ovis answered. "We hunt the Skull Tribe, not the rest."

"You reckon we'll run into more of them?" Nithan asked.

"Don't know," Arlon mused. "I've never been to the Savage Land."

A moment of silence. Sharla realized that Jyrak watched her.

"Neither have I," she finally said.

"Brilliant," Keryn said. "A crew of seven goes into Laken, wants to find toughs to follow them into a land no one's been to so they can find a tribe no one can track. This gets better and better."

Chapter Ten

BY THE TIME THEY SAW LAKEN, KINE ALREADY ITCHED TO escape Senit's men, who filled the road behind the Watchmen in a spread of dark coats and hoods. The Watchmen grimaced and licked chapped lips, frowning at everything and nothing. Understandable when considering that a host of dangerous men rode behind them.

But no one appeared as uncomfortable as Gashar, who rode beside Kine without making eye contact.

The newfound army of Watchmen and bandits planned to mobilize fresh forces in Laken before heading east to Senkha, and from there to Marast. Kine knew an exhausting several days loomed before them, and they'd grow even more wearisome if he were forced to endure this same, uncomfortable silence.

"You're not taking this very well," he told Gashar.

The younger man didn't answer, watching the descent before them. It was one of several slopes in the mesa, the most traveled highway from Keth to southern Low Country. The differing elevations grew absurd when one thought about them, as the truest "low country" existed at Tigon Land.

When one reached Thakan at Benania's northern shore, the ground instantly rose toward snow-capped mountains and frigid tundra, alpine forests and highland meadows. The farther south one rode, the more the land dipped, at times so gradually you'd never tell the difference, and at others dropping through features like the Great Canyon. Everything fell from High Country toward the first mesa populated by Keth, Laken, and Mela, which then dropped to Tigon Land. Only Low Country's peninsula of badlands lay to the east. One visit to the region had been enough to tell Kine why the Owl didn't care for eastern Low Country: the land was nothing but sand, rock, and scorched earth.

Ultimately, that visit should've been enough to tell him it probably would've been better to leave all Low Country alone. Perhaps he never should've encamped the Watchmen so long. Perhaps he should've abandoned Low Country and sailed south when the king first turned his gaze from the region. Maybe that was what bothered Gashar: that Kine had agreed to leave Low Country in the first place.

"The Watchmen won't die," Kine finally said.

Still, Gashar held his silence.

The men started down the slope. Desert juniper and rock nettle tangled the road, made the work tedious. Ahead of them, Laken shimmered in the heat. The surrounding buttes also appeared to waver, erupting from the landscape in all shapes, with squat, bulbous forms over here and taller spires over there. Sentinels to oversee Low Country, staking their territory before the terrain dropped to Tigon Land and the Great Canyon.

The scenery had never looked more desolate. Kine regarded it with a disappointed sigh, and he wondered how he'd ever thought he could bring order to the region. The ancestors couldn't rule this. Maybe not even the dragons. Why would they have tried? Why did anyone?

"The Watchmen won't die," he repeated, but now he said it to himself. A declaration of identity, a promise he hadn't lost himself in the pursuit of revenge and past regrets.

"Then you've paralyzed us," Gashar finally said. "You cut off our hands and feet, made us useless."

"You're being dramatic."

"You're being cruel." Gashar glared at Kine. "You agreed to walk away. You gave away everything you've worked for, everything *we've* worked for."

"I didn't."

Gashar stared at him for a long moment.

"You think I'd really do any of that?"

Gashar blinked. "You lied."

"I said what I had to."

"You think that's a good idea, lying to someone like Senit?"

"What else would you have done?"

"You're in bed with wolves, Colonel," Gashar said. "We've always known that, just like we've always known not to upset them. You mean to start playing games with them, teasing them by telling them you'll back down when you never planned to?"

"I've teased wolves for forty years," Kine muttered. "Ever since starting the cartels."

"What will you do? Kill them all, just like Senit said?"

"I don't know yet," Kine admitted. "I just had to get us moving."

Gashar glowered at him for a long moment, turning back when his horse stumbled on a rock. "You're dangerous, Colonel."

"And well that you remember it, Lieutenant Colonel. It's necessary in such times. If the wolves see weakness, we're dead."

"How long before they figure out you're lying?"

"Long enough," Kine said. "We just need to make it to the Savage Land. We need to kill Dormun."

"Will that give you peace?"

Kine frowned at the younger man. "Who said anything about peace?"

"Will you be satisfied?"

"I've always been satisfied."

"You've always been a drunk who doesn't sleep well, who drives away every whore he beds with, who stirs up every town he rests in until it rebels." Gashar shrugged, avoiding eye contact. "I've heard that it's…different from how you used to be."

"Don't believe everything you hear," Kine muttered. It was harder language than Gashar typically used. The conversation with Senit must've rattled him.

Chapter Ten

Kine grimaced at the thought and eyed the younger man. "You weren't going to die, Gashar. I wasn't going to let them kill you."

"You said nothing."

Kine hesitated and swallowed his response. He didn't have an answer for that.

"It doesn't matter," Gashar continued. "It's not that I almost died. I knew that could happen when you first said we'd speak with Senit." He shook his head. "It's that you treated the Watchmen like trash. You disregarded the Owl."

"What does it truly mean, Gashar? Why does the Owl matter?"

"It's the reason I'm in Low Country, the reason all of us are. The reason we've all left High Country to live in this wasteland, a place our spouses hate and our children fear. You'd take that purpose away from all your men, all your family?"

Kine didn't have a true family; not anymore. He'd lost all that when Dormun slew his wife, and then again when his daughter ran away. Good riddance to the lot of them. They'd never wanted Low Country. They'd never understood what he tried for, the peace he'd always envisioned. He knew there could be coexistence between Claws and Low Countrymen. He'd *lived* in that coexistence for the first several years, at least before he knew Dormun raided towns behind his back. He knew what the Owl could've done in Low Country, and he'd attempted to accomplish it himself, to usher in the peace the land deserved. It wasn't his fault that Low Country hated him for it.

Kine scowled. Nobody understood. Nobody but him, the only one prepared to see this through. Aye, he'd told Senit what the man wanted to hear.

At the same time, Kine knew he'd started something irreversible. It wouldn't end when Dormun died. Gashar and Senit were right: this would likely end with himself or Senit or others dead and bleeding in Low Country's dust. But then again, perhaps that had always been the conclusion of the cartels. Such governance had never been attempted in Freytilia, and likely wouldn't be tried again. Never mind the fact that it would've worked if Dormun hadn't messed everything up again.

Kine simmered over the familiar thoughts as they approached Laken. They passed ranches along the way, stunted crops that scrabbled over red soil, tiny homesteads that appeared long abandoned. Cows dotted the flat, lonely shapes that formed meager herds. They watched the riders from afar, as though confused by the momentous gathering of people.

Aside from snorting horses, creaking saddles, and rattling plate armor, the desert was quiet—as though all Low Country held its breath over the approach of the Watchmen and the bandits. Kine supposed their force had simply become another cartel, here to challenge the rest. That's what it would be seen as, at least at first. Thank the ancestors Senkha lodged closer to Mela rather than Laken.

The town nestled itself near the mesa's edge. Springs ran from the surrounding buttes to nourish the town's outskirts, transforming a desert oasis into a bustling, teeming crowd of pests, all clamoring for the same water source. Laken possessed several inns, a Lodian monastery—every town in Low Country seemed to hold a monastery these days—and a few market squares. Construed of pinewood and imported oak from High Country, the town's dull coloration of dusty yellow and muddy brown blended with the surrounding desert. Only the monastery dared anything different—as monasteries usually did—composed of sandstone bricks colored the same tan as the buildings of Senit's village. Bubbled stained glass windows depicted the Earth King and his abundant harvests, startling pictures when contrasted against the dry streets around them.

The townsfolk wore simple garments. They hugged their baskets or hunched against their wagons as the Watchmen entered the street. Children stared from alleyways or were shooed inside by their parents. Men on horses dismounted, led their mounts to the roadsides. All eyes fell on Kine's helm, the Owl insignia across his breastplate, the yellow cape that billowed behind him. After a time, Kine saw their gazes move past him, down the ranks of Watchmen to the bandits. The expressions began to change, moving from curiosity and surprise to horror and disgust. For some, it confirmed that the Watchmen worked with cartels.

Chapter Ten

For others, it simply offered another reason to stay away from Watchmen and everything they represented.

A hush followed Kine wherever he rode, and he struggled not to squirm in the silence. When someone finally did break the quiet, it was a simple man in unassuming, dusty clothes. He appeared exhausted, as though he'd ridden for days, but that didn't stop him from hurrying across the street to rush for Kine's horse.

"Sir," he said. "Sir, I must ask for your assistance."

He approached too fast for Gashar's liking. The younger man gripped his sword hilt, drew an inch of steel. "Watch yourself, citizen."

"It's okay, Lieutenant Colonel." Kine waved the man closer, relieved to have someone to talk to who wasn't a Watchmen or a bandit. "What's wrong?"

"There's a woman in town who murdered my friends. She got here not long before you arrived. She has a crew with her, and a Claw among them."

"A Claw." The cold fire crackled in Kine's chest, cooling his heart and constricting his lungs. "Does he wear a skull?"

"No, but he has the bone claws in his ears."

Kine nodded and swallowed, willing his blood to settle. "She murdered your friends?"

"She has stolen treasure in the desert. We saw her digging it up, and she killed two of my friends before I got away. She tried to hide the treasure and the money, but now she's here with a crew and I'm afraid she's here to kill me for what I've seen."

"How big is her crew?"

"Looks to be seven, including her."

Kine frowned and considered. Not big enough to represent a cartel. Sounded like another group of toughs—irrelevant. "Where'd they ride from?"

"From Mela, I assume. I first saw her east of Mela."

The crew had ridden through Senkha's territory, and he hadn't done anything about the Claw? Either he didn't care or his network had relaxed. Neither was a good sign, but a Claw thrown into the mix certainly lent an element Kine needed: potential knowledge of Dormun and his crew.

Besides, his Watchmen and Senit's army had planned to stay the night, so Kine had time to ask for details, potentially finding information to help him prepare for fighting Redskull.

"Lead the way to her, sir," Kine said. "The Owl's justice will be done."

Chapter Eleven

Laken struck Sharla as a friendly town. She'd been here once before—what felt like years ago, but what had more likely been a couple of months. She couldn't remember the exact details. Time on the road had blurred them together. What she did remember was that she'd kept to Laken's outskirts, only hopping in and out for supplies while she'd camped a mile or two outside town.

She normally knew better than to stay long amounts of time in *any* location, but perhaps riding with a crew had softened her edge: she'd found herself lounging in an inn, the "Wet Cask," before wandering off to find a new coat, leaving recruitment to the rest of the crew. They'd all proven themselves by agreeing to the job and fending off Senkha's horde, so she figured she could trust them to find anyone else they thought would fit in.

Yes, she'd softened a bit, but she was content with that. She'd often romanticized running away and living on the road, but after she'd tried the lifestyle, she'd hated it. Even so, how couldn't she have idealized the freedom of the open road when she grew up in hell—her father beating her mother, her mother never lifting a finger to stop him, and the fact that both parents wore Watchmen garb that meant nothing at all? No one had cared about their household, and they had never said anything until Sharla finally took matters into her own hands.

Of course, following the familiar trail of memories jeopardized Sharla's newfound calm, and she struggled to bury them again. The past was the past, and she'd finally be rid of it once she used the rest of her blood money to pay off the crew. All they had to do was find the Claws, find Renn, and everyone would escape. Everything would go back to the way it was.

"I'm coming, Renn," she said, willing herself to believe the words and ignore her creeping doubt. "I'm coming."

She raised her gaze to a commotion at the far end of the street. People cleared a path, moving to the sides of the road with hurried glances at something behind them; a procession on horseback. Plate armor glinted in the afternoon sun, and a bright cape billowed behind the lead rider. Her heart plummeted even before she saw his face—even before she recognized those cold, blue eyes and those weathered, grizzled features.

Kine Tarroful. He could only be here for her.

She turned and forced her way down the street, shoving past townsfolk who hadn't caught on, who still hadn't realized the colonel of the Third Regiment rode Laken's streets. Angry mutters and exclamations followed her, but she heard nothing from Kine. He hadn't seen her yet, so she ducked lower and wove through the crowd, hurtling across porches and vaulting crates to keep herself behind wagons and people.

She cut through an alleyway and pushed herself into a full sprint, dry air whipping her mouth and blowing through her hair, boots tromping through red dirt and spitting dust in her wake. A few children scampered from her path, and then she'd burst into another street, skirted a market square, and bounded through the door of the Wet Cask.

She entered a common room as busy as before, with raucous shouting all around. Well, *that* part was new. Much of the yelling sounded excited, but the further into the room she pushed, the angrier the noise.

She finally emerged closer to the bar, where she'd last seen Keryn, Hesher, and Nithan. The commotion came from the right, where a group of men crowded a table full of cards and stacks of coin. Ovis sat in the press, with sunlight from a window glowing across his wolf pelt and

Chapter Eleven

turning it fiery. His scarred face wore a stupid grin, and Sharla couldn't tell which bottles around the table where his. The other men jabbed their fingers at him, shouting and spraying spittle, while he gestured at the table with an incredulous expression. No, Ovis never did *anything* incredulous. That must have been his mocking expression.

"Blood and ashes," Sharla muttered.

"He's cheating, and they know it."

Sharla turned to see Keryn behind her. The woman lounged against the bar with her arms across her chest.

"You watched it all happen?" Sharla asked.

Keryn nodded.

"Is he sober enough to run?"

"Run?" Keryn narrowed her gaze, noted Sharla's flushed face, her heaving chest. "Ancestors above, who'd you piss off?"

"Watchmen." Sharla hesitated. "Kine Tarroful."

"As in Colonel Tarroful?" Keryn blinked at her. "You wanted by the law?"

Sharla winced. "You could say that."

"You never thought to warn us?"

"I told you to take the job and find out for yourself."

Keryn leaned forward, her face inches from Sharla's. The movement was so fast and unexpected, Sharla fell against a stool beside her. "Think this is some kind of joke?" Keryn hissed.

"Arlon decided to prove himself by fighting an entire town," Sharla said. "If this is a joke, the punchline happened a while ago."

"Watchmen and thugs are very different."

"Not anymore. And we should probably run."

"He saw you?"

"No, but he's coming this way."

"Someone told him we were here." Keryn inhaled, leaned back, and shook her head. "Or someone told him *you* were here."

"Yes."

Keryn turned to the table of cards, where the men had stood, kicked their chairs aside, and started waving onlookers over. "An escape, then."

"Any new recruits?"

"It was just starting to look promising."

Sharla shook her head. "Then it's the six of us."

"What a happy family we make."

"Get the others," Sharla said. "We leave out the back."

She moved toward the table, trusting the other woman knew where to find the rest of the crew. Ahead of her, Ovis fumbled for the bottles at the table, apparently searching for one that still held liquor. When he found one on the table's opposite side, he made a show of admiring it, holding it to his lips while gauging the other men's reactions. The men roared, pounded the table, and began circling it.

Sharla reached Ovis first, blocking the other men and grabbing his shoulder. "This is how you find new recruits?" she asked. "Offending everyone you meet?"

Ovis eyed her. "Needed to see fighters."

As if in answer to his statement, a hand grabbed Sharla's shoulder and wrenched her backward, sending her tumbling against the bar. She fumbled for balance before she slipped around Ovis to grab his shoulder again.

"We need to leave," she said. "Now. Through the back door. Watchmen are coming."

He'd barely heard the words before another hand grabbed her shoulder again, throwing her backward. This time it was a veritable *toss*, and she went sprawling. Picking herself from the dusty, stained floor burned the last of her patience, and before she quite knew what had happened, she'd drawn her remaining steel battle axe.

"That wasn't very nice," she said, and drove the axe into the man's boot, likely cutting off several toes and making blood spurt from the leather.

The man howled and leaped backward, a movement he surely hadn't thought through. The motion landed him on his bad foot and his leg folded underneath him, collapsing him into his friends.

The common room exploded into chaos. Chairs scraped and boots shuffled as men and women jumped up, all eyes landing on Sharla's

Chapter Eleven

bloodied steel and Ovis, the Claw in a wolf pelt, around whom all the confusion occurred. Obviously enjoying the attention, he decided to up the drama by clambering atop the table and shouting.

"Spirits save us! The Watchmen come!"

He jumped off and overturned the table, sending coins and cards flying, bottles exploding. The table collided with the men on the other side, forcing them back into the crowd. Sharla tugged Ovis around the bar as men and women pressed against its other side. Despite the chaos, at the far side of the common room, Sharla saw Ovis had spoken truly. She glimpsed a steel helm in the doorway, a yellow cape, but by then she'd tugged Ovis into the kitchen.

Other bodies scrambled through here: Keryn, Nithan, Arlon. Jyrak's bulk already blocked the outside door. Sharla and Ovis moved after them, loping between tables of chopped vegetables, pots of simmering meat and ovens of cooking bread. A few women tumbled from their path, and someone kept yammering in Sharla's ear. A man wearing an apron matched their pace and shook his fist at them. Ovis hurled him into a rack of pans and laughed as Sharla shouldered through the door, following the rest of the crew around the back of the inn and toward the stables.

"That went well."

Jyrak's voice from somewhere in the gloom. Sharla found Nun and struggled with the saddle, hoisting it over her horse and tightening the straps, her fingers fluttering across leather and hot skin.

"No recruits?" Nithan asked.

"Almost had them," Ovis boasted. "Had men ready to talk, but Sharla cut someone's foot off."

"I didn't," Sharla snapped. "Only a few toes."

"Why are we running?" Hesher asked.

"Sharla brought Watchmen here," Keryn hissed.

"Watchmen?" Arlon asked.

"I didn't bring them," Sharla answered. "Someone else did. But we don't want them following us."

"They're following *her*," Keryn declared. "We should leave her and ride our own way."

"We're not leaving anyone," Arlon said, even as Ovis shouted, "I don't leave without my gold!"

"The job's off," Keryn said. She'd already saddled her horse and ridden to the stable entrance, silhouetted by the afternoon sunlight. She looked back at them, her face shadowed. "It should've been called off when she mentioned Claws, but now she has Watchmen chasing us? No way this ends well."

"Watchmen are always chasing us," Arlon answered. "That's nothing new."

"We've never *seen* live Watchmen, Arlon. We've never had to deal with them."

"Doesn't mean we've never been on the wrong side of the law."

"There's only a law where the Watchmen want there to be a law, and they're fine with Senkha. They're not fine with Sharla, and that should tell you enough. It's over, Arlon. Let's get out of here and be done with it."

Sharla clambered atop Nun and examined the crew, all of whom sat in the gloom, watching each other, expectant. Arlon's horse stood beside Keryn's and the two stared at each other.

"We need the money to get us to whatever's next," Arlon finally said. "If Senkha's out, Low Country falls with him, and we'll need coin to pay our passage out. Maybe it's Odonia or Lhoria or Fahria, or maybe it's even another continent, but we need that money."

"Just like you wanted, eh?" Keryn sneered. "Locked us into this thing good and tight."

"I haven't locked anyone in." Arlon paused. "But I'm getting paid." He turned and beckoned. "Let's go, Sharla. Anyone else who wants coin, follow us."

Sharla spurred Nun forward, following him into the sunlight. Ovis whooped behind her and Jyrak muttered something. Sharla didn't look back as Arlon rode down the street, peering at the inn beside them. The crew's discussion had cost them time, for a slew of Watchmen had

Chapter Eleven

gathered around the inn. One of them looked over, saw Arlon and Sharla, and pointed, shouting something. Steel helms turned and reins flicked.

Arlon kicked his horse forward, and Sharla followed. They were in central Laken, moving southward but matched by the Watchmen's horses. Every time they looked down passing alleyways, Watchmen looked back, their plates flashing in the sun and their horses kicking up dust. The crew wouldn't outrun a legion of Watchmen, not across the bare flat outside Laken—and this time there wouldn't be a herd of bison to intercept.

"What do we do?" Sharla asked.

Arlon didn't answer. He examined an alleyway to see that Watchmen funneled down it, riding to intercept the crew. Sharla heard rumbling orders from the other side of the block: Kine Tarroful. She'd know his voice anywhere.

Watchmen poured into the street ahead of them, cutting off their route, and Arlon turned toward another alley, pulling his horse into the tight corridor. Sharla followed, catching her breath as windows clattered open and heads peeked out to observe the commotion. She ducked the swinging wood and heard exclamations and shouts behind her. One of the shutters crashed, splintered as another of the crew rode through it.

Ahead of her, Arlon exited the alley and tumbled a barrel that nearly felled Nun. Sharla followed him into another street, where Watchmen already clamored at the far end. Arlon rushed into another alley while Sharla tore her gaze away from the flashing armor. Ancestors above, the Watchmen were so fast!

No, she reminded herself, *the horses are probably just fresh.* Arlon's crew had already flogged their mounts in the escape from Mela, and there'd been little rest since then. Already, Sharla felt Nun ailing, shuddering. She patted Nun's neck, leaned to her ear, offered gentle, reassuring encouragements.

The crew traveled busier streets now, toward the eastern side of town. Arlon's company dodged and wove through townsfolk, sending people running from their path. On either side of them, Sharla saw

Watchmen struggling through the press, confusion milling around them. The crew rode through two more alleyways, and they saw less Watchmen. Another one, and they saw nobody. They slowed between the buildings, straining to listen.

"Your escape plan?" Keryn grunted.

Sharla turned to see all Arlon's crew had followed him, even if Nithan, Keryn, and Hesher looked significantly less comfortable.

"Southeast," Arlon announced. "We go southeast."

"Brilliant." Keryn tossed her hair, unslung her bow, and drew its string tight. "Another ride through the desert."

"Only the best for you." Arlon waved them forward. "Let's go."

* * *

A CART HAD UPENDED AND THROWN SACKS OF FLOUR ACROSS the street. One of them had burst into a white cloud that coated faces and streaked hair. Kine urged his horse away from the throng, waving his hands at the townsfolk and urging them to make way. He knew his tone was furious, knew he'd shout until his voice became hoarse.

But he'd also seen Sharla.

He knew it was her. That blond hair and those blue eyes were unmistakable, and she'd obviously recognized him, too. Indeed, she appeared terrified of him, fleeing the inn as soon as she'd seen him through the door. *She should be terrified,* he thought to himself. *She owes far more than she'll ever be able to pay.*

"Clear the street!" he shouted. "Make way for the Watchmen!"

New shouts from the other side of the wagon. Kine turned to see other Watchmen slogging through the crowd, waving for people to move and shouting as ineffectively as he.

"Colonel Tarroful! They're riding the next street over, toward the southern monastery!"

Kine flicked his reins and spurred his horse forward. "Go! We'll catch them in the flat."

* * *

THEY'D ALMOST ESCAPED LAKEN. SHARLA SAW THE FLAT behind the monastery ahead of them.

Chapter Eleven

"Another monastery?" Jyrak muttered. "Laken has two?"

"A lot of ranchers here," Arlon answered.

Sharla opened her mouth to say something, but saw dark riders at the other end of an alleyway. She blinked and squinted down the next alley they passed, saw more of them. Riders with tattered coats and hoods, as though direct sunlight would burn them. Mages? Other cartel riders?

"Arlon..."

"Whose are those?" Keryn asked.

Sharla turned to see the other riders approaching from the front, milling around both sides of the monastery like a black tide.

"Senkha's?" Arlon suggested. "They've followed us?"

"Clear the way?" Sharla asked Jyrak.

He frowned at her, shaking his head. "I can't clear a path. Only fire, wind, or earth would do that, and none of those guarantee us safe passage."

The group thundered toward the riders, pressed for space and running out of options.

"The monastery," Arlon declared. "Inside, and quickly!"

Protests from Nithan and a shocked response from Keryn, but Sharla blocked them all out, hunching low to Nun and clenching her jaw. They were trapping themselves to stall for time until they could do...what? But she saw their options as clearly as Arlon: namely, that there *weren't* any. Mystery riders ahead and Watchmen behind. Where else to go but a monastery? Maybe the Earth King would smile on them.

Sharla followed Arlon up the stairs, through the oaken doors, and into the cool sanctuary.

*   *   *

KINE SWORE AT THE SIGHT OF SENIT'S MEN. HE SPURRED ahead of the Watchmen and approached Senit, fighting the urge to draw his sword and flay the cartel leader.

"Senit," he said. "Why are you here?"

"What's that supposed to mean?" The other man had the audacity to look confused. He already had his pipe out, puffing smoke rings while the rest of his men bunched around him and glared at Kine.

"This is Watchmen business," Kine said. "You were supposed to enter Laken behind us and find lodging for your men."

"I didn't like the idea that you were up to no good." Senit shook his head and observed the monastery. "Besides, my men wanted a detour, some fresh air after breathing your dust. It seems we've done you some good because we've trapped your fugitives in the monastery."

Kine struggled to keep his hand from his sword pommel, to breathe evenly, to slow his racing heart. Ancestors above, Sharla wound him up as easily as Dormun Redskull. "They're in there?"

Senit nodded, a thoughtful expression on his face. "Six of them in all, I think. What did they do?"

"They're a crew of toughs up to no good."

"Come now, Colonel. You rode with *all* your Watchmen to follow six people?"

"And you rode to meet me. We shouldn't be seen together; you said so yourself."

"Impossible to avoid it now that we're riding together." Senit shook his head. "Suddenly, you're the hypocrite. My interest abounds. Colonel, I'd like to offer my continued assistance in this endeavor. I'm curious as to which of those men you seek." After a moment, he winked. "Or which of those women."

Kine fumed, aware men on both sides were watching him. All the secrets of his life, thrown into the mud for the pigs to slobber over.

"Nothing to it," he finally said. "It's a stalemate. We wait them out."

"I love those," Senit answered. "Refreshingly easy after a hard day's work."

"Easy." Kine snorted and spurred his horse forward. "We'll see about that."

* * *

"BY DECREE OF BENANIA'S LAW AND IN ACCORDANCE WITH

Chapter Eleven

the Owl's oversight, you are under arrest for attempted evasion and resistance of the king's men!"

"Attempted evasion and resistance." Keryn snorted. "There's a new one."

Sharla couldn't answer; her heart filled her throat and shook her with every beat. Kine spoke the words, and it sounded like he'd ridden to the front steps of the monastery to do it. The monster of her past, mere feet from her. No set of doors could keep that man at bay. She'd seen his resolve before, and she'd no desire to see it again.

She'd unconsciously backed Nun away from the door, behind the rest of the crew, down the line of pews and toward the altar where the monks crowded. They huddled in their robes like mole rats and stared at the group with wide eyes, colored motley blues and purples by shafts of light through the stained-glass windows.

Arlon turned and noticed Sharla's movement, considering her with a furrowed brow. She shook her head, as if answering a silent question. All it really meant was she wouldn't go out there, wouldn't face that man. He must've read the desperation in her gaze, for he turned to the door with a grim expression.

"If you don't come willingly, we'll resort to deadly force," Kine said.

Arlon rode his horse to the door. "A moment, good sir. We're considering our options."

"You have none."

"All the same to you, we'd appreciate a moment. If we're all to face the gallows, we'd like a moment to prepare."

Silence, while the rest of his crew exchanged bewildered looks.

"Who said anything about the gallows?" Kine finally asked.

"You have a battalion of Watchmen after us," Arlon answered. "That proves the severity of your charges, even if I don't know why you're hunting us."

An exasperated breath from outside. Sharla's heart plummeted as she realized what Arlon had done. He'd encouraged Kine to reveal her past, to expose it for everyone to hear.

"You're riding with a woman who's murdered several men in the desert, who's stolen the Owl's money and hidden it for years."

Murdered several men in the desert? Sharla gaped. The third man to escape her when she'd fought the bandits south of Opek, he'd ridden all the way *here*. Did the ancestors know no shortage of cruel, sick irony? To let Arlon's crew fight an entire town only to arrive on the western reaches of Low Country, where a mob of Watchmen would be waiting with the one man who could reveal her sins?

"We don't know this woman," Arlon finally said. "I don't think you have the right crew."

"But you fled."

"Because you chased us."

"Innocent men don't run from Watchmen."

"*Everyone* runs from Watchmen." Arlon snorted. "Be reasonable, Colonel. All Low Country knows your men carry enough blood on their hands to satisfy a Kanian priesthood."

Silence from outside. Kine inhaled. Ancestors above, he must've been right outside the door for them to hear him so clearly. Sharla shuddered, hunching closer to Nun.

"I've seen her, sir," Kine said. "I saw her with my own eyes. I know who she is."

"Who is she, exactly?"

"Her name's Sharla." A pause, as though Kine debated whether to spill the whole truth. "But I don't know what she calls herself now. Could be anything. She's the younger woman in your group. Blond-haired. Blue eyes. On the shorter side."

Arlon turned to Sharla. "I know her."

"Bring her to me, sir, and I give you my word the rest of your crew rides free."

"How much is your word worth, Colonel?"

"I swear it on the Owl itself. On the king himself, if the Owl doesn't convince you."

"I've seen what the Owl allows, Colonel. I've seen what the king overlooks. You and your men don't convince me."

Chapter Eleven

"Would you rather we ride in and kill you all?"

"Such escalation."

"You try my patience, sir. You stand before the law and the oversight of the Owl."

"It must have been a lot of money for you to want her so badly."

"Will you bring her out?"

Arlon paused and locked gazes with Sharla again. The rest of the crew had moved beside the pews, as if to offer him clear sight of her. They all watched her now, as though they saw through her smokescreen of lies. As if they confirmed she could never outrun her past, never become a new woman. That would be forever denied her, dead and buried with her father, and her mistakes still bound her like shackles. Maybe she could've started over somewhere else, in another time. But never in Low Country.

She should've left when she had the chance—should've followed her mother. Instead, she'd stayed like an idiot, fearing she'd never escape the Owl, that she'd never be prepared to face the rest of the world. Or had it been the hope she could change things? That she could rejoin her fellow Watchmen and become something among Low Countrymen to atone for the legacy she'd soiled?

It wasn't fair. It wasn't right. Kine had done far worse to her and her family than she'd ever done to him. The ancestors had pitted them against each other from the start, but Sharla also knew this wasn't a battle for the rest of the crew. As desperate as she was, she knew she hadn't fallen low enough to willingly drag them down with her. She'd hired them to help her rescue Renn, but if her mission crossed the Watchmen—crossed *Kine*—it left her no choice. The colonel had always been her battle, and hers alone.

"What will it be, sir?" Kine called.

Sharla watched Arlon, bit her lip, and nodded. Arlon turned to the door. "A moment, Colonel."

"You have five minutes," Kine declared. "After that, we're kicking those doors down, marching inside, and dragging you out."

While the hoofbeats of Kine's horse departed, Arlon moved toward Sharla. The tall, dark-skinned man rode through the multicolored lights of the stained-glass windows, a shadow with a brooding gaze.

"I'll go," Sharla said. "I'll face him. This isn't your fight."

"She's right," Keryn grunted. "It never has been. Send her out so we can get out of here."

Arlon frowned. "We agreed to help this woman."

"*You* did!" Keryn hissed. "For all of us. That's not how this crew operates."

"Yes, it is." A grin broke Arlon's expression, as though the entire scenario were a joke. "It's how we've always taken jobs."

"Arlon, don't do this," Keryn said. "Don't drag us into a duel with *Watchmen*. This was supposed to be a ride against Claws. It wasn't supposed to pit all Low Country against us."

"It's not all Low Country," Arlon said. "It's the Watchmen. And they *don't* represent Low Country. We all know this. Perhaps it's time to stand against them, too."

"You're fighting the Owl?" Nithan asked in disbelief. "When did this become a war?"

"It's not. It's an escape." Arlon turned to Nithan. "You saw the colonel? You know what he looks like?"

Nithan stiffened, clearly not liking where the conversation headed. "Yes…"

Arlon nodded, turning to the rest of his crew. "We're going to ride out of here. *With* Sharla. And this is how we're going to do it."

* * *

"SHARLA."

Kine ignored Senit, or tried to. Impossible to ignore that name, and even more so when spoken by Senit's ilk. The cartel leader ran his tongue over his teeth as though he tasted the word. He puffed his pipe and eyed Kine. "Seems like a lot of effort for one woman," he finally said.

"This woman is one of Low Country's most wanted."

"Funny. I've never heard of her."

"Few have."

"Unless they're Colonel Tarroful, apparently."

Kine clenched his jaw. "If you have something to say, you might want to say it."

"Nothing to say." Senit shook his head and turned to the monastery. "Just...interested in this woman, that's all."

*   *   *

THEY LEFT THE HORSES WITH JYRAK, HESHER, AND NITHAN IN the monastery while Keryn, Arlon, and Sharla climbed the steps to the belltower. Dust motes winked through sunlight from the window at the top, and they filtered into the monastery's depths like snow.

"This is a mistake," Keryn said as they climbed. "It won't go well."

"You never think *anything* will go well," Arlon said. "It's one of the reasons we pair so nicely. The optimist and the pessimist. Idealist and realist. See how that works out?"

"It doesn't work out unless you listen to me, and you never do," Keryn growled. "We can't fight bandits, Watchmen, and Claws at the same time."

"Sure we can. We are." Arlon gestured to the trapdoor above them. "We just take it one step at a time."

He eased the trapdoor open. Daylight flooded the belltower, brilliant and warm. Sharla shielded her eyes as Arlon crawled underneath the bell, crouching by the side of the belfry as he beckoned the two women to follow. She held her breath and clambered up, with Keryn coming after. She huddled against the wall while Keryn and Arlon pressed themselves to the other side. The trio watched each other over the trapdoor, quiet as the moments stretched by.

"We'll only get one shot at this," Arlon said.

"Don't act like you lot are doing anything," Keryn answered. "I'm the one who takes the shot."

"Look for a yellow cape," Arlon said. "That's the colonel. Take him in the head, and we run. Ovis will do the rest."

The three waited in tense silence. All was quiet but for murmurs from the street below them—townsfolk and Watchmen who shuffled around and waited for their exit. At least the townsfolk had stayed, interested by the commotion. The more bodies there were, the more confusion the crew could create. The more confusion they had, the better their odds of escape.

And the odds weren't good.

Sharla found herself watching Arlon, who stared through her. She cleared her throat and sought words: some sort of thanks or an apology. But nothing came, and she finally abandoned the effort, her throat tight.

His gaze met hers, and he nodded. After a moment, she returned the gesture.

It was enough.

* * *

"FIVE MINUTES YET?" SENIT ASKED.

"I don't know," Kine said.

"Huh. I suppose we're waiting on you, Colonel. Show us the Owl's justice."

Kine swallowed a bitter response and moved his horse forward. "All right, sir. You've had your chance. Now—"

"Coming out!" someone shouted from inside. Not the same man as before.

Before Kine could question the change, the doors slammed open. Figures hurried down the steps. Not the crew, and not anyone Kine expected. Just a crowd of monks waving their hands to declare their innocence, robes flapping behind them, and hoods drawn back to reveal squinting, terrified faces. They moved as though they were chased by someone…and they were.

It was the Claw Kine came for—the Claw who could lead him to Dormun Redskull. The man hurried after the monks, slapping them with the hafts of bone battle axes. He wore a wolf pelt, and his face was covered with scars. Bone claws tugged his earlobes as he ran. He shouted something in his guttural language, laughing at the terrified monks.

"Wait!" Kine shouted. "Stop!"

The Claw didn't let the monks listen to Kine. He kept shouting and barking at them, whipping them into frenzy. They ran toward the

Chapter Eleven

Watchmen, as though pleading with them to save them, to kill the Claw and free Laken.

Kine swore, enraged that *nobody* was listening to *anything* he said, and spurred his horse to meet the monks, drawing his sword with a whisper of steel.

* * *

ARLON, KERYN, AND SHARLA PEERED OVER THE SIDE OF THE belfry once they heard Ovis enter the street. Keryn raised her bow, already nocked, but Arlon froze and gripped her shoulder.

"Wait," he said.

She swore at him. "You want me to shoot him or not?"

Arlon's throat bobbed, his face tight. "Different target."

"What? Who?"

Arlon pointed to the street, to the cluster of dark riders beside Kine and the lithe, still man at their center. "It's Senit."

"Senit? Are you sure? What would he be doing here?"

"I don't know. But it doesn't matter. Shoot him."

"You want to further ruin Low Country?"

"We already wrecked Senkha's empire. Kill Senit, and we rid Low Country of their entire family."

"What about the colonel?"

"Nithan's our backup," Arlon answered. "Shoot Senit and do it *now*. Then, we're getting out of here."

Keryn inhaled, adjusted her aim, and loosed. Arlon grabbed her, nudging Sharla. "Go!"

The trio left without seeing Keyn's result, but they heard the shouts easily enough.

* * *

EVERYTHING WENT TO HELL AT THE SAME TIME. SOMEONE moved across Kine's peripherals, hurtling fast enough to make him turn, to raise his sword against a blow. A tumble of sprawling bodies filled the street, with Senit at the bottom. One of his men had tackled him from his horse, rewarded for his efforts with an arrow through the skull. He bled over the bandit leader while the rest of Senit's men thrashed, and Kine turned toward the belltower.

Empty.

He looked back in time to catch a glimpse of a smaller man, just beside him. As unnoticeable as a child, as unnoticeable as—

A mage?

Kine dove into the strike, felt the blade graze off his pauldron as he ran the small man through the chest. The man's face bulged, and he coughed blood across Kine's breastplate. An ordinary-looking man with simple clothes, he sagged from Kine's blade as the life escaped him.

No, nobody magical. Merely someone skilled at their job: blending into the crowd and hiding in a group of monks until they'd moved close enough for him to strike.

Someone sent to assassinate Kine.

Chaos everywhere. Men shouting and Senit roaring, shoving at the corpse on him. Laughter from somewhere ahead. *The Claw*. He ripped into Watchmen with his bone axes as horses erupted from the monastery behind him—the rest of his crew.

As if on cue, the Claw turned and ran. Kine swore and shoved the corpse of the smaller man aside, raising his sword and struggling through the press of monks. Ahead of him, the Claw leaped to grab the saddle of a passing horse, the reins gripped by an equally bulky man who nodded at him.

Kine howled at the accomplice and swung his sword in challenge. The brawny man turned his gaze to Kine, and then to the corpse of the smaller man. Something in his expression hardened, and he looked at the building behind the Watchmen. He waved his hand, furrowed his brow, and closed his eyes in concentration. The air before him shimmered. Kine heard a low buzz, like the droning of bees, and felt goosebumps prick his skin as the wind shifted.

Then, the building behind him exploded.

* * *

SHARLA SHOUTED AND DUCKED HER HEAD AT THE SUDDEN blast. The building behind the Watchmen had ruptured, porch, walls,

Chapter Eleven

and roof spraying outward as though a massive tidal wave had crushed it. Splinters hissed through the street like arrows, felling Watchmen and bandits alike. Sawdust and dirt clouded the sky, fogging the area as Arlon turned the horses around, galloping toward the flat on Laken's southern side.

After a moment, Sharla managed to put two and two together. She turned to Jyrak, whose face was pale. He slumped across his horse and breathed heavily, wiping sweat from his brow.

"Was that an earth rune?" she asked.

He shook his head. "A sequence of wood runes. Lots of them to affect something that big." He shook his head and turned her way; his eyes were slightly unfocused. "Shouldn't…do something that big again."

"Hang on," she urged. "We're almost out of this."

She saw the horse with the empty saddle, looked behind them, and frowned. "Where's Nithan?"

"Dead." She turned to Jyrak in shock. The mage shook his head, his eyes sad. "The colonel killed him."

The Colonel. Kine Tarroful.

Sharla's grandfather.

Chapter Twelve

THEY HAD A HEAD START ON THE WATCHMEN AND SENIT'S men, but only the ancestors knew if it would be enough. Sharla didn't want to look, tried to keep herself from looking, but couldn't stop herself. As the crew approached the mesa's edge, clattering into the descent toward Tigon Land, she risked a glance backward.

No Watchmen yet, but a storm of dark riders instead, coats rippling behind them as they stormed the desert. They rode faster, well-rested horses, and the dust trail behind them could've been smoke.

She swore, briefly made eye contact with Jyrak, and turned ahead. The mage couldn't help anymore. Indeed, he appeared as though he could barely keep himself awake, the same as last time. That meant the crew's only escape depended on them reaching Tigon Land before the bandits.

"We'll lose them in the canyons!" she shouted at Arlon. "It's our only chance!"

She couldn't tell whether he heard the words, but her tone prompted him to look back, to see the other riders for himself. He turned and flicked the reins, kicking his horse to go faster—a precarious decision when descending the mesa slopes. Their horses skittered over scree and leaped about tangled junipers. They'd started across what might've been a footrail, but it rapidly collapsed, fragmenting into sheer drops and broken talus. A hazardous route on a good day, but when you charged down it for dear life? Suicidal.

Chapter Twelve

The horses squealed, bucked, and pranced, eyes rolling in their heads. Sharla lurched like a drunkard, squeezing the saddle for dear life, nearly biting her tongue off with every drop. Hooves clattered and scraped, skidded and slid.

Jyrak grunted, nearly falling from his saddle, and finally released the reins of Nithan's horse to grip his own with both hands. The riderless horse, freed of the press, pranced sideways, away from the riders behind them, and toppled over a precipice to their right. Squeals echoed around them, along with the crunching of breaking bones.

An arrow hissed past her ear, so close she felt the wind of its passage across her cheek. She yelped and ducked, fumbling for her crossbow. In front of her, Keryn turned and aimed her bow, nearly flying from her horse as it jerked into a sudden pitch. She released her arrow too low and nearly struck Ovis through the throat. She swore, Ovis bellowed, and Jyrak moaned.

Sharla finally freed her crossbow, holding it in a death grip. Her finger danced around the trigger as she looked for a smooth patch of ground from which to fire. The terrain continued to crumble. Arlon's horse skidded from a precipice and collapsed half the slope, a fragmentation of an entire rock face that sent boulders flying in a cloud of dust.

The roar of sliding rocks nearly drowned out the snorting of a horse directly behind Sharla. She turned to find a rider right beside her, flashing a blade. Thank the ancestors he didn't have a bow, or she'd already be dead. She leaned sideways, nearly rolling off Nun as his knife tore into her coat. She felt no pain; he'd missed her.

She swung the crossbow around, leaned toward him, and fired into his chest. He hooted, twisted as though trying to escape a swarm of bees, found himself rolling into the hooves of a rider behind him. His body went under and tripped the horse, sending all the bodies crashing into the rocks. A cloud of dust and broken limbs, flopping over the landscape to ruin the other riders. The passage was too narrow for all of them, and their horses struggled to stay upright, to ride clear of the wreckage.

Hesher shouted, nearly thrown into space as his horse pranced over a ditch. The dark man flailed with one hand, rewarded for his efforts by the slap of a branch he'd just swatted at for balance. He roared and clutched the hand to his chest, nearly bouncing into Keryn. She'd been attempting to draw another arrow from her quiver, but was jounced in her efforts and spilled several arrows to the rocks.

She swore as Ovis laughed—the idiot was *still laughing*—and he swiped behind him to catch a bandit's horse with his battle axe. He blinded the horse and sent it shrieking into the abyss. For an impossible moment, its rider tumbled *above* the crew as they flew down another pitch, and then he crunched somewhere behind Sharla, a victim of the dreadful slope.

Someone started screaming, a dreadful shriek that welled from everywhere at once. Sharla realized it was herself, helpless in the cusp of terror, thrashing in every direction as Nun fought for balance.

They couldn't take much more of this.

*   *   *

KINE COULDN'T TELL HOW MANY MEN HE'D LOST. HE couldn't tell who was wounded, dying, or already dead. Wreckage covered the street: broken boards and mutilated bodies. The only reason he'd survived without injury was because of the Watchmen behind him. They'd unintentionally protected him from the deadly spray, and all of them were now collapsed and bleeding beside his horse.

The splinters had ripped through their skulls, throats, and limbs. The Watchmen's horses had fared little better, strewn through the street with their entrails hanging out and their blood soaking the dirt. Blood was everywhere, as red as the soil until no one knew the difference. Red dirt and red blood mixed to produce a dark mud, coating everything and everyone.

"Colonel."

Kine turned to find the one man he'd hoped to see dead. Senit had mounted a new horse—his own lay as quiet as most of the rest—and the man turned to survey the aftermath.

"They have a mage," Senit said.

Chapter Twelve

"And you don't?" Kine asked. When compared to the prior roar of breaking wood and rushing air, everything sounded strangely hollow. He shook his head, smacking his fist to his forehead.

"He's already in pursuit." Senit pointed past the monastery, where a dark tide of his riders chased the crew. Kine's Watchmen were noticeably absent from the crowd, but most of them had been caught in the blast from the exploding building.

Kine coughed, attempting to spit the remaining sawdust from his throat. "We follow them," he declared. "After this, that crew deserves worse than the gallows. Now you see why Sharla is so dangerous."

Senit didn't answer, staring at his departing riders with a thoughtful expression. "They tried to kill me."

"And me."

Senit shook his head. "They shouldn't know who I am. I've barely left the Great Canyon in years, and I've never traveled far enough east for anyone to see me."

"We'll catch them and question them," Kine answered. "We'll finish this." He kicked his horse forward without waiting for Senit's answer, trusting the rest of his Watchmen to follow. Even if they didn't, he could ride with Senit's men, at least until the crew was captured.

Until he had Sharla and the Claw.

The rest would be ridden down and slaughtered. No mercy or mistakes, not when they revealed themselves to be so dangerous. Here, justice shone its brightest: it didn't matter whether judgement came by the sword of a Watchmen or the arrow of a bandit. The Owl approved of it all the same.

*   *   *

IT HAD BEEN CLOSE. THE HORSES SHUDDERED, STAGGERED, running on their last reserves. Hesher's mount had entirely collapsed, and he'd barely escaped in time, forced to ride behind Keryn and add to the burden her horse already struggled to carry.

Against all odds, what remained of the crew finally reached the desert floor. Jyrak roused himself for a last attempt, turning to face the bandits and waving his hand before Sharla could stop him. The air around them shimmered for a moment, like summer heat radiating from the landscape. A low buzz sounded in her skull—perhaps more felt than heard—and goosebumps tingled her skin.

Behind them, the talus erupted in a spray of dust and debris, knocking riders clear and throwing horses through the air. The slope beside the explosion shifted. Cracks spiderwebbed the mesa as an entire face dislodged, released by Jyrak's magic. It slid in an overwhelming spread, burying most of the riders. Horses squealed and stumbled in the rising dust. Only a few shapes emerged, escaping the cloud to chase the crew.

Jyrak slumped again, nearly toppling from his saddle. Sharla grabbed his shoulder and pulled him toward her, centering him as best she could. The mage was mumbling something, and she leaned closer to hear him.

"What a ride."

Ahead of Arlon, the canyon disfigured the desert flat. A perimeter of white sandstone etched its profile, a pale expanse that starkly contrasted the surrounding browns. Arlon rode straight for the sandstone, disappearing over the slope. Sharla followed without giving herself time to think. The second slope was hardly better than what they'd left, with the addition of rock pinnacles that rose from the canyon floor as if to skewer the crew. Pillars and rock fragments formed irregular angles, strangely isolated after prior erosion. Below them, she saw this stretch of the canyon was long dry: nothing but an old wash greeted them when they finally reached the floor.

They hurtled through the space, into the deepening shadows as late afternoon transitioned toward evening. Never in her life had Sharla desired to spend any evening or night in such a place, especially not near Tigon Land. But with the bandits still in pursuit, there was little choice.

The crew continued into a broader canyon, where a river still flowed. Other gorges opened around them, numerous tributaries of the River Shapan that spread into the canyons bordering the Savage Land. All of them appeared equally dark, sheer, hateful. Enclosed spaces where any number of creatures or strange magics could lurk.

Chapter Twelve

The walls spread so high above them that Sharla only saw a sliver of daylight now, twisting fingers of sunlight as the canyon warped around them. The sandstone walls caught the light in hellish tones, as though reflecting firelight from an oven. The display might've amazed her if she hadn't heard bandits behind them, galloping closer.

Sturdier ground here—that was something. She struggled to load her crossbow again as Keryn drew another arrow, peering around Hesher, who blocked her view. Ahead of them, Arlon continued riding.

* * *

KINE REINED UP AT THE EDGE OF THE MESA, STARING AT THE devastated slope below them. The crew's mage must've continued his work, for a pile of talus blocked the entirety of the slope's base. Another path would have to be forged to Tigon Land, somewhere further along the mesa.

All this for Sharla? Kine scowled and stared across the brooding, darkening canyons. How quickly everything fell to pieces. How instantly he'd committed to hunting her down and bringing her to justice, scrambling his own plans.

Then, he reminded himself there hadn't really been other plans; just the thought that they'd ride to Senkha, and then to Marast. Join forces and ride into the Savage Land together, meet Dormun with a force he couldn't hope to survive. A message would be written across the Savage Land, a statement of blood to irrevocably solidify Low Country's border. Perhaps it was Kine's own pride that made him seek the other cartels, for the force he presently rode with would surely be enough to handle Dormun's men. Such an army hadn't entered the Savage Land for as long as he'd been alive.

Yes, they could ride into Tigon Land, round up Sharla, and head to Dormun with the knowledge they tortured from the Claw in her crew. Kine would settle both demons of his past in one swoop, restoring Low Country for all time. He'd—

He blinked, peering closer. A thunderhead loomed over Tigon Land; a massive, blackened pillar that forked with lightning. Rain poured from its depths in a sudden torrent, a dark curtain that drew over the westernmost reaches of the canyonland in an inexorable smear. It hadn't been there moments before, nor did the cloudless sky support its presence.

This was magical, and not the crew's doing. The storm would start a flash flood through the canyons to drown them all. Kine needed information, not their deaths. This was likely caused by Senit's mage, another of Senit's accomplices trying to ruin everything, hiding the chess pieces while Kine tried to make sense of them.

He examined the riders along the mesa's edge. All of them were Senit's men—Kine's Watchmen were still well behind them—and they moved across the mesa, peering at the thunderhead. Some of them whooped in victory while others nodded and muttered what might've been approval. He flicked the reins and thundered past them, moving east.

A mage would go somewhere private, somewhere to concentrate while they casted—or at least, that was the usual practice. Most mages required time and concentration to do their work, but the mage in Sharla's crew had cast a massive amount of magic with little effort. Kine didn't know how; he only knew Senit's mage had to be stopped, and immediately.

It was past rationality. Kine knew this, but didn't care. The cold anger had risen too high, squeezing his throat and clutching his lungs. Memories of his dead wife and his countless failures had exploded into the world with Dormun's reappearance. And now to find Sharla involved as well? Kine needed justice, needed to *see* it.

There were fewer riders here, scattered between the desert junipers and rock outcroppings. A few paces further and he found what he sought: a small gathering of riders behind a broken rock spire, watching the spectacle over the canyon. They turned as he dismounted beside the spire, tying his reins to a juniper.

"What are you doing?" he roared.

The riders stepped to meet him, seeing the blackness in his gaze and the anger in his face. They gripped hafts of battle axes, poleaxes, and even a halberd or two as the mage—a slight man with a shaved skull and swirling tattoos around his ears—regarded Kine as though he were a pestering insect.

"Ending those riders," the mage said. He turned back to his work and squinted, raising his hands.

"Under whose orders?"

The mage shook his head, barely present. "They tried to kill Senit. That must be answered."

"By the Owl's justice. Not yours."

The slightest grin, as though the mage thought this all a humorous joke. "We *are* the Owl's justice."

Kine didn't see it happen, didn't *feel* it happen. It was instinct now; the caged animal released, the starving wolf unleashed. One moment, he was walking toward the mage. The next, he'd drawn his sword and chopped in one motion, decapitating the first man he came across and spraying blood in a torrent. The headless trunk staggered sideways as the other three raised their weapons.

Kine stepped into their midst, pivoting with his yellow cape billowing behind, bright with sunlight. He caught the poleaxe haft across his left pauldron as he stepped into the strike, rending the man's chest with his blade. Blood sprayed up his side, misted his eyes as he stepped underneath the halberd, a massive arc of metal. He drew the knife from his belt with his left hand, punching in and out of the man's side, twice, before he could step further. The bandit floundered, waving his halberd as though stunned it had been so quick, so easy, and he accidentally blocked the strike of his friend. The friend shouted and flailed with his dying comrade as the mage finally turned to Kine, abandoning his former efforts.

Kine rushed forward, aware he'd found himself in dire straits as the mage channeled. He dropped his knife and fumbled for his shield, barely wrestling it around as he dove. The air shifted; goosebumps rippled across his skin as something *changed* directly beside him. An opening of space, a drop in pressure as fire exploded in a torrent, blazing close enough to singe Kine's hair and bake his skin. The shield came around in time to catch part of the pillar, blocking the closest flames while they licked underneath and around, reaching for Kine's head and legs. He stumbled and found himself in the dirt. The mage had ceased his attack, eyes widening as he stared at his burned comrades, now turned into shrieking, leaping spectacles while fire contorted their limbs and consumed their hair.

Kine forced himself upright, running at the mage as he stepped backward. Too close for magic, too quick an attack to concentrate on more runes. The mage drew his own blade, a longsword hopelessly ill-suited to the present task. Its reach nevertheless forced Kine to raise his own blade, and the weapons' edges grated against each other as he continued forward. The mage tripped and brought both men to the ground, rolling toward the edge of the mesa. Kine dropped his shield, reached around their blades, and smashed the mage's head with a gauntleted fist. He grabbed a fistful of the other man's hair and crashed his head against the ground.

"I'm the Owl's justice," Kine snarled. "*Me.*"

The mage's body slackened, his limbs flailing with every report of his head against the rocks.

"You have no authority here," Kine said, all his frustration, anger, and regret pouring out like hot lava. "Senit has no authority here. Low Country is *mine*. I *made* it."

He finally stopped, blinking at the blood that splattered his face and armor. He pulled himself away from the ruined mage—now possessing a cratered skull—and panted. Ahead of him, the thunderhead dispersed. The sky emptied of rain, clouds, anything unnatural. The evening glowed as before, with nothing changed but for what they couldn't see: the phenomenon surely caused by the rain that had fallen in the canyons.

"Ancestors help us all," Kine whispered.

"No. I think we're past that."

He turned to see Gashar beside the pillar. He watched Kine as though Kine was a snake he'd stumbled onto, a serpent with bared fangs.

"Lieutenant Colonel."

"Colonel."

Chapter Twelve

The men stared at each other while Kine waited for Gashar to speak, be it to condemn or affirm his actions. When the younger man said nothing, Kine finally stood, wiped his blade on the mage's coat, and sheathed it, going to pick up his shield and knife. The burned men had finally stopped shouting, laying together in what might've been a peaceful embrace if their skin hadn't been charred as black as pitch.

"Lieutenant Colonel," Kine repeated. "Help me throw these men over the edge."

* * *

SHARLA'S BOLT MISSED. RIGHT WHEN SHE RELEASED, NUN skittered over a rock and sent the shot wide. But it wasn't a rock; Nun stumbled everywhere now, too exhausted to continue. Sharla swore and dismounted, abandoning Nun and diving to the side as the bandit thundered past. Steel flashed, whispering over her neck—he'd barely missed her. He tugged on his reins, turning his horse for another pass as Nun stumbled toward the river in the canyon's center, desperate for a drink.

The bandit came at Sharla again, his sword poised for a downward chop. It was a massive blade, likely stolen from some convoy of military armaments. She stepped backward, briefly considering her options before drawing one of the bone battle axes and tossing it. She hadn't intended to hit him, merely to disrupt his charge, but it appeared to do the trick. He reared and chopped at the flying weapon, knocking it from the air in a move that unbalanced him and hung his head low enough for a chop from Ovis's own battle axe to trench his forehead. The bandit dropped with a moan and his horse continued past, crazed and disoriented.

Sharla turned to see four more bandits, two of whom already harassed Keryn and Hesher as the woman missed her shot. Jyrak slouched nearby while Arlon turned his horse to face the riders, drawing his stiletto and snarling.

"Wait here, little lady." Ovis turned to face the bandits, kicking his horse forward with a shout.

Sharla frowned at the comment and drew her other axe—the beautiful steel one. She stepped forward, but something changed. *What happened?* She stared around the canyon, watching the riders as they fought, struggling to stay atop their saddles while steel clashed and men spat. They circled each other, swiping blades while their horses splashed through the river.

Sharla took a step and felt it again. No, it had been there all along—something under the earth. Something of the earth itself. She crouched and put a hand to the sand. She heard it now; a dull roar from the other side of the canyon, like all the bison of Low Country stampeded. A chill ran down her spine.

"What—"

A shape. Colossal, fluid, undulating. Swaying and rocking across the far side of the canyon as though the walls were collapsing. It consumed the river and roiled several men high, sweeping away trees, rocks, brush, and anything else in its path. It was colored a dull red, like rotting tomatoes, carrying grasses, tree limbs, and the broken bodies of horses and bandits. It was preceded by a strange dust, a haze kicked from the canyon floor as the torrent washed away entire banks of mud and shelves of rock.

Sharla finally recognized it for what it was: a flash flood that filled the canyon, rolling in an unstoppable tide. But there hadn't been any rain, had there? She'd seen no clouds.

She wasted precious seconds considering the impossibility of such an event. Old wisdom finally kicked in, trickling through her shock like sand through an hourglass. *Find the high ground.* Aye, but there was none around her.

She frantically searched the canyon, seeing nothing but the same, flat stretch everyone presently fought in. No change anywhere but—

There. Behind her, the slightest rise anchored a cottonwood beside the river. There was a ledge beyond it, but she doubted she could make it that far—and certainly not with Nun. The horse was already exhausted.

She sprinted for the cottonwood and abandoned Nun, yelping prayers for her as she ran. "Sorry, girl. I'm so sorry. I'm so—"

Chapter Twelve

Men shouted as the roar grew louder. Their screams suddenly ceased, swallowed into nothing. Jyrak said something somewhere beside her. Arlon and Ovis and Keryn all yelled while Hesher moaned. The combined noise drummed Sharla's skull, slamming in alongside the roaring water.

"Sharla!" She turned to see Arlon leaning, reaching for her from atop his horse. "Here!"

A shape behind him, closing fast, made her jerk away from him. "Look out!"

He spun and avoided a chopping blade as he struggled to retaliate. The bandit's horse surged against Arlon's, pushing them toward the river. Sharla ran again, refusing to look back, refusing to acknowledge how close the water had grown.

"Little lady!" Ovis hesitated, kicking his horse forward and abandoning her. The water was too close now—she felt it through her entire being. The ground trembled and the air rushed as though it moved against the tide, struggling to counteract it. Jyrak and Keryn rode by on the other side. A glimpse of Arlon and the bandit on her peripherals, and then—

She dove the final few paces, scrambled behind the cottonwood as the canyon darkened. She fought for a handhold, leaping as high as she could and grabbing the uppermost branches as the world *surged*. Floodwater streamed around the cottonwood in an ugly mud, thick and dark. A horse floundered past, swept away, and a hand grabbed Sharla's boot. She kicked it, struggled upward, and the entire world twisted as the tree plunged, caught in the swell and uprooted as though it were a rotten fence post.

She squeezed the tree for dear life. It rocked and swayed, but impossibly, it didn't roll over. They were moving too fast to comprehend, bucking and roiling as though she rode an enraged horse. She spared a glance sideways to see the roots of the tree splayed around her, anchors in the current that functioned as outriggers to keep the cottonwood upright. It heaved and shook, following the floodwater as it coursed through the canyon.

Her breath hitched in her throat, a terrified half-laugh of relief before the hand grabbed her boot again. She arched her neck to see a man behind her, his eyes wide and his face stretched with terror. He clutched her boot while his other hand gripped a knife, his arm wrapped around a tree limb to keep himself steady. He swayed with the branch and struggled for balance, hissing with the effort.

Sharla tried to kick him but lurched and nearly lost her grip on the tree. He howled something as they tumbled through the canyon. The walls were blurring past them, the sky twisting and arcing.

She tried to kick him again and one of the branches underneath her snapped off. She slipped, scrambled for a new handhold, and slid down the tree, finding her legs across the bandit, who shrieked as he fumbled for her limbs. He gripped her pants while he fished with his knife, scraping tree bark and wavering dangerously close to skin.

She screamed a wordless prayer to the ancestors and let go of her remaining handhold. She chopped her battle axe down as she slid forward, mashing his hand before she abandoned the weapon to grab another cluster of branches. For a nauseating moment, she found nothing but tree leaves, catching herself in the eyes, the mouth. She tasted dirt and dust and mud, seeing nothing but green, bark, water. Both arms strained against the branches she'd tangled in. Her hands clenched the bark, drawing blood from her palms as she hugged the tree for dear life, heedless of the branches or the knotted surface that ground against her ribs.

She found herself looking down the tree and caught a glimpse of the man as his mouth gaped, letting out a howl she never heard. He waved his mutilated hand while bloody fingers tumbled around him like pebbles. He lost his balance, sought it again, and reached for her.

One of his boots touched the water. He blinked, and the current drug him under the mud.

Sharla buried her face into her shoulder, all efforts and sensations focused on her lifeline: the tree trunk. She grasped it for dear life, squeezing until flesh could've melded with wood, until all time and

Chapter Twelve

meaning lost itself in the shape of the tree. The water churned underneath her, drowning her thoughts and consciousness.

For a time, she knew only the tree, the water beneath it, and the reality that she was still alive.

Chapter Thirteen

STILLNESS. EVERYTHING HAD STOPPED.

You sure?

No.

Maybe try looking around?

Sharla hesitated, cautiously raising her head to look. Her cottonwood had lodged between the trunks of several other trees, its roots tangled about theirs and holding her against the current. The water had slowed but still carried a red color: mud and dirt and sediment swirled against the banks. The canyon was quieter, gentler.

Overhead, dusk colored the sky purple and pink. In such light, the canyon walls were menacing and foreboding, as though they could topple over Sharla. After everything she'd just seen, she wouldn't have been surprised if they had—wouldn't have been surprised if all Low Country suddenly caved into itself, swallowing her to the underworld. Ancestors above, she'd fallen past her depth.

Past my depth? She stared at the tree she hugged, at the steel battle axe still embedded in the wood. Bloodstained, with a scrap of flesh pinned underneath it. *What depth? Blood and ashes, what am I doing here?*

She tried to focus on retrieving her axe and climbing down the tree. It made sense to return to stable ground, to get her bearings and think on what came next. She crawled backwards and winced as stiffened limbs flared with pain and aches all over her body—the results of pressing herself against knobby wood for too long. She crawled steadily, nearly

Chapter Thirteen

slipping into the water several times, but finally reached the shoreline. She attempted to stand, to take a few steps forward, but her legs shook too badly to go far. She finally sunk against a cottonwood and fell to her knees.

Something rose from her chest: a low moan. A terrified sound in the vast, empty canyon. Only the sighing wind answered her. Everyone was gone. Everything had washed away. She was starting over at the bottom of the world, lost in a sudden nightmare. She'd hired a crew, but now she'd probably gotten all of them killed and stranded herself in the middle of a labyrinth with no way out.

What am I doing here?

She was succumbing to hysteria, taking frantic breaths as though she couldn't get enough air. The canyon walls were suddenly closing in, pressing her, squeezing the life from her body. The world reared taller than she'd ever seen it: trees, rocks, even the sky stretched impossibly high. She recognized herself as she really was: a speck of dust before eternity's curtain. That curtain drew over her soul: a black cloud of doom and despair.

She found herself on the ground, breathing too fast to call for help, for someone to save her from the sudden panic, the rushing despair. She cowered in the blackness, choking and spluttering, hugging herself until every limb shook, ached, froze.

Ancestors, help me. Blood and ashes, somebody, please.

* * *

SOMETIME LATER—SHE DIDN'T KNOW HOW LONG—THE PANIC subsided, leaving her exhausted and cold on the canyon floor. Above her, stars blinked down, piercing the night to herald the coming moonrise. They were cold, distant things watching over the cruel landscape.

She stared at the sight, licking her lips and pulling herself upright. She shoved herself against the tree behind her and struggled to think. *What now?* Well, she had water...of sorts. She needed food, but maybe that could wait until tomorrow? First, she had to find someplace to take shelter. Maybe the trees could work?

She examined the length of the canyon, seeing nothing else. The trees, then. She'd stay right here. She'd stay until—

Something moaned from downriver with the magnitude of grinding rocks, but with the pitch of something higher, like shrieking birds. Equal parts hissing, slithering, and cawing all rolled into one, a noise that sent chills down her spine and shivers through her limbs. She grabbed her battle axe and froze.

She waited, staring down the canyon. The water reflected the growing night, blackening as though stained by ink. The shoreline darkened alongside it until the shapes of trees and brush appeared as twisting silhouettes, tortured people who'd clawed free of the floodwater.

The wind sighed; maybe that's what she'd heard?

A second utterance of the noise, but louder—and this time from somewhere behind her. She moved into a battle crouch, both hands clenching the axe until it trembled. Memories of legends and myths filled her head before she could block them out: every tale she'd heard of travelers who wandered Tigon Land and never came back.

Another noise before her, but this time it sounded closer, as though something were *communicating*. She shrank against the tree and examined both sides of the canyon, nauseous and dizzy. Ancestors above, it wasn't fair. She'd survived the flood and Kine Tarroful only to find herself in this? Chased by...what?

Indecision plagued her. Move on? Wait for whatever was calling to show itself? Should she fight it? *Impossible.* Run? *Can't make it.* Give up?

She focused on her frustration and anger. She gripped it as tightly as she could and reveled in its blaze. She'd made it to Mela, found a crew, fought off a town—*two* towns by now—and survived a flood. She wouldn't go down without a fight. Even if she had no idea *what* she fought.

A moment of silence. She waited in the quiet, then clenched her jaw and stood. She stepped forward—

Chapter Thirteen

A hand clapped over her mouth, and another on her shoulder. She screamed into the hand before she recognized Arlon's voice in her ear. "Don't do anything stupid."

Her heart raced alongside her breath, almost as fast as before, but she forced herself to nod, to relax. After a moment, Arlon released her. She turned to him and sought his eyes, but she could barely see him in the night.

"What is it?" she whispered.

"Tigoras. A few of them, at least."

"What?"

"Older Common for, 'canyon creatures.'" He paused and stared down the canyon. "A better description would probably be 'canyon serpents.'"

"That supposed to be better?"

"It's supposed to be more serious. They're said to be kin to the dragons of old." He shook his head. "Don't make unnecessary noise."

She looked behind him and saw the rest of the crew shambling from the darkness. Their faces remained shadowed, and their postures were slumped, mirroring her exhaustion. Their horses hung their heads in the same manner, reminding her of Nun.

She trembled with the memories, and she forced herself to speak before she collapsed again. "You made it."

"We were lucky. Reached a ledge before getting swept away. We saw you ride the tree out and we feared the worst."

"*He* feared the worst," Keryn hissed. "I knew with our luck we'd find your sorry hide sooner or later."

"You came looking for me?" Sharla asked.

"You promised us payment," Arlon answered.

She wished she could see enough to know whether he offered his sly grin, whether he made a joke of the notion, but a bellow interrupted her thoughts. This one was close enough to rattle her bones and echo from the canyon walls. Rocks spilled, trees rustled their branches, and water stirred to lap the shorelines. The horses were either too exhausted to care or better trained than Sharla could've imagined, for they shrank under the touches of their riders, all of whom walked beside them and whispered into their ears.

"They're closer now," Arlon said. "We should move out of sight."

"Where?" Sharla asked.

He looked around them. "Good point."

"We stay where we are," Jyrak whispered.

The crew stopped and waited, listening. The moments oozed past like the mud at the banks. Sharla found herself holding her breath, her lungs squeezing her chest until she thought her ribcage would burst.

They finally heard another roar. It sounded—or felt—quieter, and this time, no rocks fell, nor did the trees shake.

"Moving away," Ovis said.

"It seems so," Jyrak agreed.

"Why?" Sharla asked. "What are they doing?"

"If they're tigoras, they're just restless," Jyrak said. "The flood probably woke them, combined with the magic required to create it. Like Arlon said, they're thought to be descendants of the dragons. They're just as sensitive to magic."

"You know all this?" Sharla asked. "And you and your bloodkin still choose to stay here?"

"Tigoras hibernate just like the dragons." Jyrak shrugged. "If you don't disturb the tigoras, they don't wake up. They usually don't move around like this."

The thought of resting so close to a tigora made Sharla's heart lurch, even if the serpents usually slept.

"We should stay here for the night," Jyrak said. "Let them settle."

"And then what?" Hesher demanded.

Silence filled the canyon, a wonderful quiet without the tigoras' moans.

"Let's decide tomorrow," Arlon finally said.

"How convenient," Keryn muttered. "Gives you time to find your next idea."

"Would you rather us hash it out now?"

"It needs to happen at some point, doesn't it?"

Chapter Thirteen

Arlon's lips thinned. "You keep bringing it up, and yet you never do anything about it."

For the second time in the gang's company, Sharla found herself wincing, stepping back from the brewing conflict. The moon had finally edged over the canyon wall, and its light washed their faces silver, glinting in the hard set of Keryn's eyes and tracing the shape of Arlon's clenched jaw.

"I'll wait a little longer," Keryn muttered. "Mostly because I'm curious to see what fool plan you'll come up with."

"You just want to get paid, same as me. Same as the rest of us."

"We're owed *something*," Keryn answered. "Especially after Nithan."

This brought another moment of silence. The crew hung their heads, looked at the dirt, grimacing or frowning. Hesher gritted his teeth, and when she looked closer, Sharla thought she saw tears across his cheeks.

"He never wanted any part of this," Hesher said.

Some of the crew sniffed, as though fighting their own tears. Unable to bear the moment any longer, and all too aware she'd been the cause of Nithan's death, their hasty escape, and everything else they'd suffered over the past several days, Sharla finally retreated to a safer distance. She sought the blessed quiet and struggled to leave the rest behind.

Chapter Fourteen

KINE AND GASHAR LED THE RIDERLESS HORSES BACK TO where Senit and the rest of his company waited at the mesa's edge. The cartel leader examined the animals and his eyes narrowed.

"Where's my mage?"

"I guess the spell was too powerful for him to wield," Kine said. "He lost control and blew out the rock shelf, knocking himself and the others down the mesa. You can still see their bodies if you look close enough."

"Why would I look for their bodies?"

"For proof. Should you have any need."

"Afraid I don't trust you, Kine?"

"I *know* you don't trust me, Senit. And the feeling's mutual. It should stay mutual if you know what's good for you."

Senit thought through this for a moment. Finally, he turned to the canyon. "I needed that mage, Kine. He was a hard man to find."

"You don't need to tell me; I've searched for mages for decades. Never found any."

"I don't think Senkha has one," Senit mused. "I never hear anything about Marast. So…we're at an impasse."

"We can fight Claws without a mage."

Senit pursed his lips. "I've heard people say the Claws have their own mages. They call them shamans—men who can enter the spirit world."

Chapter Fourteen

Kine grimaced. "All the more reason we should follow that crew into the canyons. They had their own mage with them—a runemaster, by the looks of it. He had to be one who destroyed that building. He looked at me, waved his hand, and it was done."

"After you killed one of their men."

Kine hesitated, unsure of how to respond. "Yes."

"When one of their men sought you out. And one of their other men sought *me* out." Senit shook his head. "I don't like this, Kine. They shouldn't know who I am."

"They planned an escape. They tried to assassinate me. When we all moved, in the heat of the moment, how can you be so sure they weren't aiming for *me*? That they didn't just…miss?"

Senit said nothing. His displeasure smoldered like a black cloud, a smoke that stirred his men. They drew themselves upright, gripping their sword pommels.

That familiar trickle of sweat returned to Kine's spine, and he scowled. "Senit, I ask you to take me seriously when I say we can catch their runemaster. He'll lead us to others. Those canyons are full of them; we've all heard. Where one goes, more will be found. Plus, the crew has a Claw with them. He can tell us about Dormun Redskull."

"And they have a girl with them." Senit finally turned and locked gazes with Kine. "A girl you seem to know. We all know what you're after, Kine."

Bitterness coursed through Kine. "Please, enlighten us."

"You're after her. You're after…*Sharla*."

"She's a wanted criminal," Kine said. "Plus, she has a Claw with her. None of this would've been a problem if it hadn't gone wrong at the monastery. *You* weren't supposed to be there, and you startled them."

Quiet stilled the riders. Senit grinned.

"Blaming everything on me, Kine?"

Kine clenched his jaw. "I'm telling you we should follow that crew. Let their runemaster lead us to the others. There'll be more than enough mages for you then."

Senit considered for a moment. "Very well. Find us a way down, Colonel."

* * *

THE ENTIRE CONVERSATION HAD HAPPENED HOURS AGO, long before the riders had traveled westward along the mesa and found a solitary trail down—one that looked as treacherous as what Sharla's crew had taken. They'd made it as far as a canyon's edge before deciding to make camp, for the crew couldn't go much farther than they, especially not after the beating they'd given their horses. Besides, navigating the canyons by nightfall was suicide; everyone knew that much.

Or at least, Kine *hoped* it was suicide. He hoped Sharla's crew would wait the night out just as he did, that there would still be a chance to catch them before they found their way out.

The thoughts so consumed him, he never heard Gashar approach until the younger man stood beside him.

"Colonel."

"Lieutenant Colonel."

"Can't sleep, sir?"

Kine exhaled and stared across the rim of white rock. "The night's still young."

Gashar appeared to ponder his words, a silent sentinel that stayed long enough for Kine to squirm. "You have something to say, Lieutenant Colonel?"

"You have that look again."

"What look?"

"You're thinking. Planning something. Given what you've already done, I'd say it's something dangerous."

Everything *he'd* done? Since when had Gashar looked for reasons to question Kine, to throw doubt on his judgements? Kine examined the man, irritation rising. "If you have something to say, you should say it."

Gashar hesitated. After a moment, he sat beside Kine, easing backward to rest against a rock. "Just a question to ask. Who's Sharla?"

"A criminal."

Chapter Fourteen

"We both know she's more."

"Because Senit said so?"

"Because you aren't yourself, Colonel."

"You're the one who said I was known as a drunkard who stirred up every town I lodged in, who made enemies of every whore I bedded," Kine said. He couldn't entirely succeed in keeping the bitterness from his voice.

"You're a different man in peacetime than in wartime. Isn't that the same with all of us, Colonel?" Gashar shifted in place, clearly uncomfortable with the role of interrogator. "But you were always so calm when you wore the Owl plating. So tactful. Now you seem…impulsive. Angry and reckless."

"Dormun killed my wife."

"I'm sure he's killed a lot of people."

"He was my friend," Kine growled. "A friend who abused my trust." He turned to Gashar, snarled at the man. "Have you ever known love, Gashar? *True* love? Love that makes you promise yourself to follow a woman to the ends of the earth?"

Gashar looked beyond Kine to the canyon, his gaze distant in the light of nearby campfires. "Reckon I haven't found the right woman, Colonel."

"Low Country, then. Do you love this country? Would you sacrifice for it, bleed for it? Die for it?"

"I suppose that's what we all agreed to do when we took the Owl's mantle."

"Imagine someone treading on what you love. They take your wife behind your back, abuse her night and day, all while smiling at you and sharing in your ale. They have you thinking it's bandits or lowlifes or someone else who does it, and by the time you've realized what's really happening, your wife is dead from their torment."

"You think Low Country is dead? That Dormun could kill it?"

"I think Low Country has suffered long enough. Ignored by the king, dismissed by the Owl. No one cares for this land, Gashar. No one did anything until I put my foot down. Someone had to."

Gashar fell quiet for a long moment. "You feel you're owed more? Is that it, Colonel? You feel you should have gotten a better deal, so you gather these men to take back what's yours."

"It's not mine. It's all Low Country's."

"It was your wife." Gashar inclined his head. "And now it's Sharla."

"Sharla." Kine spat into the brush, looking around to ensure no other men were close enough to hear. "What do you know about it?"

"Nothing but the rumors." Gashar folded his arms across his chest, exhaled like he was preparing to dive into a freezing river. "Stories about the Tarroful family."

"The Tarroful family." Kine barked an empty laugh. "We're a byword now. A story used to frighten children."

"Please, Colonel. You're worrying your men. You're erratic, and some of them are saying you've gone crazy."

"Finally cracked under Low Country's sun, eh?" Kine eased himself against a rock opposite Gashar and stared into the canyon. Somewhere in that darkness, Sharla rested, even now. Almost within his grasp, as she'd been all those years before. "I reckon this place eventually does it to everyone."

"It doesn't have to."

"It deserves more, Lieutenant Colonel."

A moment of silence, broken only by the sounds of conversation and crackling wood from other campfires.

"It's a desert, Kine," Gashar finally said. "Perhaps it would be best if we just let it be."

"Only a day ago you scolded me for thinking of leaving."

"I didn't say we should leave it. But maybe we should return to our original purpose as Watchmen. We watch and police. We don't conquer and rule."

"We aren't ruling. We co-control it with the cartels."

"This is your new love," Gashar said quietly. "You said as much yourself only a few minutes ago. When your wife died, you married yourself to this country. You've fought to control it ever since."

"It's not about control."

Chapter Fourteen

"Then it's about policing? Keeping the innocent safe? Not lording over your personal empire?"

"You want the men to hear what you're saying?" But Kine knew it didn't matter, not anymore. It'd been so long since the king sent reinforcements that the remaining Watchmen had formed their own brotherhood, their own alliance. The former hierarchy established name and loyalty merely for the pecking order, or so Kine suspected. He'd long ago known if the going grew tough, he wouldn't gamble on his men to back him up. No, they'd probably sooner join arms with Gashar. A civil war within the Watchmen.

Kine shook his head and looked to where the moon should've been, now covered with clouds. Who would've imagined it? Watchmen turning against each other? But then, who would've imagined the Watchmen still rode Low Country, especially after so long without word from the king? Kine had been the one to strengthen the Watchmen, steeling them for the test of time. Of course he was owed more. Look at what he'd done.

"When my wife died, I arranged the cartels," Kine said. "Hard enough in those times. Little peace and little honor among Watchmen. I don't know how many of those early days you remember, Gashar, but our Watchmen handled themselves little better than bandits.

"My daughter was Hari Tarroful. She married a Watchman of questionable character, someone who would've made you rethink the king's judgment. But the king hadn't been around in so long that this man was allowed to wear the Owl's mantle. He was a drunkard, a thief, and surrounded by rumors. I have no idea what she saw in him; she'd made poor decisions since her mother died.

"They had a daughter—Sharla—and for a while, everything was quiet. Everything was peaceful." Kine shook his head. "But Hari had learned from her man. She'd been stealing from me, slipping coin from under my nose. All the money earned since negotiating the cartels and cashing in on the new drugs, every coin that would've been used to set her and her daughter up away from Low Country, away from the fighting and strife. She stole it like a common thief, stabbing me in the back just like Dormun."

Kine's hands had started trembling, itching for conflict, burning for justice. "Maybe she learned it from her man. He'd become abusive, but she wouldn't tell me. He beat her, and she explained all the bruising away as sparring accidents. I was too busy with the cartels, so how could I have known? How could I have changed anything?"

Kine hesitated, aware he was verging on information he'd never shared with anyone. He'd obviously heard the whispers; a strange thing to hear stories about your own family, your own flesh and blood. Nobody ever confronted him on the matter, never asked him what became of his family. Did Low Country truly think him such a monster? Did it fear him, the drunkard colonel of the Watchmen who proved himself dangerous to every town he visited?

"Sharla killed him—Hari's husband. Stabbed him in the chest. I suppose she couldn't watch more abuse and took matters into her own hands when Hari wouldn't." Kine held his breath, as though he feared Gashar's judgement. He felt little better than Hari in that moment, cowering under the hand of her husband, stealing from Kine rather than asking for help or aid. Little better than her daughter, Sharla, who killed a man and ran like a coward, a common criminal.

"Hari ran away, but not before she gave Sharla the money she'd stolen," Kine said. "Sharla learned from her example, and she ran east when her mother went west. She saw Low Country as her home after all, and according to the man who spoke to me in Laken, she's buried the rest of my money somewhere in the desert. Little better than bandits, the lot of them. And now she's down there, in that canyon below us. I've finally found her."

Gashar still kept silent, but Kine felt his gaze all the same, burrowing through his skin.

"This is all for money?" Gashar finally asked. "You're after Sharla to get your money back?"

Kine stared at the other man. "This is about my legacy. The legacy of Kine Tarroful: the man who resurrected Low Country, built it back better

Chapter Fourteen

than before. That man will not be known as the patriarch of a family of thieves."

"I thought Low Country was your legacy. The land itself. Isn't that what you wanted?"

Kine glared at Gashar, but turned away as the younger man's gaze tore something inside of him. "I want Sharla and Hari back," he growled. "I want my family whole again. Ancestors only know where Hari went, but Sharla's still here."

"That's why you're after her? To welcome her back?"

Kine couldn't answer that and couldn't meet Gashar's gaze. "Once, I tried to teach this country about mercy. When I let Dormun go, I tried for a new age between Claws and Low Country, an example Low Country could learn from. But once the people saw our new age, they didn't want to listen to me anymore. Maybe they never did. Maybe Low Country has always been doomed. Maybe I've only delayed its collapse. I've allowed too many mistakes, failed to bring justice."

Kine found that his hand traced the pommel of his sword, rubbing it between his fingers as though it were a charm. "Judgement must start somewhere, Gashar. Even if it's judgement for my family."

"Then we chased this crew for Sharla, not the runemasters."

"We chased this crew for the runemasters and the Claw," Kine answered. "Sharla is just a complication."

He trailed off, uncertain what else to say. Their conversation had already touched precarious topics he'd never wished to stumble through, perhaps because he hadn't navigated them himself. How could someone manuever the stormy waters of their family, the darkest secrets of their loved ones? How could anyone stand the truth?

"Do you see us as friends, Colonel?" Gashar asked.

"Of course."

"Then may I speak to you as a friend rather than as my commander?"

Kine hesitated, but nodded. "Please."

Gashar cleared his throat, weighing his words. "I've never seen Low Country as you have. I know that, and so do you. I understand this land

and its people less than you do. But it seems to me you've shown the rest of us something. You've shown us a man's legacy doesn't come from the things he's accomplished. Those all fade, given time. Low Country is a wasteland. It'll forget you once you're gone."

Kine turned to the man, who shook his head as though Kine's gaze unnerved him. "You've supported me through difficult seasons, sir. You've helped me through times no one else could, and for that, you've earned my respect. You've impacted my life, and I believe that's the truest legacy we leave. It comes from the people you impact; from how they remember you. It isn't measured by Watchmen or what they've done. You're not the Owl. You're not the king. You won't be remembered as either."

Gashar's voice trailed off, and he looked to the canyon as though forgetting what else he meant to say. "We're all here today, gone tomorrow. But I'll remember you by how you made me a better man. That's the legacy we leave, not the state of a country or its borders." He shook his head. "And I know you're not the man Low Country makes you out to be. I've ridden with you long enough to see that. You want something better for us."

Kine watched the man, his mouth sinking into a frown. "That's supposed to comfort me? You're telling me I should let Hari and Sharla go free? That I shouldn't try to catch them?"

Gashar exhaled. "I know you want the right things. I just…don't want to see you throw everything else away."

For a moment, Kine's resolve wavered. But then he thought of his family again and his blood boiled anew. "No. Justice will be done. It must."

A long silence fell between them, and after a moment, Gashar nodded. "Of course, Colonel."

Kine nodded, as if they'd concluded the matter. Gashar's words bit deeper than he had expected, likely deeper than the younger man imagined they could. They threatened to shake Kine's belief, to wriggle through the cracks and upend everything he knew. Was this all a mistake? Were his efforts to end Dormun and bring Sharla to justice

Chapter Fourteen

merely a result of his own selfishness, as though he were an impudent child who pleaded for his way?

No. This was Low Country. It didn't want mercy—not anymore. Low Country deserved justice, and he'd give the people what they wanted. He'd do it for his wife, for Hari…for Sharla. In the end, they'd all thank him for it. In the end, the land would know peace. His legacy would be affirmed, fulfilled. Everything would be restored.

Kine Tarroful wasn't the forgiving kind. He couldn't afford to be. Not when the fate of all Low Country rested on what happened next.

Chapter Fifteen

THE CREW HEARD NOTHING FROM THE TIGORAS FOR THE REST of the night. When Sharla woke, blessed daylight burned from the east, glowing off the canyon's sandstone walls in fiery reds and oranges. The colors shimmered in the river, granting it a beautiful warmth now that the mud appeared to have dispersed. The water tasted crisp, refreshing, better than anything Sharla remembered. It seemed things might be looking up.

At least until she saw the rest of the crew, and remembered where they were and what had happened. Nithan was dead. They'd found no new recruits to help them in their fight against Dormun. They'd been chased into a canyon and their pursuers probably camped somewhere above them, waiting for them to exit.

Breakfast was a quiet affair. The crew passed around dried beef and biscuits Jyrak bought in Laken before Sharla's past chased them out. When they finally stashed the remaining rations, the silence deepened. The crew eyed each other, waited for someone to ask the question they all dreaded.

"What now?" Keryn finally asked.

Sharla felt eyes on her, and she struggled not to look at anyone. Arlon cleared his throat and spoke. "I reckon we keep going."

"And do what?" Keryn demanded. "How long will we do this, Arlon? How long will we ride for this woman?"

Chapter Fifteen

"You can turn back and ride away," Arlon said. "Forget you ever saw her."

"You still planning on fighting Claws with this crew?"

"It won't only be us," Sharla said, unable to hold her silence any longer. She forced herself to make eye contact with each of them. She struggled past Hesher's haunted features, Keryn's embittered expression, the somber eyes of Jyrak, Ovis's unreadable look, and finally, the distant gaze of Arlon. "The riders who chased us from Laken. All of them are riding to fight Dormun."

"How could you know that?" Keryn asked.

"Their leader, Kine Tarroful." Sharla hesitated. "He wouldn't have joined Senit's bandits for any other reason." She turned to Arlon. "You're sure that was him?"

Arlon nodded. "I'll never forget his face. Saw it long ago, when I rode the Great Canyon. I knew who he was because he looks so much like Senkha."

Sharla returned the nod. "Kine is the Colonel of the Third Regiment, the only regiment the king stationed in Low Country. I don't know how he convinced Senit to ride with him, because doing so would only communicate an alliance to the other cartels. It would probably force the others together and there'd be civil war. There might still be one. Kine wouldn't risk that unless he was desperate. There's only one thing he could be after to take a risk so large: Dormun's head. The cartels and Watchmen have banded together to form an army to match Dormun's own. They're going to fight him...meaning we can still do what we came here for."

"Save everyone from Opek?" Jyrak asked.

Sharla nodded.

"You really think they'll still be alive?" Hesher asked.

"Why would Dormun kill them?" Sharla hesitated for the briefest moment. "It doesn't make any sense—not if he did this to bait Kine. I don't see why else he would've done it, knowing how the Watchmen would react. He wants hostages to barter with, to negotiate with."

"He's a Claw," Keryn scoffed. "He wouldn't know a thing about Kine. But you seem to know all about him, and he knew you by name. He brought his riders to kick down the monastery doors, and he said it was for money and murdered men? No. He knows you, Sharla. We all see it. Care to explain?"

Sharla squirmed; she'd known this would come sooner or later. Still, that didn't make the sharing any easier. She'd hoped that by riding with a crew of strangers, she'd be able to blend in without sharing her past. So much for that. "Kine Tarroful is my grandfather."

Keryn leaned against a tree, as though stunned. Ovis looked confused, Jyrak's eyes widened, Hesher shook his head, and Arlon watched her with an intense expression.

"Fabulous," Keryn muttered. "So, what? You ran away from home?"

"Something like that."

"Stole all his money?"

"Basically."

"The money you were going to pay us with?" Jyrak asked. "That's *Kine's* money?"

"The money I *am* going to pay you with," Sharla answered. "And it's not Kine's money. It never was. It was coin that came from the new drugs off the borders, through Keth from over the Shapan River. It's money from the black market made off the backs of addicted men, women, and children who never would've suffered so much if he hadn't formed cartels who terrorize as much as they keep the peace. Cartels who have their bandits fighting over territories just as much as they all fight the Claws on the borders." She shook her head and spat into the bank. "It's blood money. It's terrible. And it was all given to me by my mother."

"Who stole it from Kine?" Keryn prompted.

"Yes."

"And where is she now?"

"She ran away."

"Runs in the family, I suppose." Jyrak raised an eyebrow at his own joke, but nobody acknowledged him.

Chapter Fifteen

"It's not his money," Sharla insisted. "It belongs to Low Country. It belongs to you."

"You ran away from him because of what he'd done?" Arlon asked.

"I ran away from him because I can't stand him. Never could. I ran away because…" Sharla trailed off, aware she'd stumbled deep into her past—deep enough that she couldn't return unscathed, not without soiling herself.

So, she told them about her mother. She told them about the father who beat her mother, the mother who never defended herself until Sharla finally killed her husband for her.

The same mother so stricken by shame that she gave Sharla all the money before running and leaving her to fend for herself.

The memories stirred up Sharla's old anger toward her father that had fueled her self-imposed exile. It smoldered through her until her hands trembled, and she glared at each member of the crew in turn, as though spiting them for the truth they'd forced her to uncover. "I don't want to see her again. Didn't want to see Kine, either. I thought I could take the money and use it to sail out of Low Country. Start somewhere new."

Now, she felt herself dipping into the familiar well of regret, and she trailed off, uncertain.

"But you never left," Arlon noted.

"No."

"Why?"

"I couldn't. Didn't know how." Sharla huffed. "I don't know why I didn't."

"How old were you when you killed him?" Jyrak asked. The man seemed quiet, almost sad. Pitying, perhaps? Sharla scowled at the thought. She hadn't shared everything just to receive pity.

"Fifteen," she said.

"And you've traveled Low Country for…"

"Four years." Sharla shook her head, staring into the river. "I carried that money for so long. I finally had to get rid of it, so I buried it. I just wanted to start over. But there's no fresh start in Low Country. No new beginnings."

"Only demons to burn," Arlon said quietly.

"Yes." Sharla looked him in the eye. "That's right."

"I sympathize," Keryn said. "I think we all do. But you can't be certain Kine and Senit are riding for the same reasons we are."

"They are," Sharla insisted. "Otherwise, Kine wouldn't do it. He's obsessed with his territory. He thought himself to be a king, the face of the Owl itself. No way he would side with Senit unless he wants to fight Claws." Sharla shuddered at some of her other memories, the drunken rages Kine had terrorized her with. "He *hates* the Claws."

"You think he'll just let us join him?" Hesher asked. "He tried to kill us."

"He tried to kill *me*," Sharla said. "But maybe we don't have to join him. Maybe we just use him."

"Use him?" Jyrak asked.

"He already has the army we don't. So why not let him fight the Claws for us? We round up the captives after Dormun and his tribe are finished, and we get them back to Opek? Everyone makes it out alive."

"He would never let us," Keryn said. "He's probably above us right now. Waiting for us to try and ride out somewhere."

Sharla hesitated. "Maybe, but we have a head start. Jyrak blocked our path down the mesa with magic. If we keep moving, we'll stay ahead of their group. Their horses won't be in any better condition than our own…I mean, yours. We can beat them out of the canyon, find somewhere to lay low, and follow them the rest of the way to Dormun. Let them finish him off, and we go from there."

"And if they're faster than you think?" Jyrak asked. "If they meet us when we try to leave the canyon?"

Sharla scrambled for a response and finally found one she wasn't certain she liked—not when she'd already landed the crew in so much trouble. Even so, she found her gaze settling on Ovis.

"We have a Claw, too," she said. "We'll use him as leverage."

Ovis blinked. "What?"

Chapter Fifteen

"You have information on Dormun's tribe. You know them from the inside out. You know where they'll be, how they'll act." Sharla shrugged. "Even if that isn't true, Senit and Kine wouldn't know it. They'd just believe you're helping us fight a crazy tribe. If worse comes to worst, you're our bargaining chip for safe passage. You keep the Watchmen and cartels off our backs until we reach Dormun. You can say you left your tribe, and now you're helping us fight them."

Ovis shook his head, confusion twisting his expression. "Why would I fight my tribe?"

"You told me so yourself: the Skull Tribe is made of crazy men and women. You realized Dormun was crazy, so you left. Now, you're helping us remove a tribe that threatens both Claws and Low Countrymen."

Ovis grinned. "That makes sense."

"Okay, so you have a way to reach Dormun," Keryn said. "But what about after? When we've fought the Claws—assuming everything you said works and we even find them. You think your grandfather will let you just walk away? That he'll forget why he's after you?"

Sharla frowned. "I already asked you to give me up at the monastery, and you didn't."

"Arlon didn't," Keryn corrected her. "The rest of us were still thinking about it."

"The point is that it didn't happen." Sharla spread her hands. "I know we're in this canyon because of me. I know everything went south because of me. If Kine wants me again, just give me to him. I've run for long enough. Maybe I should stop being my mother and just face what happened. I'll tell you where to find the gold, and you can have it. All of it."

Keryn frowned, as though she hadn't expected Sharla to give a credible response. The rest of the crew shifted where they sat, eyeing each other.

"It does makes sense," Hesher finally said.

Jyrak grunted, a sound that might've been agreement. Arlon watched Sharla with an unreadable expression while Ovis continued to squint. "You small people are stupid," he finally declared.

"We don't know Claws like you do," Sharla said. "Senit and Kine will accept whatever you say to them. Probably."

"This could work," Jyrak said.

"It's barely a plan," Keryn answered, rolling her eyes.

"You haven't left yet," Arlon said.

"No." Keryn scowled at him. "I haven't."

"And?"

She glowered at him for a long moment. "I want to see how this plays out."

"A head start, then?" Jyrak asked. "We keep moving?"

"At a slower pace," Arlon said. "The horses can't take anything else."

The horses. Sharla blinked and stared at the river, reminded once again of Nun. Her loss still brought an ache to Sharla's chest. It felt like too ordinary a pain to know, something she should've outgrown—just like she'd outgrown her parents, her grandfather, and all Low Country. But then why had she never left? She shook the thoughts away to find Arlon still watching her.

"It's a good plan," he said, as if reassuring her. "You might've given us a way through this."

Sharla swallowed and nodded. Her plan was the only chance they had. She'd robbed the group of everything else, and now they traveled on borrowed time. Either Kine caught them, or they found Dormun, but whichever turned out to be the case, Sharla couldn't shake her suspicion that more of them would die before everything was settled.

Chapter Sixteen

A SLOWER PACE APPARENTLY MEANT THE CREW WALKED alongside their horses. To Sharla, it felt as though this brought travel to a snail's speed, and she grew increasingly uncomfortable. She squirmed in the light as the sun crept over the canyon walls, as though walking in the shadows could keep her hidden from the world—or from Kine, should he ever look over the edge.

The canyon was a labyrinth; she'd seen that from the mesa. She doubted Kine would know where to look for her, or that he'd find her before the crew exited the canyon. Even so, she frequently caught herself watching that faraway rim, frowning at the sheer walls and the crumbled patches.

She found herself walking beside Arlon with Hesher, Keryn, and Ovis close behind. Jyrak led the group after explaining if they held a consistent pace, they could reach his bloodkin by nightfall. Apparently, his "family" stayed in a network of caves nearby, and they could offer the crew a safe place to spend the night. He was in high spirits, buoyed on the promise of good company, and his cheer spread to the rest of the crew. Hesher didn't seem so torn over Nithan's absence, and Ovis grinned at more of the crew's words. Even Keryn seemed to have softened, regarding Sharla with a calmer demeanor and speaking with Ovis and Hesher as though everything were normal.

Conversation was still light and sparse. The stillness of the canyon pressed down on them, with nothing but the sighing wind or tinkling water to disturb their passage. Occasionally, they crossed other tributaries and streams that fed into the central river: cool spaces crowded with lush grasses and cottonwoods. These inviting hollows looked more than adequate for a resting place, but Jyrak never slowed, and Sharla began to wonder if this day of "slower pace" would do anything for their horses after all.

The heat rose with the sun, a stifling blanket. Sharla occasionally took off her boots and waded into the river, savoring the instant relief that flushed her skin. This helped take the edge off, and as the afternoon hours approached, she welcomed the shadows that stretched from the westward wall of the canyon as the crew migrated toward them. Now, there were only insects to worry about. Sharla soon tired of waving them away and accepted her lot of itching hair, a crawling neck, and the occasional intrusion to her ear or eyes. With company, something she'd rarely enjoyed, and the shade of the canyon wall, the trek still made for better conditions than she'd enjoyed in the desert flats.

Arlon said little, and she didn't encourage more conversation. He'd risked his neck for hers on two occasions now, and she didn't know what to make of it. Since leaving her household, she'd met few friends or allies; even considering someone in such a manner left her suspicious of their motives. Regardless, from what little Arlon had said, it seemed he carried as wounded a past as she, and she supposed that maybe he felt himself drawn to her as a fellow damaged spirit. Kindred souls in a quest for redemption and healing—and all this for a man Sharla thought she'd loved after knowing him for less than a week.

Would he do the same for her? Would he be wandering a canyon with a crew of exhausted toughs, marching southward on a desperate quest to find a single tribe in the Savage Land? Since leaving home, she hadn't met anyone who'd cared a lick for her one way or the other, and even if she thought they had, they certainly wouldn't be scouring Low Country to find her. What made Renn any different, truly?

But she had to find him now. She *had* to. She'd sacrificed too much, traveled too far. It wasn't just his life now, but the lives of her crew and

Chapter Sixteen

the lives of everyone who'd been stolen from Opek. It was bigger than anything she'd known.

"Don't worry," Arlon said.

She blinked herself from her thoughts and stared at him, finding he wore his tiny grin. "What?" she asked.

"I said, don't worry. We'll find your man. We'll get him back."

She frowned and nodded. It didn't comfort her to think more on the topic.

* * *

THE CAVE OF JYRAK'S BLOODKIN WASN'T INVITING, especially not in evening light. Set in the canyon's depths well beneath the sun's reach, it stretched across the wall in a dark mouth, a sinister space.

"This is it?" Keryn asked. She sounded as skeptical as Sharla felt, but Jyrak didn't seem to notice.

"The one and only," he proclaimed. "We've held this place for years. Avoided the tigoras, the bandits, Claws, and everything else. There are other tunnels in the back that open into country near the mesa, places we've hunted and even traded with a few ranchers. My family might have food for us, and it'll be better meat than anything we've had."

"It looks abandoned," Hesher said.

"Sure does," Jyrak agreed. "And the rumors of runemasters and tigoras help keep it that way."

"There aren't other runemasters," Sharla said. "Right? You said you were the only one."

Jyrak winked at her and stepped toward the cave, leading his horse by the reins. He snapped a branch from a nearby cottonwood—a dead, twisted shape—and fumbled in his saddlebag for flint.

"Mages spare their magic wherever possible," he explained in answer to Sharla's questioning gaze. "Especially runeborn like me. If you have a limited library of runes, one meant to last a lifetime, why throw them away when you can just as easily use other means?"

"'Easily,'" Keryn scoffed as the mage struggled with his tool.

"Oh, hush," he muttered. "You have no idea what you'd do without me."

When the branch finally lit, Jyrak pocketed the flint and led the horse inside, waving for the rest to follow. Sharla raised her eyebrow at Arlon before she went after the mage, stepping into the coolness of the cave. It stretched into an impressive space with yawning walls, a ceiling too high for the torch to illuminate, and stalactites that loomed from the heights. Ovis and Keryn had lit their own torches, but even their combined light couldn't reach all of the cavern. Sharla had to admit Jyrak's bloodkin had stumbled onto an impressive find, and she stared about them as they traveled deeper.

Shadows danced in the flickering light, crawling around rocks and shivering from stalactites. Everything glowed in ruddy tones, reflecting the firelight from water-slicked surfaces. It wasn't long before they'd left sunlight far behind, and despite Jyrak's reassurances, Sharla couldn't help but wonder over the presence of his bloodkin. She saw no signs of life, no evidence of campfires, foot traffic, or animal droppings from horses. For that matter, how did Jyrak's bloodkin find light? How did they keep from going blind down here?

"You're certain we're in the right place?" Hesher asked from behind. His voice echoed in bizarre fashion, bouncing from the walls until it died somewhere above them.

"I wouldn't forget it," Jyrak answered. "Been here often enough."

"Your family must stay deep underground," Sharla said.

"They stay far enough from the canyon entrance that no one would find them unless they walked for a while," Jyrak answered. "With talk of runemasters and tigoras to keep them away, my bloodkin have never had trouble. The occasional rancher finds the tunnels at the other end, but we make sure they leave everything alone."

"It seems lonely," Sharla said.

"It has its disadvantages," Jyrak agreed. "But there's nowhere better for my family, not without their magic. They're not entirely defenseless—we can still hold swords and shields—but once you've traded your magic away, nothing is ever as easy."

Chapter Sixteen

Sharla frowned at his words. It seemed a terrible way to live, even with the promise of Jyrak's coin. Would it be enough for her to sit and wait, to trust that her friend would one day bring enough treasure to charter them a boat for Liadinia? It didn't seem likely, but she'd traveled on her own for so long the thought of settling anywhere didn't seem possible.

They walked deeper, following twisting tunnels through countless caverns, all of them rendered in the same hellish tones. Contorted walls with shadowed ceilings, dark spaces behind stalagmites, various side tunnels Jyrak ignored. All the while, the crew's torches burned lower, their patience grew thinner, and their unease loomed larger. Sharla felt it among them as though an illness spread across her skin, a toxin in the air that filtered from the rocks. Jyrak apparently noticed it, or else felt it himself, because the mage stopped talking. Indeed, he stopped looking around as he walked, and his attention grew more direct, more focused. He marched ever onward, guiding his horse in a relentless slog.

A smell grew, something Sharla couldn't put a name to. Something old and sickly, with a strange hint of something sweet or molding. It was a confusing odor when mixed with the stale air around them, air that had rapidly dried and grown heavier when they left all traces of water behind. There were no slickened surfaces now, no drops from above. There were only the tunnels of abandoned habitations, places where one stored forgotten things or relics of bygone ages.

Or at least, places people were meant to stay out of.

Sharla couldn't ignore the notion anymore and found herself considering the likelihood—again—that something was wrong. "Not too much farther?" she asked Jyrak's back.

The mage stopped in place, his torch burning low—almost low enough for the flames to lick his fingers—and stared ahead. Had he seen something? Heard something? He stiffened, and now Sharla caught it, too: a stronger whiff of whatever smell had grown. Now, it carried the unmistakable scent of rot and decomposing matter: the smell of a decaying corpse. Sharla had smelled one or two of those in her day.

"Something is wrong," Keryn said.

Jyrak stepped forward and stumbled, sending something skittering across the stone. He crouched and swung his torch to follow the sound, and jerked backward with a cry. His torchlight revealed a glimpse of pale shapes, small and stunted, tumbling from Jyrak's boots like broken pottery.

Bones.

Hesher swore; the dark oath from the quiet man would've been surprising enough if Jyrak hadn't charged forward, a motion that sent his horse jerking and whinnying. Sharla hurried after him, suddenly terrified of losing him to the darkness, but she needn't have bothered. He stopped a few feet further, staring at mottled shapes strewn across the floor: half-eaten corpses, with scraps of rotting, dead flesh that barely covered the remains of entrails and ribs. Everything half-decomposed, half-shaped, nibbled and gnawed at until whatever attacked the victims had grown bored and left.

Jyrak moaned, a guttural sound from the depths of his chest. He sank to his knees and the torch fell away, rolling across the floor as the flame guttered and winked out. Sharla stared at the remains in shock, sudden fear squeezing her chest as she recognized the one thing that could've caused such death in these tunnels: tigoras.

"Jyrak," Arlon cautioned from behind her, apparently reaching the same conclusion. "Jyrak, we have to—"

He stopped; they'd all heard it. A clattering, scraping sound, as though many armaments were dragging across stone. It echoed from the depths of the caverns, from the shadowed spaces ahead of Jyrak. Another sound accompanied it soon after: a squeaking, squealing noise. It also bore resemblance to what Sharla had heard the prior night in the canyon: the grating undertone of rocks smashing each other. The sound grew until the floor vibrated with it, until it dropped debris from the ceiling and spilled dust over the crew.

Tigoras were coming, probably several of them. Surely they wouldn't be as large as those in the canyon? Arlon wasn't taking any chances: he'd stepped past Sharla to where Jyrak slouched, lit from behind by the torches of Keryn and Hesher. He knelt beside the mage and shook his shoulder, spoke into his ear.

"Jyrak, we need to leave. Now."

Jyrak mumbled something incomprehensible, and then Sharla saw them. Ahead of the two men, barely on the edge of torchlight as though the shadows themselves were writhing. Snatches of ghostly shapes, apparitions that scuttled around the crew, passing through shadows and behind stalagmites, weaving in and out of existence. Most of them were dull, but a few caught the firelight, reflected it in gleaming shards as though they wore molten skin. The light defined serpentine bodies, sinuous tails, folded wings no bigger than those of a bat. Long faces with reptilian eyes that shone in the torchlight, flicking tongues and serrated teeth that overhung the jaws.

Wyrms—the spawn of dragons. Perhaps related to the tigoras, which meant they really were related to dragons after all. They were the dragons' kin that roamed Low Country's depths, long after their ancestors had fallen into hibernation.

The horses shrieked, leaped backward, and pranced about. Torchlight danced as Keryn and Hesher fought to control their horse while avoiding the kicks of Ovis's mount. The cavern exploded into chaos: the sounds of frantic horses, squealing wyrms, shouts from Arlon and Jyrak. The two men finally launched into motion, running toward Sharla while she turned and floundered after the rest.

All order was abandoned as everyone ran from the monsters, fleeing for their lives. Their torches sputtered in the sudden motion, threatening to die as the shadows writhed around them. The wyrms mottled everything, crawling on the stones, emerging from shadows, glinting here and there as they approached the light.

Something brushed Sharla's leg—a wing or a snout. She screeched, drew her battle axe, swung at the darkness, and caught nothing. All visibility decreased to shaking, fragmented light dashed with the glinting scales of wyrms. She saw them everywhere: close beside her feet, ahead of Keryn and Hesher, behind rocks and stalagmites where their eyes reflected light and their scales betrayed movement. The screeching rebounded from everywhere, a primal cry that squirmed through Sharla's ears until it was all she felt, all she knew.

She swung her axe at another body against her legs and hurried after Keryn and Hesher, both of whom floundered in the encroaching dark. One of the torches sputtered in the sudden motion, failing. The other crashed into a stalagmite, spat sparks onto a horse, and threw flaming sticks into the dark. They clattered across gleaming bodies—several of them, too many to count.

Ovis shouted from somewhere to Sharla's right. Brief torchlight revealed him to be swinging his own axes, one hand on his horse while he snarled at something on his trousers. Wyrms bunched over his limbs like wriggling maggots, as though he'd mutated and sprouted new growths. A burst of flame bright enough to shock the whole cavern—Jyrak finally using his magic—and the wyrms across Ovis's legs shrieked and scattered. Jyrak had lit a few on fire, turned them into flaming specters that tumbled into the blackness, demons trailing sparks.

The crew bunched against each other. Sharla supposed closer proximity made for safer passage, but it also meant she couldn't swing her axe. She focused on running, following the dimly-lit path around Keryn's torch, the only remaining light.

Sounds of swearing, shouting, and squealing wyrms and horses were everywhere. All reality became the flickering light, the dancing shadows, a weave of shapes and rocks that accompanied their flight through hell. How did they know they were headed in the right direction?

Something glowed ahead, a precious light in the infinite dark. Something colored differently from the red and orange—a glimpse of evening twilight. Someone shouted—from relief or pain, Sharla couldn't tell—and she redoubled her pace, eager now that she could finally see. She practically ran over Hesher as they stumbled into the cool of the canyon, floundering down the shore and splashing into the water.

They shook under the call of another tigora, one of the larger ones they'd heard the night before. The same magnitude of noise made Sharla tremble, rippling the water. She staggered sideways and readied her

Chapter Sixteen

battle axe—a useless motion when facing something so massive—as she turned to the tunnel they'd just exited.

Wyrms poured into the evening; strange, mutated creatures from the world below. Some of them glinted with scales while others wore the pale, mottled skin of grubs, maggots with flashing claws and snapping teeth. They wove after Jyrak and Arlon—the last to exit the tunnels—and both men looked exhausted from their flight. Sharla moved to intercept, frantic to defend them. She'd barely taken two steps before she stopped, staring in terror.

She saw scales in the tunnel as something uncoiled from the ceiling: something so massive, so unreal, that it appeared to shift the canyon itself. She only saw a stretch of a mouth, a glimpse of serrated teeth wide enough to fill the tunnel entrance, and she understood what she witnessed. A fully-grown tigora, disturbed from its slumber and ready to eat. Something large enough to constitute the tunnel *itself*. The crew had wandered under a massive tigora without knowing it.

Jyrak turned and saw the creature, shouting something to Arlon as he waved his hands. Sharla felt the buzz of magic as the tunnel entrance burst like a cracked dam. Rock, sand, and dust sprayed from the walls as the tunnel folded on itself, collapsing to bury the emerging tigora. Wyrms shrieked and scattered in the collapse, most of them retreating into the depths while the rest were crushed by debris. A few remained outside—Sharla hacked them with her battle axe. The blade glanced off scaled bodies while shearing into others, sent limbs tumbling in spurts of green blood. The rest met Arlon's stiletto or Ovis's axe, and after a few frantic moments, the remaining wyrms had either retreated, wriggling into the pile of debris and slipping away, or had been dismembered.

Sharla had just breathed a sigh of relief when the pile of debris shifted. Another bone-shuddering roar from the tigora prodded everyone backward, and Arlon exchanged glances with Jyrak. The runemaster frowned, waved his hand, and more magic filled the canyon. Sharla saw the shape of it from upstream: a funnel of wind that gusted cottonwood leaves, sticks, and dust in its wake. A horizontal tunnel of detritus whipped along the river, following its contours, until Jyrak muttered something else, wincing under the strain of his effort, and a streak of flame billowed through the funnel. It created a flaming tornado, a torrent of fire that cut toward the collapsed tunnel, flying across the river to blast a gout of steam. The elements pounded the rock with steam as thick as smoke off a wildfire, and the tigora's roar became a scream of pain—or perhaps just rage.

Wordlessly, unanimously, the crew decided it was time to depart, and turned their mounts from the chaos. Sharla found herself scooped up behind Arlon, wrapping her arms around his waist and ducking her head into his back as they galloped up the canyon.

More roaring echoed behind the crew as the tigora—or perhaps another one—struggled to free itself. Sharla didn't know how fast tigoras could move or how far they could chase the crew. Far better to flee first and ask questions later; ride hard and look back as little as possible.

* * *

UNSURPRISINGLY, THE HORSES COULDN'T KEEP UP THE PACE for long. The tigoras sounded distant now—Jyrak's magic had apparently hindered the first while the second might never have been close enough to pursue them—and Arlon allowed everyone to slow.

Jyrak looked awful. He slouched as heavily as before, but now Sharla couldn't tell whether exhaustion or sorrow robbed his strength. Probably both—a notion that burdened Arlon. Sharla read it from the way the man turned to the mage, how his expression fell, and his shoulders slumped. The sentiment infected the rest of the crew, all of whom regarded Jyrak with serious expressions. Hesher looked as crestfallen as when he'd mentioned Nithan's death, Keryn appeared angry enough to murder all Low Country, and Ovis wore a particularly bleak expression not often seen on the warrior.

A silence as oppressive as that of the prior night filled the canyon, and when moonlight crept over the rim, Arlon finally cleared his throat, broke everyone from their trance. "That looks like an exit."

Sharla followed his gaze to a switchbacking footrail that reared from a talus slope to circle around rock spires up toward the overworld. It looked like one of the smoother trails they'd seen, and Sharla sighed

Chapter Sixteen

with relief as they ascended. More roars breached the canyon behind them, but by now, the crew had concluded their climb.

She stiffened when they mounted the canyon rim and recognized where they were. She'd never been to the Savage Land, but one only had to see it from afar to recognize its border, its characteristics.

If one were being technical, the Savage Land represented Benania's border with Lhoria, but neither kingdom cared to stress the issue when Claws proved reluctant to leave the territory. It encompassed a stretch of arid badlands that twisted from grassy hills, patches of oak trees, and scrubland. Folds of granite and sedimentary rock molded the hills into crests, fins, and countless alcoves behind which to shelter Claws, and they knew the land far better than anyone else. Attempts to remove them had only resulted in continual slaughter of the offending parties, and the land had therefore been rendered an unofficial no man's land, a natural border neither kingdom wished to rule. No one came here willingly—at least, not if they were the "small men" Ovis derided. Of course, Sharla had hired this crew to come here—but now that they were here, on the southern side of the canyon network, how could they possibly know where to look for Dormun Redskull?

"Lion's Head," Ovis mused, waking Sharla from her trance.

"I'm sorry?"

The Claw turned to her with a serious expression. "Lion's Head. Dormun is there. The rocks look like a lion. It was my ancestors' land until the Skull Tribe moved them. Dormun cursed the land." Ovis wrinkled his nose as though he smelled an odor, and looked east. "He will be there."

"You know how to get there?"

Ovis nodded, looking at Arlon with an expectant gaze. Arlon hesitated and turned to Jyrak, who appeared oblivious to everything around him. As the two of them watched, Jyrak dismounted and led his horse to a nearby hollow, tying the reins to the branch of an oak and sitting in the grass. He stared at nothing, his hands folded over his lap. His cheeks shone with tears, and the sight burned Sharla's heart.

The death of his bloodkin hadn't been her fault, but she couldn't ignore the tickle of guilt. *All* this had been her fault, from Nithan's death to their tumble through the canyon. Ancestors above, the ruckus Kine made in his bid to capture her had been what startled the tigoras in the first place. It had probably led to the death of Jyrak's bloodkin after all. Thankfully, nobody voiced the sentiment, and it wasn't long before Arlon ripped his gaze from the mage.

"You still have friends in the area?" he asked Ovis.

Ovis blinked. "Friends?"

"Members of your tribe. Are they nearby?"

Ovis slowly nodded, comprehension filling his gaze. "They're close."

"Could you find them? Bring them here? As a buffer against Kine and his men until we reach Lion's Head?" Arlon shook his head. "We can't travel now. Not with Jyrak like this and our horses so exhausted. We also can't afford to camp tonight, but we must. If you find others and bring them here, it might scare Kine and Senit away and buy us more time. They don't know your kind any better than we do."

"Small men are stupid." Ovis chuckled. "It will work."

"It will," Sharla agreed. "Kine was afraid of the Claws. He won't follow us if we're protected by your men."

"I'll find them," Ovis declared. "They're close."

"Good man," Arlon said. "We'll wait for your return."

Ovis nodded to the two of them, turned his horse, and rode into the hills. His shadow darted over the moonlit swells, a massive shape that hurtled through the night. Sharla watched his departure and shuddered. Ancestors only knew how she would react if the entire horizon filled with shapes as large as his. Kine would have plenty of reason to fear their reinforcements.

"Do you think he'll find enough men?" she asked Arlon.

"We'll use whomever he finds." Arlon frowned. "We'll have to hope Kine and Senit won't see enough to know how badly they outnumber us."

"You think they'll catch us tonight?"

Arlon turned to Jyrak. "I don't know," he said quietly. "Jyrak's in a

Chapter Sixteen

bad way. I've never seen him like this. We'll certainly give Senit and Kine plenty of time to decide."

Chapter Seventeen

IT SOUNDED LIKE THE EARTH WAS SCREAMING; LIKE NAILS across stone, a grating, grinding noise that sent shivers down Kine's spine. That was only one part of the sound, the high pitch that accompanied the lower one, which sounded like a rumble of falling rocks or a distant waterfall. The combination jarred him awake and had him on his feet, sword drawn, staring at the canyon.

"Ancestors above," he whispered. "What's that?"

Around the camp, other men were roused and leaped upright. Steel flashed in firelight as weapons were drawn. Men shouted to each other. Another roar shook the ground hard enough for logs to shift, horses to whinny, and men to stumble.

"Something from the canyon," Gashar breathed. He'd fallen asleep near Kine, and now the two men stood side by side, as though the past several days hadn't changed either of them.

"Tigoras," Kine breathed.

"Sir?"

"A legend." Kine blinked and swallowed. "Well, not anymore. Canyon monsters."

Gashar winced at another bellow. "Can they leave the canyons?"

"Don't know."

"They always this loud?"

Chapter Seventeen

"If they were, I reckon no ranchers would settle anywhere near this place." Kine shook his head and thought. "No, something disturbed them. It's said they hibernate, like the dragons."

Both men watched each other as they arrived at the same conclusion.

"Sharla's crew woke them," Gashar said.

"Or the runemasters did." Kine sheathed his sword, grabbed the reins of his horse, and led it through camp. "Doesn't matter which. We're close."

His purposeful stride carried him through much of the bandits' territory before other men mounted their horses. Most still attempted to settle their mounts, placating them with soft pats and murmurs as the animals reared, eyes wide and rolling. A spectacle of chaos and disorder, ill-befitting any company of Watchmen, but Kine's force seamlessly fit with the rest, as though there'd never been a difference. There probably wasn't any—not anymore—but Kine refused to dwell on the notion.

It took him a few moments to find Senit—long enough for Gashar to reclaim his position at Kine's side. When the colonel finally saw the bandit lord, the other man retained an infuriating ease, lounging against a boulder with his pipe in hand, the glowing end trailing through the air as he beckoned to Kine. "Colonel, what do you make of the noise?"

"Tigoras," Kine answered. "Has to be. And that means Sharla and her crew woke them. We can catch them and the runemasters before they escape the canyon."

"Sharla." Senit grinned, his teeth flashing in the firelight. "There's that girl again."

Kine stiffened; he'd momentarily forgotten that he'd explained his past to Gashar and not to Senit, but he refused to give Senit more ammunition. Who knew what the man would do with it? Instead, he cleared his throat and nodded. "The murderer who stole gold. Yes, her crew is in that canyon. And they're formidable enough to wake tigoras."

"Tigoras." Senit peered across his camp. "And Claws. We're finding all kinds of interesting things."

"It'll be more interesting when we catch them," Kine urged. "And we can."

"So certain? None of our men or horses have had rest."

"We'll rest when we find them."

Senit evaluated Kine, noting his urgency. Finally, he stood and waved to the men around him. "Form up!" he shouted. "We have runemasters to catch."

As the men around him scurried into motion, the cartel leader eyed Kine with a significant look. "We're close to the end of your road, Colonel. Remember our deal. You're stepping away from Keth."

"I can't forget." Kine mounted his horse. "To arms, Senit. We'll catch them before sunrise."

* * *

SLEEP CAME IN FITFUL SNATCHES, FILLED WITH BROKEN dreams and panicked thoughts. Every time she closed her eyes, Sharla saw something of Renn's face, but the features were confused. As though he'd become two men, molded with someone else—a victim of her recollections. She never discerned whether the second man was Kine or someone else, but she always felt the same panic, the same desperation. Renn was in pain, wounded or dying, and she'd arrived just in time to watch him slip toward the ancestors. She maintained enough awareness to assure herself the dreams weren't real, and she clawed herself to consciousness only long enough to recognize the bitter truth: she had no idea of Renn's true condition. Every awakening exhausted her more until she fought to stay alert.

Keryn's regular breathing and Hesher's occasional snores broke the silence. Other than that, the only sounds were of distant coyotes yipping from the badlands.

Sharla sat up and hugged herself as she heard rustling; clanking bottles and flapping saddlebags. She turned to Arlon, who was supposed to be keeping watch, and saw him searching the crew's possessions. A few bottles lay on the ground behind him, all empty, but Sharla didn't recognize her own. Her mouth dried at the thought of drink, and when she moved to help Arlon search, she paused. She saw his occasional hesitation, the way his hands trembled. Beyond him, Jyrak lay on his back, but it was impossible to tell whether the mage slept.

Chapter Seventeen

"Bad dreams?" Sharla asked.

Arlon startled and turned to her with a flustered expression. "Usually."

"I have the same problem." Sharla hesitated and watched him search. She finally sat beside the saddlebag he presently emptied. "Drinking only makes it worse, you know."

He ceased his efforts and looked over his spoils with an empty expression. "It softens it."

"Like a cheap high."

"No. I'd never use ichor or gargev powder."

"You ever tried them?"

"Of course." He examined her with a wry expression. "I worked with Senkha, after all."

"How long was that for?"

Arlon hesitated and looked away. "Long enough."

"You have the nightmares because of people you lost?"

"Because of *everything* I lost."

"Your family?"

"My life." Arlon blinked, as though remembering she watched him, and he grunted. "The gift of every Low Countryman, eh? Never knowing what to do with your life, only knowing somewhere along the way, you missed something."

"I lost something," Sharla said. "I didn't miss it. I *had* it. And now, we're getting it back."

Arlon locked gazes with her and stared for a long moment. The moonlight lit his eyes silver, casting an unearthly sheen to those dark pupils, and suddenly, she felt he saw everything inside her—that he'd watched all the same nightmares as she.

"I hope you're right," he said. "I hope this brings you peace."

She snorted, struggling to ignore the doubt his words always stirred. "What do you know of peace?"

He hesitated. "That it can't be built."

That stilled her for a moment, and her gaze dropped to the ground. "Can't be built?"

"That's what Senkha's tried. That's what Kine's tried. That's what Senit and Marast and all the rest have tried. They tried to build Low Country with peace, but peace isn't built." Arlon shook his head and his gaze trailed westward. "I reckon it's found."

"You sound crazy."

"I need a drink," Arlon answered. "We're fresh out of that."

"The drink never leaves you alone?"

He offered a wry smile, but it also looked like a grimace. "Not really."

Sharla frowned and decided she didn't like the man who'd manifested before her; the broken one who seemed uncertain of himself. This wasn't the Arlon they needed. "Well, maybe it doesn't leave me alone, either. It doesn't matter. Put the bottles away and stop looking, yeah?"

He smirked, and this time it looked genuine. "That's the thing I like about you, Sharla. You're always so..." He trailed off, staring at something behind her. "Calm."

She turned at his gaze and saw the riders. It had to be Senit and Kine, a black spread of men that discolored the horizon. A lot more than had been following them from Laken—the full force Sharla hadn't seen yet. Only so many men could squeeze into a street outside a monastery, but here in Tigon Land? An army approached them, surely more than enough to rival whatever force Dormun Redskull possessed...if said army didn't destroy Sharla's crew in the process.

"You were supposed to keep watch," she said.

They sat for a time, contemplating Arlon's failure. Finally, he cleared his throat. "I see riders."

"We wake the others?" she asked.

"We'll have to ride south." He turned to the hills behind them. "Deeper into the Savage Land."

"And if we don't find Ovis?"

The question sank between them, and they finally rose, stuffing possessions into saddlebags and readying their horses. No sense in wasting words on the answer.

Chapter Seventeen

Keryn and Hesher were already awake when Sharla and Arlon stepped toward them. Several paces distant, Jyrak still hadn't moved. Arlon met Sharla's gaze and exhaled. He turned and approached the mage while Sharla turned to Keryn and Hesher.

"Riders," Keryn stated. "Your grandaddy dearest and all his tin soldiers."

"They're not all his," Sharla answered, waiting on Arlon. After all, she didn't have Nun anymore. "Senit's also riding with him."

Arlon returned, with Jyrak some distance behind. The mage wore the same expression as before, unreadable and alien in the moonlight. He stared southward, as though completely uninterested in the men who approached them. Sharla ached to see the sight of the sturdy mage so reduced from what he'd been, but no words of comfort came to mind. Indeed, she feared her efforts would only reveal how her involvement had doomed everyone from the start. It likely *had* been the flash flood that roused the tigoras who butchered Jyrak's bloodkin, and the flood had been her fault.

Arlon caught her expression, shook his head, and pursed his lips. "Don't," he said. "You didn't do this."

He'd apparently recovered from his prior lapse in confidence, and Sharla found herself anchoring to his newfound presence, though she knew it to be false. They were both fake, the two responsible for the crew's dilemma, and the thought nauseated her. "Okay."

He turned his horse southward. "We have to ride."

"Fast?" Keryn asked.

"Don't think the horses can handle it." Arlon paused, glancing at Jyrak. "Don't think *we* can handle it."

"I'm fine," Jyrak said, toneless.

Hesher frowned and nodded. "I just hope we find Ovis in time."

"Or rather, that Ovis finds us," Arlon said. He slipped into a darker coat and threw a hood over his head.

Sharla mounted behind him and wrapped her arms around his waist, pressing her head to his back. Ovis *would* find them. After all, he'd said the other Claws would be close. They *had* to be.

* * *

KINE KNEW SHARLA'S CREW COULDN'T OUTRIDE HIS OWN. Their horses had to be worse off than his or Senit's, and a group that small couldn't stay abreast of Senit's force. He watched them grow closer as his own horse pounded alongside Senit's.

The rest of his army filled Tigon Land behind him, a mass of black or silvered riders. Plated Watchmen and dark bandits, all of them glowering in the moonlight. Leather saddles creaked, hooves thumped the earth, and no tigoras disturbed the night. It felt solemn, something that unsettled Kine. This was his chance: a chance to right all the wrongs Hari committed, all the bad fortune that plagued his family. Sharla lay within his grasp…so why did it feel so grim?

They entered the Savage Land, and grasses reclaimed the terrain. At first patchy, then more abundant, a rippling spread that covered hills and occasionally fragmented into slopes of granite and sedimentary rock, badlands that carved furrows, ridges, and buttes or pinnacles more reminiscent of Low Country. It was as though the riders traveled through old ruins of prior settlements, isolated rocks that jutted from grassland and scattered oak trees.

Kine felt the restlessness of the riders around him; he knew it grew like summer heat. Nobody rode into the Savage Land if they didn't have to, not with all the stories. He'd never been back, not since leaving Dormun with his ultimatum decades before. Claws could be anywhere here; behind any hill, butte, or hoodoo. Some people even said they'd seen Claws leap from the ground like gophers.

"The Claw in this crew had better be worth it," Senit muttered.

"Runemasters," Kine reminded him. "Don't forget the runemasters."

"Assuming you were right about them, too."

Ahead, Sharla's crew appeared to have slowed. Kine lost sight of them moments after they crossed a rise. This formed a pattern where Sharla's crew would disappear over the next one and leave Kine hoping he followed the right path for long, terse moments before they ascended the hill to see the crew summiting the next. He grew close enough that he never lost sight of them, tracking the group up the next rise and down

Chapter Seventeen

the other, until they'd finally drawn close enough for Kine to raise his voice and shout to them.

"Sharla, this is pathetic! You're not even trying. Turn around and come quietly."

The riders slowed, stopped. He recognized Sharla's figure at their head; she rode behind a cloaked, hooded man who didn't turn. Two other horses rode beside her...but only *two*? One of them bore two riders, while the other held the man Kine recognized from Laken—the runemaster who'd destroyed the building behind him. Momentary confusion escalated to frustration and anger. Kine snarled at them.

"Where's the rest of your crew?" he bellowed.

The riders watched him in silence, apparently waiting for someone to speak. The woman to Sharla's left turned to the cloaked figure behind Sharla, as if expecting him to do so. When no response came, Sharla finally cleared her throat.

"You sound disappointed, Colonel," she said. "Is this too easy for you? Scooping up strays like you're shoveling dung? Too demeaning for Watchmen?"

Kine heard the muttering around him. They'd gone to a lot of trouble to catch Sharla's crew, and for what? A handful of toughs, each of whom looked as though they'd just ridden through hell and back, literally collapsing from exhaustion? Most notably, the mage looked like a walking corpse, defeat and sorrow etching his face.

"Where's your Claw?" Kine finally demanded.

Sharla frowned and turned around, as though she sought him on the horizon. After a moment, her shoulders visibly slumped—with relief or anger, he couldn't say—and she turned to Kine. "On that hill."

Kine looked to the hill behind her crew to see a rider silhouetted at the summit. He recognized the Claw's broad profile even from this distance, but before he could say anything, other riders crested the hill: a row of them, each as broad as he, and the realization rocked Kine at the same time as it did Senit and the men behind him. Kine felt the wave of panic break over his riders, shocking them into awareness.

"Claws," someone hissed.

"An army."

"More of them behind the hills?"

Senit muttered something under his breath. From the corner of his eye, Kine saw the cartel leader edge closer to him. "Peace, Senit," he breathed. "We retain the upper hand."

The bandit lord gritted his teeth. "You led us into a trap, Colonel?"

Kine spat and spurred his horse forward, shouting at Sharla. "What is this?"

"The makings of a deal."

"Watchmen don't make deals with your ilk."

"I see more than Watchmen in your army, Colonel." Sharla paused, tilting her head. "And everyone here knows the hypocrisy of your words."

"She's an educated little brat," Senit breathed from next to him.

Kine frowned, unaware that Senit had matched his motion forward. He spurred his horse another step and outdistanced the cartel leader. "You have nothing to bargain with, Sharla."

"I have the location of your man, Dormun Redskull."

Kine froze, his mouth agape. "You…" A garbled sound tangled in his throat, and he barked it into a cough. "What do you know of him?"

"I know your Watchmen wouldn't be riding with cartels unless it was for something big. I know that almost a week ago, Dormun Redskull rode all the way to Opek, raided the town, and took captives. I know I've never heard of Claws doing that, and I'm betting you're after him the same as we are."

All her words rang true, as though unraveling Kine and exposing his core for everyone to see. He struggled not to shrink from her voice, to recoil as though it were a whip to his face, and he grabbed the only response he could think of. "Just your crew? You thought six of you could face a whole tribe?"

This stilled Sharla for a moment. Beside her, the mage drew himself upright.

"The plan was to hire more men," Sharla finally said. "But you chased us from Laken before we could."

Chapter Seventeen

Kine struggled for composure, aware of how quiet his voice had grown. "And what gold were you going to use for that, I wonder?"

Sharla spat. "Here's how this goes. Our Claw has a whole company of riders over that hill—more than enough to handle you and your men. You want Dormun the same as we do. I know you want me, and I'm willing to give myself up. Freely. Willingly. But not until Dormun's dead and Opek's people are safe.

"So, you let us go ahead. We cross the Savage Land, scout Dormun's position, and tell you everything you need to know. We attack together, end Dormun, and rescue the captives. After that, I'm yours."

"And the money you'll use to pay your crew?" Kine asked. "I assume it's payment on completion?"

"Are you here for Opekian captives, or for gold?"

"You're wanted for robbery and murder, Sharla. The Watchmen can't let that slide."

"Are you sure you just can't ignore my name, Kine Tarroful?" Sharla shifted in her saddle, eyeing the men behind Kine. "After all, it's Sharla *Tarroful*, in case you've forgotten. *Grandfather*."

When the murmurs spread behind him, Kine bit his lip hard enough to taste blood. He squeezed the pommel of his sword until his fingers could've snapped. Another mark against him, another tally to blight his record. After everything he'd sacrificed for Low Country, it would only remember his runaway daughter, his outlaw granddaughter. A rule of the ancestors: Low Country remembered you for your worst offenses, never your greatest successes.

Senit whistled. "Everything makes sense now."

"What will it be, Colonel?" Sharla asked. "The lives of a town, or justice for a single woman?"

"That's the Watchmen's money, Sharla."

"It's blood money, Colonel. Collected from deals with cartels, from drugs across the border. I reckon your Watchmen haven't seen honest, Owl-issued gold in a long time."

That struck a little close to home. It was unimaginable that Kine found himself bartering with this insolent wretch, a granddaughter who knew *nothing* of what he'd sacrificed, of how he'd bled for Low Country's formation.

Senit had ridden beside him, quiet again: waiting for his next slip, his next mistake, drinking the spilled secrets between Tarrofuls. Kine inhaled and fought to relish the cool air, to find clarity in the heat of anger.

"How do I know you'll keep your word?" he asked.

Sharla shrugged. "Maybe I'm just tired of running."

"And Dormun's location? How do I know your Claws won't lead us to a trap?"

"Do any of us look like Claws to you, Colonel?"

"Why has one been riding with you?"

"He hates Dormun as much as we do—he told us himself. Apparently, all the Claws think Dormun and his tribe are a pack of madmen."

"And your Claw knows where he is?"

"Says he's at a place called Lion's Head."

Of course. Kine's breath hitched again, and he struggled to swim clear of the nostalgia for happier seasons when Claws and Low Countryman coexisted. He'd often sparred with Dormun at Lion's Head, and had spent many evenings watching the sunset from atop that granite formation. He'd enjoy the view of the badlands around them; the ridged hills, the patchy forest, and the long prairie grass.

Dormun had been a friend there, and he'd obviously chosen the formation because of his history with Kine. Everything he'd done was a setup, a ploy to goad Kine to action. The knowledge that it had worked didn't matter; with Sharla's Claws added to their crew, the Watchmen would crush Redskull. They'd rid the world of his stain, finishing what should've been concluded decades before.

"I know the place," Kine heard himself say, as though from a distance.

"You know how to get there?"

Kine winced. "Not from here."

"Then you follow us. What other choice do you have?"

Chapter Seventeen

Kine turned to Senit, who watched Sharla with a tiny grin. Kine turned to examine the rest of his men, each of whom had just learned more than Kine wanted to admit. There was no going back now, and it didn't make sense to postpone their attack. If they rode with other Claws, their best advantage would be to attack Dormun as soon as possible.

Besides, Sharla had just offered to turn herself in. He could correct his past, salvage his legacy, and change everything in the same day. Kill Dormun and bring Sharla to justice. Everything remedied and returned to normal.

"We'll follow you," he said. "You'll take us to Lion's Head."

"You'll follow at a distance. Only close enough for you to see the last of our party."

"We ride together."

"No. You keep your distance, Colonel. Otherwise, the deal's off."

"You don't trust my word?"

"I don't think it's wise to trust someone with more men than me."

Kine clenched his jaw. His own granddaughter was thinking like an outlaw, evading Watchmen and dangling him as though he danced on strings. "Fine. At a distance."

"Our man says Lion's Head is close," she said. "When we reach it, we'll send a man back with a better read of what we're facing. We'll attack it together, and we'll finish this quickly."

"The sooner the better."

"Aye."

Silence fell between the groups. The other riders turned to Sharla, expectant. She finally nodded and patted the rider before her on the shoulder. Their horse started forward, and the other riders followed.

"Wait." Senit spurred his mount forward, raising his voice and shouting at her. "The man in front of you. Why doesn't he speak?"

Her horse stopped, but the cloaked man didn't turn.

"Someone recognized me in Laken," Senit said. "It must've been him." He gestured to himself. "I'm Senit Blackhair. You clearly know me, and you know my cartel. But I don't believe I've had the pleasure."

The cloaked rider tilted his head, as though considering whether to give Senit an answer. He finally muttered something to Sharla, who turned and shook her head. "He can't give you that, sir. Says he fears for his life and for those of his friends."

Senit opened his mouth to say something and stopped as recognition swam over him.

Sharla seemed unconcerned. "Follow us to Lion's Head and help us kill Dormun. He claims he'll answer you there."

"Clever," Senit muttered. "Hinting at traitors in my own cartel. My own men making plans with her crew." He turned to Kine with a grim expression. "Trouble is, she might be right."

"She's saying whatever she needs to in order to stay ahead of us," Kine answered. "I'd take any of it with a grain of salt."

"But of course." Senit grinned, all teeth and no humor. "After all, she learned from the best."

Chapter Eighteen

"IF SENIT FALLS, WILL YOU KILL MARAST TOO?" SHARLA ASKED Arlon as they followed Ovis and the other Claws.

"Might as well," Arlon muttered. "Why not give Low Country the chance it deserves?"

"You mean a chance to find peace?"

"A chance to try again. Shouldn't we all have that?"

"Works better for some than for others, I reckon." Sharla turned at Jyrak's voice and found the mage riding close beside them. The man still wore an unreadable expression, staring over the moonlit hills with slackened features. He didn't cry anymore, but the prior pain still lingered in his gaze, often rendering it unfocused or hard. Sharla winced at the sight, and she regretted the departure of the Jyrak she'd gotten to know.

"I'm sorry," she said quietly. "Sorry for those you lost."

"The tigoras never bothered anyone before," he muttered. "They might roar when thunder or a storm broke. But they always went back to sleep. Never made trouble. None of us could've imagined they were breeding in those tunnels."

Silence fell over the riders. It covered the Savage Land the same as in Low Country, but here, the quiet maintained an eerie edge. As though Claws waited under the trees, behind the rocks, watching the crew as they rode further. No one rode this deep into the Savage Land, not when talk of shamans and monsters and spirits cloaked these hills, or when any incursion of Claw territory could spark raids of ranchers along Low Country's border.

Sharla struggled not to think on the latter: that their arrival could threaten more Low Countrymen, that it could start another war between Benanians and Claws that lasted years. That is, if they hadn't already been enduring a cold war, one that had lasted since before she was born. Would this attack make everything worse? No—Dormun made this inevitable when he raided Opek.

She turned to look at the army behind them. Kine followed at a distance, a precarious notion when considering Arlon's crew had bluffed: Kine trusted that Ovis really *did* have an army of Claws, and perhaps that was what kept him back. If Kine knew Ovis had only brought five other riders with him, perhaps things wouldn't be going so smoothly. In that scenario…

Sharla turned from the army, refusing to dwell on the magnitude of the force behind her. It would be more than enough to handle Dormun and his crew; it *had* to be. They would free the Opekian captives. They would free Renn. And then she'd…turn herself in.

She scowled at herself, glaring at Arlon's back. She hadn't known what else to say. In the heat of the moment, she'd given Kine what he wanted: he'd have her and Dormun. Arlon's crew even got the treasure she'd promised, for Kine had agreed to take her without commenting on the rest of the crew.

Of course, Kine could be lying. He might still order the Watchmen to kill Arlon's crew, take Sharla, *and* have her lead him to the gold. She wouldn't put it past him.

She squirmed in the saddle, grimacing at the thoughts. "You might have to leave before the attack," she said. "Escape while Kine and his men fight Dormun. Leave the rest of us. I don't need you anymore. We've found an army, Dormun will die, the captives will go free, and the rest of you can get away. Don't stay and wait to wear chains with me. Kine will take all of us if he can."

Chapter Eighteen

Jyrak pursed his lips. Keryn and Hesher rode in silence, apparently waiting on Arlon's response. Ahead of them, Ovis rode with the other Claws, too distant to hear their conversation.

"What the rest do is up to them," Arlon finally answered. "They've already said this is their last ride with me. They don't have to stick it out...but I'm with you to the end."

"Your loyalty is misplaced."

"Because you wouldn't do the same?"

For people she didn't know? For townsfolk who'd never done anything for her? Of course not. Sharla was only here for Renn, and now, she didn't even have him. She'd traded him for strangers, and Renn would never know.

"I wouldn't," Sharla admitted. "I don't even know why *I'm* still here. I could ride away with you. No sense in me staying, not when I'll become Kine's prisoner. I meant to free Renn, and now I won't even have that."

"Then we all ride," Keryn said. "We all leave. As soon as we find Lion's Head and they start the charge, we leave."

"I'm riding your horse," Hesher said. "I reckon that puts me wherever you go. And Ovis?"

"Ovis can do what he wants." Keryn snorted. "He might even stay here."

She looked to Arlon and waited. On Sharla's other side, Jyrak did the same.

Arlon inhaled, drew his hood back, and regarded the mage. "Jyrak?"

"I've always been with you," Jyrak said. "You know that."

"I do." Arlon turned back to the Claws. "I reckon I'm in this to the end."

"Blood and ashes!" Keryn exploded. "What's wrong with you? You have a way out. You can leave. This has never been your fight; *none* of this has. You think yourself to be Low Country's guardian, and for what? What has it ever given you?"

"Nothing."

"Nothing!" She spat and led her horse away.

Sharla watched the other woman keep her distance. "She cares for you."

"She shouldn't," Arlon answered. "We promised each other to end things should we lose our way."

"And what was your way?"

"Good question."

"She sees you as a friend. You must understand that."

"We all say we're friends." Arlon shrugged. "Maybe it's true. Maybe we found something good in this."

Sharla recognized the pain under his words, the guilt and resentment. Or maybe she merely imagined it, heard it in what everyone else said because it was all she'd known. "Was everything always bad?" she asked.

He paused for so long she wondered if the timid, anxious Arlon had revealed himself, the one who scrambled for alcohol to soften the past and ease the night. "Not always," he finally said.

They fell silent after that, and the hours ran together. All was quiet hills, granite ridges, buttes, and spires rising from prairie grasses: dark splotches in the silvered grass, tall and imposing amid the softer shapes of oak and shrubs. A soundless country of whispering wind, pale moonlight, and distant stars.

Everything felt closer here, as though the landscape squeezed the crew after they'd endured the vastness of Low Country. The horizons were condensed, shrunken by vales between hills and spaces between ridges. After so long in the open mesas and the vast canyonlands, Sharla almost felt claustrophobic.

Without realizing it, she found herself squeezing Arlon tighter, hugging him closer. His presence comforted, warmed, and stilled her. It felt as though she'd anchored herself to him, a secure foundation in the wilderness of the Savage Land, a bright spot in the night. Though he wore a dark coat, burnished by dark hair and darker skin, he could've been a beacon to her, a companion with whom to share this ride—a ride that might be their last. Perhaps, it could even be a last ride for Kine, and everything would be settled.

Chapter Eighteen

She drifted, swimming in and out of consciousness. More fragments of Renn, but the images kept changing. Now, she couldn't tell whether she saw Renn or Arlon, and in the haze of her dreams, she couldn't tell whether she disliked the idea.

A tug drew her from slumber, and she raised her head to find Arlon leaning toward her. "Time to dismount," he said.

"We're here?"

She squinted around and saw the east bore the telltale lightening skies of dawn, while the moon hung fat and ripe over the western hills. It caught the haze in a peculiar ambience, shining orange and amber through the badlands. The spectacle reminded her of shamans and spirits. Myths, all of them—but then again, that's what people had said about the tigoras.

A new formation lay east of them, one barely seen over the highest rise but unmistakably unique. The jutting, granite bulge of a snout with a ragged ridgeline that ran across it to the grassy slope it emerged from: what could've resembled a mane atop a lion.

"That's it," she breathed. "Lion's Head."

"The one and only," Arlon said.

She shook her head in disbelief. "Dormun rode from here just to raid a town?"

"All a show," Ovis said. He finally trotted back to the crew with the other Claws behind him, each of them similarly broad and scarred, with bone claws through their earlobes and war paint across their faces, streaks of white and blue on their cheeks and foreheads. "Dormun wants spirits to see him, but they'll judge him. He brought northerners into the sacred lands."

"So we get closer?" Sharla asked.

"We already did."

She blinked, looking at Arlon as she dismounted.

"You were sleeping," he explained. "Ovis and his friends looked it over."

"Oh." She swallowed. "What do you think?"

"Most camp below Lion's Head," Ovis said. "They keep watch, so we charge them. We have more warriors. Better fighters."

"You're certain?"

"Better fighters," Ovis insisted. "It's easy."

"Why?" Sharla asked in bewilderment. "Why would Dormun do it if he knew this would happen?"

"Probably didn't know Kine would come with so many people," Arlon muttered.

"He must've known. Claws know not to invade Low Country. Why would he…" Sharla trailed off as her eyes met Jyrak's, and she knew they thought of the same thing.

"The chaos mage," Jyrak said. "He's over there, somewhere. I feel his power. Aether has been distorted here, channeled in huge amounts."

"A shaman?" Ovis asked.

"That's one word for it."

"He lets the shaman fight." Ovis spat into the grass and scowled. "Dishonorable. Cursed."

"Their mage will do serious damage." Jyrak exhaled and stared at Lion's Head. "Our charge will be a distraction, no way around it. If the mage is distracted for long enough, I can get close enough to kill him."

The crew fell silent, contemplating his words with somber expressions. Arlon was the first to break the quiet, regarding the mage with a grim expression. "Are you up to it, Jyrak?"

"I'm ready for payback. One man makes a poor trade for a family, but if the ancestors have decreed it, that's the way this will go."

"Not trying to ride off and die on me, are you?"

Jyrak managed a broken grin, but only barely. "One of us will die. I plan to make it him."

"How much of a distraction do you need?"

Jyrak turned to the men several hills behind them, where Kine had obediently halted. "An army should do the trick."

"You'll have it."

Silence drifted over the hills as the crew regarded each other, wordless. Sharla recognized this was the last time she might share their

Chapter Eighteen

company, the last time she might thank the ancestors for such allies. Maybe even…friends? But here, when it mattered most, she found herself speechless. Emotion choked the breath from her throat. Was it guilt? Anger? Sadness? Fear?

Keryn finally shook her head, leading her horse a few paces to the side. "You lot are crazy," she muttered. "The woman's giving us the chance to leave. You should take it and let her grandaddy's army take care of things."

Sharla turned to Jyrak, who still looked as impassive as a wall of stone. He'd said he'd follow Arlon until the end, even if it killed him, which meant everything depended on Arlon's response.

She swallowed and faced the dark rider, who calmly watched her. The opposite of the broken man who'd fumbled for bottles only a few hours before, the confident presence now returned from the first day she'd sat across from him in Mela. When he'd taken on an entire town just to prove he could: to prove he was ready for a change, something different from Senkha's empire. He'd traded his life on her promise of coin?

No, it was something else. She could see it in the way he watched her, the way the moonlight caught the emotion in his eyes. As though they were mirrors to reflect the anger she'd bottled for years, the pain that stoked her determination. It was understanding that drew him to her, a recognition of someone who'd fought the same battles. They'd bonded somewhere along the way, and she didn't know how. They understood each other, but she couldn't describe it.

"Please," she heard herself say. "Please leave. Before it's too late."

He tilted his head, and his mouth curved into the wry grin he'd offered her in Mela. "Do you love this man?"

"Renn?"

He gave a single nod with those eyes that understood her, that grin that tugged her heart. That easy, self-assured awareness with which he regarded the world, with which he'd looked through her past and seen something she hadn't seen, known something she hadn't understood.

Maybe he'd been here once, too? Maybe he knew exactly what she felt, what she fought for? *Impossible.*

He'd never known anyone as she'd known Renn. Never known anyone as she'd known a man who…she'd slept with, gotten drunk with, and spoken to for a few days. The man who'd unlocked her heart, who'd given her the world…all over shoddy, splintering furniture and cheap drinks in an inn no one had heard of in the farthest reaches of Freytilia.

Yes, it all sounded hopelessly romantic. But undeniably true, real.

Then he'd been taken, and she didn't know whether he still lived. She'd come all this way for him, but she'd already changed from the woman he'd known. The question that suddenly froze her heart, the question that terrified her more than the tigoras, the army behind them, or the Claws before them was whether Renn would still understand her. Whether he could ever understand her as this crew did. She'd told them about Kine, her mother, and her father, but Renn didn't know everything. Only that she'd run away from home, that her father had died…but not that she'd killed him. She didn't even know why she'd told this crew the truth; only that Arlon had watched her with this same gaze and spilled everything from her like a burst dam.

She didn't trust herself to speak, so she forced herself to nod.

Arlon turned to Keryn. "I'm staying," he declared. "Reckon I'm going to help Sharla find her man. About time I did something good. Something that matters."

"As if any of this ever mattered." Keryn turned and led her horse away.

"It was all just for the coin, eh?"

"Shut up, Arlon." She shook her head and watched the eastern horizon, now turning a pale blue. "We can't all be as noble as you."

That sobered Arlon, and he finally cleared his throat. "Then do me a final favor: ride to the Colonel and give him the news."

Keryn frowned at him. "They'll take me in."

"They won't. Not until Dormun is finished. Not with Sharla still here." Arlon shrugged. "Tell them to give you time to catch up with us.

Chapter Eighteen

Tell them to delay their attack until you return, and once they start, you can leave."

Keryn examined the crew and shook her head. "Don't run off on me now," she said. "I want to know where the gold is."

"There's a footrail from Opek," Sharla said. "You can't miss it. Used to be one of the main highways through the flat between Mela and Adron. When rumors of the Claws got worse, it became less traveled.

"You follow it about a day, and you start reaching sand dunes. The trail gets more difficult to follow, but once you hit the dunes, you go around them to the east and break away when you start finding scrubland. You'll find sandstone stacks. Follow these to a sand wash with a wall around it, sort of a crescent shape." She nodded to Keryn, to Ovis, and to Jyrak. "That's where you'll find the treasure."

Ovis's eyes grew wide and round. He grinned as Jyrak pursed his lips. Arlon said nothing, while Keryn merely watched her.

"Take it," Sharla said. "Take all of it. It can't go back to Kine, and I don't have any use for it. Not anymore."

With a final shake of her head, Keryn flicked the reins and cantered toward Kine's army.

Ovis watched her depart with a wicked grin. "Here at last," he breathed. "Spirits bless this day."

"I reckon spirits have nothing to do with it. Not anymore." Jyrak scowled at Lion's Head and flexed his fingers. "This is about revenge."

The fire in his tone unnerved Sharla, and she shivered. "Just don't kill yourself, yeah?"

"I'm not dying today." The runemaster shook his head and clenched his jaw. "At least not before their mage dies. Then, we'll go visit my family."

Chapter Nineteen

Senit was quiet, watching Sharla's crew with an unreadable expression. He was apparently deep in thought, which never boded well. Kine reckoned he should probably watch for a knife between the ribs.

What Sharla's companion had said about himself and his friends fearing for their lives was probably a ruse, one that would have Senit searching his cartel for the traitors who'd concealed the man's identity and conspired with him. Sharla probably lied as smoothly as Kine, and incredibly, he found he almost respected her for it.

She'd clearly taught herself a thing or two, even when living on her own. Maybe there was still a chance that he could bring her on as a Watchman. They could serve Low Country together, defending his borders, and she'd be the better for it. She'd already proven herself a better learner than Hari, and maybe she could help him redeem their family.

There was no denying it: in a way, Kine admired his granddaughter. She was a survivor. Maybe he could even impact her, as Gashar suggested? Maybe there was still time to influence her for the better, to leave his legacy with her if he couldn't leave it with Low Country.

Senit shifted. "Riders."

Kine blinked and refocused on the horizon: a single horse shambled toward his army, one that carried the other woman and her dark-skinned friend.

Chapter Nineteen

"Not your granddaughter," Senit noted.

"Not yet."

"All this to recover your broken family." Senit tsked. "You might have said something about it."

"We came to kill Dormun. I didn't know Sharla would be here. But now, we can fix both problems."

"You keep saying *we*." Senit regarded him with an amused expression. "Don't forget you already traded your livelihood, Kine. You gave me Keth and the rest of your territory. Sharla joins you on the street. More baggage to carry around."

"Yes," Kine breathed, his throat suddenly tight. "I haven't forgotten."

Senit grunted, switched topics. "You know of Lion's Head?"

"I used to be friends with Dormun. We camped together at Lion's Head." Kine frowned at Senit. "This is where Low Country used to begin. By all rights, it should still start here, but the Owl never cared enough to settle the details and we never had the men to maintain the border. Dormun and his Claws pushed north, all the way to the mesa south of Mela. But when he decided to come into Opek?" Kine snorted and shook his head. "The fool thinks all Low Country is his. Thinks all Freytilia is his."

"It used to be."

Kine scowled. "It wasn't all *his*."

"No, but it belonged to the Claws."

"What's your point?"

"I'm just reminding you of what the country used to be." Senit put his pipe in his mouth and grinned around the edges. "Nothing but a bunch of men who fought for scraps. Then we came along, saying we could build a new country and bring peace. Today, Low Country is still a bunch of men who fight for scraps. Best not to think of ourselves as much different from them. Your dreams for a noble country, one the Owl's proud of? You've stretched too far for too long."

Kine clenched his jaw. Senit spoke as though Kine's reign already ended, but it hadn't. This wasn't over.

"Colonel," the woman said. She regarded Senit with a cool gaze. "Senit Blackhair."

Senit puffed his pipe and blew a smoke ring before whistling. "And who do we have the pleasure of addressing?"

"Keryn," she stated. She gestured to the dark-skinned man behind her. "This is Hesher."

"A Claw?"

"Kathagonian," Hesher answered

Senit's grin widened. "A crew of all flavors."

"What did you see?" Kine asked the newcomers.

"Lion's Head is encamped by the enemy," Keryn explained. "They're below the rock while their sentries are stationed around the hillside and on the summit. They're watching every direction, so our only chance is a direct charge. We have superior numbers, and we'll overwhelm them before they can defend themselves. We plow straight to Dormun, and we end this quickly."

Kine frowned. Something wasn't right. Dormun must've known Kine would respond with superior manpower. Maybe he'd simply underestimated Kine's response?

"Is this your strategy or Sharla's?" he asked, stalling for time.

Keryn regarded him with the same calm as before. A strikingly beautiful woman when seen up close: long black hair to complement dark, inviting eyes and features even more alluring when tightened by the thrill of battle. "Our crew works together," she finally said.

"Really?" Senit laughed. "You're already turning on each other."

Keryn scowled at him. "There was never anything to turn on." With a final snort, she turned and flicked the reins. "We wait for your charge," she said over her shoulder as they rode away.

Senit watched her go, and his prior humor faded. "That was strange."

"They're on edge." Kine squinted at Sharla's crew. "This isn't the way they thought it would go."

"Why? They have an army."

Chapter Nineteen

Yes. But Kine suspected Sharla hesitated for all the same reasons he did. Dormun had something up his sleeve—something Kine's army wouldn't like.

"Doesn't matter." Kine gestured behind them. "You take your men that way. Attack the hill from the south. I'll take my Watchmen this way and attack from the north. We pinch Dormun between us and squeeze him out."

"Classic." Senit nodded. "A bit of steel to root out the rats."

"Unless you have a better idea."

"None." Senit turned to Kine and nodded. "Enjoy the ride, Kine. It'll be the last you have with your men. At least, the last as a Watchman of Low Country."

Kine scowled at him and flicked his reins, turning north. "I will always be a Watchman, Senit."

* * *

THE MOMENT HAD ARRIVED. KINE'S ARMY GATHERED BEHIND them, the crew was prepared to charge, and Sharla's own future hung in the balance. Everything had built to this moment, this morning; almost the same number of days apart from Renn that she'd spent with him. She'd free him, secure their futures, and everything would go back to the way it was. Everything would be normal.

Everything, but for Kine.

She had to run; she knew that now. The decision had struck her in an instant, the same moment as she'd watched Keryn reach Kine and his men. She couldn't go back with her grandfather. After escaping his shadow, she'd come too far and learned too much.

"Are you okay?" She stiffened at Arlon's voice and was afraid to meet his gaze. Afraid to face Jyrak, who rested nearby, or Ovis, who lounged with the rest of his riders. The crew she'd assembled, everyone who'd abandoned their former lives just to help her and a few others they'd never met—all the dregs of society from families no one would remember.

"You shouldn't stay," she said.

"You keep saying that, but every time you do, I think you really want the opposite."

"You have no idea what I really want."

"Then spell it out for me."

"No."

"Call it my payment. You can keep the rest."

She blinked and turned to him. He'd approached from where he'd tied his horse to a nearby juniper, and he stood behind her with that knowing expression she'd grown comforted, ashamed, and nervous of. "You'd give up your share of the gold?"

"I never came this far for gold, Sharla."

She stiffened, thought of the bottles he'd fumbled for and the pain he'd drunk away, same as her. "You have your own demons to burn."

"We all have regrets." He shrugged and stepped beside her. "Wouldn't be a Low Countryman without them."

They watched the distant army and she swallowed, found herself trembling. She wasn't the only one to notice.

"You fear him?" Arlon asked.

"Of course," she whispered. "I hate him."

"You still turning yourself in?"

"No. I'm going to run."

"Where to?"

"I don't know." The words sounded frail, weak, and she hated herself for them. Hating herself was nothing new, and she waited for that familiar fire to burn through her, to rejuvenate her. She waited for the rage to smolder in her heart and stoke her determination, but this time, it flickered and died, leaving her hollow and cold.

She sat on a granite outcropping, her legs dangling over the hillside below. She stared at the landscape, silvered by moonlight and glowing under the eastern sky, marveling over what a fool she was.

"You've been running for years," Arlon said. She nodded, unable to form words. "Maybe you just need to stop running."

Chapter Nineteen

"I ran here, didn't I?" She swallowed and couldn't stop her hands from shaking; sudden tears moistened her eyes and blurred her vision. "Fine, I admit it. I didn't know where else to go, or what else to do."

"Your world was taken from you."

"It happened a long time ago." She shook her head and closed her eyes to escape from everything, to leave it all behind. "My family were Low Country's proudest leaders, or so Kine thought. And look where it got us.

"All this time, I thought I was angry at Kine. I thought I was mad at him and my mother. She ran away like a coward. Gave me his gold and left me to die with him."

She opened her eyes and glared at Arlon through a veil of tears. "You know what happened to me, that first night in the canyon, after the flood washed everyone away?"

He stared back, silent and knowing, that dreadful gaze that both tore her apart and patched her together.

"I panicked," she said. "I had some sort of...attack. I couldn't breathe, I couldn't think. I sat on the canyon floor and wept like a child. Renn needed me, Opek needed me, and the best I could do was stop and wait to die." She shook her head, numb. "I thought all this anger was for Kine," she whispered. "It's really for me. I hate that I've been running because I'm scared. I hate that I've been afraid to leave Low Country, but I'm afraid to stay here too. I hate that I'm afraid of *everything*."

The confession didn't surprise her, not when she'd known it ever since that first moment in Opek, when the sandstorm had lifted, and she'd looked across the desert for any sign of the Claws. It had been the moment when she recognized she'd sought an escape in Renn, that she'd hoped for him to lift her from her life, to take her somewhere new, to blind her to herself. He'd been her salvation, and with him stolen, she'd been left with nothing but her own skin. Her own wasted life.

After a moment, Arlon sat beside her. "That's understandable," he said. "You were young when you killed your father."

"That supposed to be encouragement? Would it have been easier if I were older?"

"It would've helped."

"Have you killed your father? Are you the reason your family broke apart?"

He shook his head. "My family was dead before I came of age."

"Of age to do what?"

He watched her for a long moment, frowning as his eyes drank her in. They were beautifully dark, swallowing her vision. "To make a difference," he said.

"Aye, making a difference." She snorted and tried to wipe more tears from her eyes. "Look where that gets us."

"You're trying to build peace," he said. "Just like your grandfather. But still, I reckon you have to find it."

"How do you do it?"

He frowned for a moment, and when he finally broke eye contact, she couldn't tell whether the action relieved or discouraged her. "I reckon you give something away," he finally said. "Release your life. Stop trying to control everything. Because you've seen the way Low Country is. You've seen how we fight for nothing, how we settle for the cheapest victories. This country can't give us more, Sharla. Maybe we just stop trying so hard. We let go and…enjoy what we have."

His words drifted now, trailing over themselves. She frowned and waited for him to turn back to her, wanting to see his gaze. "You sound like you're making this up as you go."

When he spoke again, his voice had softened. "I fought as hard as you. When I sought a place for myself in Low Country, I was as ambitious as any man. Maybe I even rivaled your grandfather. The problem was, I was born south of Mela: slums on the edge of the mesa, a bunch of failing ranchers and farmers. The rest of my family left, one by one. Sought places for themselves in Low Country, tried to make a life of it. My brothers became…very successful.

"It was black work, Sharla. Bunch of killing and looting and stealing and torturing. Sending a message. We worked with Senkha's men." He hesitated for a long moment. "At least, I did."

"This crew?"

Chapter Nineteen

He shook his head. "They came later. After Senkha was dead."

Sharla frowned. "But Senkha's not dead. You're confusing me."

"It's not difficult once you piece everything together." He smiled, but this time the smile was grim. "I hid it from everyone. Only Jyrak knows what really happened."

He hesitated for so long, Sharla squirmed on her rock.

"I killed him, Sharla," Arlon said.

"Senkha?"

"My brother." Arlon turned to her, and this time his eyes had hardened, glinting as though they'd turned brittle. "They were one and the same."

Her breath hitched and she froze, struggling to make sense of the situation. "Your brother..."

"He was paranoid. He lived in the shadows. I knew his empire would fall without him, and I wanted it for myself." Arlon inclined his head. "So, I killed him."

Sharla felt her eyes widen, her mouth gape. "So...you're..."

"I'm Senkha."

"You're his brother, Arlon."

Now Arlon's smile disappeared. "That was the name of a nobleman I picked up—some fool from High Country who visited once and never came back. Senkha took my name because he didn't like his. He was originally Henit. The name is a bad omen of sorts, the twin to our eldest brother, Senit. But my name was always Senkha." Arlon hesitated. "And then, I became Senkha again when I killed my brother."

"You're Senkha," Sharla repeated, stunned.

"I've been Senkha for years. About a decade. Started a little older than you were when you killed your father." Arlon—*Senkha*—dipped his head, eyeing her with a grim expression. "And I've seen it all, Sharla. I know what this country is, what it does to you. I know what you feel."

"But you're—" Sharla's voice broke off. She swallowed and sought words, struggling to make sense of what she tried to say. *But what? Could she say he'd seemed so different from the rest? So willing to try for change, risking his life to save a few nobodies from Opek?*

"I'm the Tyrant of the South?" Senkha nodded. "Yes, I've heard it before. And I don't blame anyone but myself for the name." He shook his head and turned to the distant army, where Senit—his *brother*—sat. The man who'd demanded Senkha show himself.

"You tried to kill Senit, too," Sharla said.

"I wanted to end our family." Now, Senkha spoke with a bite like Sharla's own. "Look at what we've done to Low Country. Look at the addicts, the impoverished, the *fear*. Look at how people live. We staked our territories, held our borders, ruled this country. Killed the bandits who threatened our trade, silenced Watchmen who were too patriotic. All of us worked together—Marast, myself, Senit, and Kine—without ever meeting each other. A network of fear and suspicion, preying on the poorest of Low Country to keep ourselves afloat. We were awful, and the country suffered for it. I think it could've been better, once. But now…I just want it to end. I needed to try something different. Maybe I thought I wanted Henit's empire, but after taking it?" Senkha shook his head. "It only sickened me. Over time, of course. But a decade is plenty of time for a man to change his mind."

"You're Senkha." She couldn't stop thinking the words. As if keeping everything simple could hide the atrocities of the man she sat beside; as if it could spare everyone the pain he'd brought Low Country. All the innocents who'd died at his hands, the bloodshed, the strife, and the chaos. Men like himself, Senit, and Kine were the ones who'd created Low Country. They were Benania's problem. And yet…

"But you want peace?" she asked.

"I didn't always. But I do now."

"You think this will bring you peace?"

"I don't know." He finally locked gazes with her again. "But it's a chance to try for something different. A chance to start over, give away what I had. Remember the happy moments on the ranch, small as they were." He snorted. "It sounds crazy, even to me…but after killing so many friends to keep myself hidden, I'm willing to bet on something crazy."

"All this time, you ruled from the shadows."

Chapter Nineteen

"No one knew who I was. Wasn't different from how Henit already operated. No one knew I sat in the open because the only way to get to me was by alleyways at night, multiple front men, letters and messages under tables; men got their throats cut if they looked too deep. It worked for Henit: I only knew who he was because I'm his flesh and blood."

She shook her head, still scrambling to put everything together. "You owned Mela."

"I owned all the south, except for Marast's territory. Everything was mine, and it still wasn't enough." Senkha grimaced. "In the end, it sickened me." He barked a laugh, something that wilted and died. "You said you run from yourself, that you hate yourself? I've done that for years. I wished I could leave Mela, but I was afraid of what that looked like. I think I can finally tell you what we both know: we won't find what we're after by running further."

"Then how will we find it?"

"I don't know." His eyes examined her, deep and potent, and they suddenly reminded her of the dream they both shared: a chance to start something new. But he'd suggested they find it by giving something away? What would that look like?

But he was still here, beside her, the only one who'd volunteered to stay. He didn't want the money, not anymore. He'd said so himself. That meant he was here for the idea of change, of starting something different from what he'd known. He was here for—

Their lips brushed. Only a touch. She hadn't realized how close they'd grown until the second of contact, the flush of heat to her face.

"Oh—"

She drew back, struggling to swim clear of those dark eyes and that brooding, serious countenance now softening with a grin. When she'd spoken to him in Mela and he'd decided to fight his own town for her cause…was it simply because she'd asked? Because he'd wanted to try something new?

"You came for me," she said. "You brought your crew for *me*."

"You were in trouble," he said. "You needed help. So I came. It sounded like something worthwhile, a difference that would matter. Ancestors know Low Country's seen too little of that."

"I came for Renn."

"I thought you came for the rest of Opek, too."

"I was just running away."

"I know."

They watched each other, and she wondered what this moment meant, where it might lead. She questioned which boundaries they'd crossed, never to look back. But that was both their natures, right? Run and forget the wreckage, at least until the aftermath. But this didn't feel like wreckage.

This didn't feel like wreckage at all.

"I came for Renn," she explained, and kissed Senkha.

She lingered this time, a flush of lips and heat that pulsed warmer energy from her chest, a stronger flow than she'd managed with anger. Something that filled her hollow heart and brought fire, something that made her want to run and laugh and dance and fight for years, for decades, for the rest of her life. A wild torrent that gripped her as effortlessly as it had when she'd slept with Renn, when they'd discussed their future dreams. When she'd met this beautiful cowboy from Low Country, someone with nowhere to be and all the time in the world.

She broke from Senkha, realizing her hands gripped his cheek, his hair. That his hands had done the same to her. She stared at him, confusion etched across her heart, and she pulled away.

"I came for Renn," she repeated, weaker this time, and turned from Senkha. She watched the moonlit hills and exhaled, her heart smashing like a hammer wielded by a drunken smithy.

"And now?" Senkha asked quietly.

"I don't know." Her hands trembled so badly that she tucked them between her legs and huddled over them, as though she could hide how Senkha affected her. As though she could hide how badly she wanted him, how she'd recognized it as instantly as she'd recognized that she'd run from Kine. It had happened over the same number of days as she'd

Chapter Nineteen

known Renn, in all the pauses between their breaths and through all the breaks in their conversations. But she'd traveled Low Country and battled through hell with Senkha. She'd only slept with Renn, drank with him, mumbled a few dreams for their future.

Ancestors above, would Renn have done all this for her?

"I don't know why I came," she whispered.

A quiet moment passed as they watched Keryn and Hesher ride back. Behind them, Kine's army split. Senit moved south while Kine moved north, an apparent pincer movement determined to crush Dormun—maybe even to force the mage to pick a group to attack.

Finally, Senkha stood and offered his hand for her. "You came to make a difference," he said. "You came to do something good. So let's finish it."

She stared at his hand, looked into his eyes. He'd grown blurry through more of her tears. She scowled and scrubbed them away. What could she be worrying about? More fear, anger, pain, or sorrow? Because now she had to choose between Renn or Senkha.

What a mess the ancestors made.

"I can't do this." She shook her head. "Don't make me leave someone again. Not when I just started to know them."

"You're not leaving," Senkha said. "You're staying. You're fighting for something. And you're not afraid anymore, Sharla Tarroful. I see it. You're ready to stand. Whether it's for your father or Low Country or something else, take a stand. Now, beside me. Let's show the ancestors we're past what we've done."

He asked her to take the same chance she'd already taken with Renn, to take the same plunge as when she'd left Opek: abandoning her former ambitions for the sake of a single, wayward soul who'd stumbled into her life.

But this time, it still didn't feel like wreckage.

She nodded, forcing a small smile. "Okay. Let's ride."

Chapter Twenty

KINE SAW IT NOW: THE EPITOME OF HIS NIGHTMARES. LION'S Head, the place where he'd shared friendship with Dormun, where they'd spoken about the lives and mistakes of their people.

Benania and Lhoria had fought with the tribes over the Savage Land for generations, the remaining sanctuary for Freytilia's indigenous population. Both nations had admitted to their faults, that they'd pushed the Claws too hard and too far. Kine had sought to explain as much to Dormun, revealing he was the colonel of the only regiment sent to inhabit Low Country. He wanted peace, perhaps more than the Owl did, and he'd hoped to build it with Dormun.

They'd agreed on their goals. They both wanted the same things: a bright future for their people, a new and promising age for Freytilia. If Claws and Low Countrymen agreed on a shared border, perhaps one day they could trade with each other. Work together to keep the peace, helping defend Claws from dhorak and Low Countrymen from bandits. It could all work, and it *should've* worked if Dormun hadn't gone behind Kine's back all the while.

If he hadn't been responsible for ordering the raid that slew Kine's wife.

The Watchmen were forced to pull back, to help their ravaged towns. Low Country's border shifted northward, and Kine finally stopped the bleeding by issuing his ultimatum: should Dormun ever

Chapter Twenty

attempt anything again, Kine would ride on Dormun's tribe until every soul had been slaughtered.

Now, the day came. Judgement turned full circle. Friendship began and ended at Lion's Head. Justice for Kine's wife, for Sharla and Hari, the family he'd sacrificed for Low Country's stability. He'd amend everything he'd lost.

He burned with the anticipation of it, itched with the restlessness of it. He hunched over his horse and watched the hills with a snarl, likely twisting his features into a hellish caricature. Gashar evidently thought as much when he flinched from Kine's expression.

"Your orders, sir?"

"We ride. Simple enough." But it wasn't. Kine knew that much. Something still wasn't right.

"Only a few men." He eyed Gashar. "We move quietly, send the rest ahead. Ask them to yell and scream as though all hell is breaking loose."

Gashar swallowed. "We won't lead the charge?"

"Senit will wait us out. He'll make sure we charge before he does, and by then, the trap will be sprung."

"The trap?"

"Dormun isn't just waiting." Kine shook his head and turned back to Lion's Head. "Something's up. There's a trap somewhere."

"But to spring it with our own men..."

"Do you have a better idea, Lieutenant Colonel?" Kine didn't have to look at Gashar to know his face had locked in a frozen expression, the mask he wore when he struggled to hide anger.

"You should have Sharla's crew do it."

"You think they'll listen to anything I say? Get too close to them and they'll probably run."

"Are you still worried about Sharla or Dormun?"

"They're both here. She already said she'll sweep in and help clean everyone out."

"*After* we spring the trap."

"There's nothing else to be done, Gashar." Using the younger man's name stilled him, as though they were still the friends they'd always been. The men who'd enjoyed each other's company before Kine nearly allowed Gashar to die under Senit's blade, before he'd traded away his position as a Watchman, before he'd likely spent all the remaining trust the younger man held for him. It was a wonder Gashar was still here, but evidently, his words outside Tigon Land were true. He thought Kine had impacted his life for the better.

Kine grunted at the thought. One tally in his favor, and he prayed to the ancestors it wouldn't be wasted.

"Spring the trap," Gashar finally muttered. "Aye."

* * *

THE SUN WAS ALMOST UP. THE EASTERN SKY GLOWED A brilliant orange, as though a rim of firelight encompassed the world, and it lent the prairie grasses a lush, vibrant cast. Sharla watched the sight and couldn't help but grimace.

A beautiful day for bloodshed.

Lion's Head caught the glow like a sentinel over the surrounding badlands, proud and noble. It arched over the huddled figures about its base, a tribe that couldn't have been more than one hundred strong. Easily enough to crush Sharla's crew, but once Senit and Kine attacked with their men, the tribe would be slaughtered. Sharla's crew would pick through the wreckage with ease…or they would after Jyrak disposed of the chaos mage.

Sharla swallowed at the thought, turning to catch Jyrak's gaze. She saw Senkha instead, who crouched just beside him. She stiffened and looked back to Dormun's camp, hating the thrill that tickled her, even now, when she was near Senkha. Ancestors above, there was no time for this. She'd come for Renn, and she had to focus on him and the Opekian townsfolk.

The crew had crept to the hillside with Ovis and his other Claws after they'd seen Kine and Senit lead their men in opposite directions. Now, they waited for the armies to attack so they could sweep in and kill the mage.

Sharla turned to ask Keryn whether she'd mentioned the mage to the other men, but Keryn and Hesher were already several hills away. They

Chapter Twenty

stood and waited in the predawn light, presumably waiting for the fighting to commence before they fled the rest of the way. Kine or Senit might mistake their leaving for an early retreat and try to stop them.

Two of their crew were down, but Jyrak, Ovis, and Senkha remained. Sharla couldn't deny she would have felt safer with Keryn's ready arrows, but now it couldn't be helped.

Sharla eased her battle axes free—one steel and one bone—while she waited for the first attack, whether it be from Senit or Kine. She could see Kine's men around the hills to the north, while some of Senit's bandits milled to the south. Both men probably waited for the other to make their move, wishing to spare as much of their own army as they could. That meant one of the men would probably have to be encouraged in their efforts.

She grimaced at the thought and backed down the hillside so she could look around Senkha. "Jyrak, I think you should—"

That's when the first shouts broke the quiet morning.

* * *

KINE HAD TO ADMIT HIS MEN KNEW HOW TO PUT ON A SHOW. He'd led his forces as close to Lion's Head as he dared: the final swell before camp. All the enemy waited on the other side, a mass of Claws he could smell from here. Or maybe he smelled his own men: horseflesh, unwashed bodies, urine, and scummy, rotten bread.

The first of his men charged, some on horseback and others on foot as they ran down the other side. Their orders were to kill and destroy, to run as wildly as possible. Should the tide appear to turn, they'd retreat, drawing the Claws over the hill. Of course, this meant Dormun's tribe would meet the rest of Kine's men, and that the Watchmen would suffer the brunt of casualties should Senit choose to do nothing.

Kine was roused when he heard the first thuds of flesh on steel, weaponry that clove a path through the unsuspecting Claws. The startled roaring of the tribe filled the air as they answered. Whinnying horses, shrieking men and women, someone bellowing orders. Kine imagined that someone to be Dormun, and he nearly abandoned his men and galloped over the hillside then and there—if only to put his blade between Dormun's eyes, to finish everything in one blow.

He locked gazes with Gashar, nodding at the other man's frown. They waited and listened.

*   *   *

"WHAT IS HE WAITING FOR?" SHARLA MUTTERED.

Below them, the camp fell into chaos. Several Watchmen charged over the hillside and into the press, swinging their blades with no apparent rhyme or reason. They massacred whomever they could, striking wildly. Spilling as much blood in as little a time as possible, apparently to goad a response.

"Do they know about the chaos mage?" Senkha asked.

"I wanted to ask Keryn if she told them, but she's already gone." Sharla turned to see that yes, Keryn had turned and started riding away with Hesher.

Senkha muttered something under his breath. "Good riddance."

"You're not friends after all?"

"Not when she leaves her crew to fight for the gold she plans on taking, no."

The air shifted. Goosebumps rippled over Sharla's skin; a humming built through her ears. A pressure, as though something fell against the world, pushing into her chest. A ripple of wind, a shrieking howl, and a storm erupted from nowhere. Gusts tore the prairie grasses to sweep clouds of dust and dirt, billowing funnels that darkened the sky with impossible speed. Energy flashed in their midst—some kind of lightning?—and they broke onto the Watchmen with a thunderous bellow.

"There's your chaos mage," Jyrak muttered.

Sharla looked southward, where Senit's men still hadn't moved. "Jyrak, could you..."

He'd lumbered forward and rested on the hillside, staring at the camp and concentrating. "Way ahead of you."

Sharla felt him channel, saw a spray of dirt somewhere to the south. A press of bodies crested the southern hill and spilled around Lion's

Chapter Twenty

Head formation, Senit's men shocked into a charge by Jyrak's magic behind them.

At the same time, the storm to the north faltered, wavered as the chaos mage evidently recognized someone else had casted. Jyrak's eyes widened, and he swore.

"Down," he said. "Get down!"

Sharla scuttled down the hillside, tugging Senkha after her, and the grass where she'd lain tore apart.

* * *

THE STORM OVER THE HILLSIDE CEASED. KINE'S SKIN CRAWLED as he felt another surge of power, an explosion somewhere to the west. At the same time, he recognized the din of other yells and screams, chaos from the south. Senit's men. They'd decided to charge after all.

Kine grinned with relief, and he turned to his men. "Senit's leading a charge." He paused and thought. "It sounds like Sharla's crew also engaged, but we'll wait for Senit to push deeper. Let them do some work for a change."

He pointed westward toward the rush of energy. "Dormun has some sort of mage. A very powerful one, by the sound of it. That must be his secret weapon, so we wait it out. Make sure it's focused on Senit before we attack."

He turned and hunched against his horse, drawing his sword and fingering the hilt. "Wait for my lead," he said. "At my signal, we charge, end this tribe, kill Dormun, and take the Opekians. For the Owl. For Low Country."

* * *

THE STORM ONLY LASTED A FEW SECONDS, BUT LONG ENOUGH to shave off the entire hillside. It looked like a rock had scraped it raw, leaving nothing but bare earth. Sharla stared at it and shuddered. The chaos mage was far stronger than Jyrak, far stronger than anything they'd seen. How could they possibly hope to match it?

She found herself locking gazes with Jyrak, and she knew he'd been wondering the same thing. "I have to get close," he explained. "I'll have to get close enough to strike him when he's unaware."

"So we wait for Senit's men—"

And then they must've been attacking, for shouts erupted from the south. Shrieking horses, howling men, steel ripping through flesh, and then the occasional clatter of steel striking bone armaments. Another roar of wind tore through the hills, and even from where they crouched under the hillside, Sharla saw a funnel spiraling through the sky, darkening the air with sudden clouds that came from nowhere. She saw pockets of dust, dirt, and debris. Pieces of armor, fragments of bone weaponry, and arrows. They rained from the sky like an awful hail, a brutal storm for Senit's men. Judging by their screams, the attack proved deadlier than anything she'd seen in Opek.

She swallowed and nodded at Jyrak. "Ride hard and fast."

Above her, Ovis practically hopped around with excitement. "Spirits ride with us," he said. "Guide us to the Third Horizon!"

"That doesn't bode well," she muttered as they crawled forward.

"Not at all," Senkha agreed. "But I reckon he's all we've got, unless you consider yourself a religious woman."

They peeked over the hillside again, witnessing a scene of pandemonium. Figures crouched atop Lion's Head—with Dormun's red skull among them—and watched the chaos below. A black mass of twisting elements absorbed the southern hill, obscuring an entire stretch of the camp. Sharla barely spotted Senit's men inside, now rendered as nothing more than arbitrary shadows. Here and there, they tried to escape, to circle the storm and come around the hill, but the storm only shrieked louder. It threw debris over the hills, sometimes sending them miles into the horizon, and ripped through the grass with brutal gusts. She watched entire swells dissolve, buffeted by an impossible assault, their turf peeling like stripped carpet and tossing sheafs of grass and dirt.

Only a few feet from the storm, the rest of the camp surged with motion. Claws scrambled from Watchmen who charged from the northern hills, their armor glowing in predawn light. Even as Sharla watched, the sun crested the eastern horizon. The Watchmen gleamed,

Chapter Twenty

their swords molten and their shields fiery. They looked like dragons, routing the Claws as they moved toward Dormun.

Directly below him, the Opekians rested. Sharla saw their huddled figures, writhing as they apparently wrestled against whatever bounds held them in place. They howled as the storm crept over the landscape.

She swallowed and looked to Senkha. "What's the best way to approach?"

"Can't go south." He shook his head at the storm. "We go north, around Kine's Watchmen. We'll circle and come at the camp from the east, find some captives who look strong enough to fight Dormun."

Like Renn.

The thought lay between them, unspoken, and Sharla tried to shake herself free of it. "Can we make it in time?"

The storm had already shifted, its elements swirling over the camp as it moved toward Kine's men.

"We'll have to move fast." Senkha mounted his horse and offered his hand to hoist her up before he turned to Ovis. "You and your friends, with us. We're riding for Redskull."

"At last!" Ovis roared. He mounted his own horse and waved at the other Claws, each of whom whooped and hollered.

Senkha turned to Jyrak and regarded him for a long moment. "Jyrak. Don't die."

Jyrak grinned, a rare gesture after the death of his bloodkin. Sharla only wished it didn't look so empty. "Don't worry about me, brother," Jyrak said. "Dormun's man isn't the only one with a few tricks up his sleeve."

Senkha nodded and kicked his horse down the slope. "We ride!"

* * *

GO FAST. GO HARD.

There'd been no time to observe the camp before he charged. Kine only knew Dormun would be somewhere at the southern end, where Senit was. Likely, he'd be atop Lion's Head itself, where he used to share meals with Kine. Where they used to spar, laugh, and joke.

How quickly everything changes.

Kine's sword split the face of one of Dormun's men, splattering himself and nearby Watchmen with red spray. Half the Claws hadn't managed to don their ram skulls, still fumbling through the process. They staggered about, wrenched from their sleep and flailing in confusion, knocking skulls over and tripping their neighbors. Kine swung his sword at every bare head he saw, with quick, brutal strikes that felt less like swordsmanship and more like he carried a mace.

He couldn't help himself; all his emotions spilled out. The same tide he'd repressed all these years, now freed to empty itself. He screamed with his wife's pain and his men's shame. Screamed for everything that went wrong in Low Country, a righteous anger that burned for retribution.

Watchmen flashed around him, blinding him with gleaming swords and shining armor now that the sun rose. An incredible sight: dusty, dirty armor suddenly appeared renewed, restored, cloaked in light. As though the ancestors encouraged the Watchmen forward, pushing them through their dirty work.

And ancestors above, it was dirty.

Claws reacted, stabbing with spears and chopping with bone axes. Kine abandoned the reins and lifted his shield, barely deflecting a blow that glanced sideways to thud against a fellow Watchmen's horse. He jabbed with his sword to tear a throat out, and swung through the gout of blood to catch another Claw in the head.

Or rather, he *tried* to, but his sword crunched against bone, ground around skull horns. It floundered beside the Claw as Kine's reach cost him his balance. A spear jabbed past his head as hands grabbed his sword arm, pulling him down. He roared as he fell, throwing himself into a roll that carried him from his flailing horse. Another horse shrieked directly beside him, almost crushing him as it toppled into the press and rolled, bloody bone fragments jutting from its sides as Claws howled and leaped onto its rider, stabbing with crude weaponry.

Kine scrambled for his footing, slashing through dust and dirt to keep Claws at bay. He'd fallen into the chaos, the heaving crowd of bodies that surged from his Watchmen, that scrambled to retaliate. Men

Chapter Twenty

jostled him from all sides, pinning his limbs. He roared and headbutted as though his helm were a club. He thumped against bare heads with ugly squelches, rattled against ram skulls with aching impacts. He hit enough people that his head hurt, that he tired of colliding with bones, but at least it cleared him room.

Now he swung with his sword, cleaving a spear in half and exposing the ribs of a nearby Claw. A spray of blood and dirt, a coppery dust that rose from the badlands and coated his mouth. He crouched behind his shield and scuttled sideways, dodging through bone weaponry and thrusting.

Block and thrust, stroke and counterstrike, dash and repeat. Mechanical movements, a repetitive, grueling game until his muscles screamed in agony and his breath rattled through his lungs. He moved on instinct, at least until he found an opening in the mob, a breather with which to assess their surroundings.

Bodies writhed across the vale: flashing Watchmen and dark Claws. They tousled like waves in ocean currents, a tide of agony that rolled toward Lion's Head. The rocks rose over the chaos, and on them, Dormun Redskull stood. Kine would recognize that skull anywhere, even after decades apart. Kine knew his old friend stared directly at him—as though the ancestors encouraged their reunion.

A wordless bellow rose from Kine's chest. He jabbed his sword toward the distant figure. Dormun inclined his head.

Kine felt the shifting air before the storm from the south moved across the battlefield. It appeared Dormun's mage could only strike one direction at a time, and with Senit's men temporarily disbanded, the mage aimed for the Watchmen.

Aimed for Kine.

Kine threw himself forward, tackling a Claw to the ground as the wind ripped over him. It howled so quickly, so ferociously, that it literally pulled Kine like a grown man, yanking as though to hurtle him through the air.

Screaming with the effort, he rolled over, pulling the Claw with him, losing his weaponry as he held the Claw over him as a body shield.

Everything howled, wind shrieking in Kine's ears as the earth shuddered. The men trembled like leaves in a sandstorm, blown about as debris swirled.

The sky darkened, the swirling dust and dirt blackening everything until Kine could've inhabited a dark room. All perception shrank to himself and the Claw, who writhed and shouted as debris struck his back. As though from a distance, Kine heard himself howling into the nether, be it from panic, agony, or rage.

After what felt like an eternity, the winds lessened. The mage turned back to Senit's men, redoubling his attack. The Claw draped over Kine, lifeless; whatever blew through the storm had flayed his body. Everything below Kine's waist was sticky and warm, and he tasted the man's blood. He struggled to heave the body off him, to roll clear as a horse fell from the heavens, dropped from wherever it had been sucked to. It crushed several men directly beside Kine, two Watchmen among them.

He swore and staggered sideways as another fell close behind. Pieces of armor, weapons, and bodies rained from the sky, crushing man and beast alike—snapping spears, pulverizing bones, bursting bodies like overripe fruit.

Kine flailed through the maelstrom; he found someone's shield and held it over himself in a frantic defense. He peered around its rim as he saw the last of the carnage fall from the sky.

A respite, but probably not for long.

He fumbled for weaponry, found someone's mace, and charged forward, waving his newfound armaments and howling. "Watchmen, to me! To Lion's Head! Press the attack!"

Survivors stumbled around him, Claws and Watchmen alike. They picked themselves from the ripped earth and looked about, dazed and confused. He dodged around their bodies, forcing his legs to pump faster, harder, as he sprinted for Lion's Head.

Someone had to find that mage and finish him.

* * *

Chapter Twenty

THEY'D ROUNDED THE HILLS TO ENTER THE CAMP WHEN THE storm finally dispersed, moving south again. Sharla stared at its aftermath: horses and men fell from the heavens as though they'd been thrown by the ancestors.

"That's impossible," she uttered.

"It's ridiculous," Senkha snarled. He sounded angry, furious. "What kind of man tries to harness that power?"

"A Claw."

"Jyrak had better work his magic."

Senkha still looked west, his attention absorbed by the storm, and he missed the incoming spear.

"Senkha, look out!" Sharla grabbed his shoulder and wrenched him sideways, knocking them from the saddle as another spear stabbed his horse. It shrieked and toppled over a granite boulder, rolling through bodies as several Claws converged. They'd apparently seen Sharla and Senkha riding for their prisoners, and they wished to keep their prizes.

Sharla stood to find herself face to face with a screaming Claw. His face disappeared with a muffled thump, warm spray and skin tackling her to the ground. She found herself under a corpse, a gaping wound in its neck, and she scrambled free to see Ovis and the other riders storming the camp. They hooted at their skulled adversaries, who hollered back. The camp filled with a cacophony of guttural growling and shouting. Riders circled and struck each other with bone axes and spears.

Sharla pulled herself upright, searching the captives for anyone who appeared strong enough to help fight. She instantly saw Renn; she'd recognize that blond hair and those bright eyes anywhere. For a moment, they stole her breath away as memories flooded her. The last time she'd seen those eyes, she'd been on a horse, leaning over to kiss, to laugh, to hug.

But now he was frowning, and then he was yelling. "Sharla, get down!"

She threw herself forward as something passed over her head, close enough to stir the hair across her neck. She toppled into another Opekian, a bound woman who thrashed against her. She fumbled with the woman, losing a battle axe as she struggled to turn. A bone axe whipped at her, catching the woman beside her and opening her shoulder with a horrid squelch. The woman shrieked as her blood sprayed Sharla, coating her eyes and mouth. Sharla spat and scrambled, struggling to see the Claw as he came again.

She parried—ancestors only knew how—and sent his bone axe sideways as she lurched upright, swung for his head. The desperate heave turned her momentum into an awkward stumble; he caught her and spun to toss her into a boulder, a dreadful impact that punched the air from her lungs and made her drop her second axe.

She turned as he came at her with his remaining weapon, throwing herself under the blow. Smashing her face into the dirt, she spit grass as she crawled, lungs aching for depleted air. She moved behind the boulder, only to meet another Claw. He lunged for her, but his grinning face burst outward, steel shining through his mouth as Senkha's stiletto sprayed her with more blood. She shrieked and jerked away as the corpse slid from Senkha's blade. He turned and dodged another Claw behind him.

Sharla ducked under the blow of the original Claw who'd chased her, pressing against his chest as she jabbed her fingers at his eyes and mouth. Her fingers bruised against a bone skull, finding no purchase as he grappled for her, wrenching her wrist and tossing her sideways. Rocks ground her back in another bruising impact as she spluttered for breath, seeking a weapon and finding a rock. She swung it as he leaned over her, dashing the ram skull against his head. A second blow cracked the skull, grinding it deeper. The Claw bellowed and stumbled. She jumped onto him and swung her rock. *Go down, go down!*

She lost count of her blows. His ram skull crumbled to bloody fragments and his misshapen face pulped underneath. It was no longer possible to tell where the ram skull ended and his own began. She rolled off the corpse and retched into the grass, looked for her battle axes. She found one and darted for it, scooping it up and raising her gaze to see Kine.

Chapter Twenty

They locked eyes, and she could've sworn he grinned before the winds picked up again.

* * *

THAT FAMILIAR SHRIEK. THE SURGE OF ENERGY. DIRT AND dust ripping from everywhere. Kine hadn't made it far enough! He raised his shield to block whatever might catch the wind, falling to his knees. But then, the howl dissipated. The winds dispersed.

He frowned and peered around the shield, daring to believe his luck. Other men cowered around him. Beyond them, toward the southern hills where Senit had led his charge, a nimbus of black cloud and dust billowed over the battlefield. Shapes moved in its midst, as two men appeared to be wrestling with glowing fists. A fight between mages?

Hoofbeats slammed the earth. A shadow reared an instant before Kine threw himself sideways. The blow that would've decapitated him bashed his shield instead, knocking him flat. He rolled and struggled to his knees, panting for breath, as the rider turned and came in for another pass. It was Senit, his face bloodied, his hair tangled around him, and his eyes wide and furious.

"You knew!" the man roared. "You knew of the mage. Led us into a trap!"

"No trap," Kine gasped. "Didn't know!"

Senit had pulled a spear from one of his men—or Kine's—and plunged it toward Kine. Kine barely pulled the shield up in time to catch the blow. His entire body shuddered from the impact, and he topped backward. He fumbled, struggling to pull himself upright as Senit rushed him again, too close to dodge this time.

He flinched as the spear came low, angling for his neck, but it lurched sideways as Senit jerked and cried out. Blood sprayed as Gashar's blade clove Senit's back. The man passed on his horse as Senit retaliated, twisting sideways and thrusting his spear. The point punched through Gashar's left pauldron and exploded from his shoulder, nearly tossing the man from his saddle. He dropped his blade, unbalanced and lurching sideways. His horse angled into the press of bodies, and he disappeared into the mob.

Senit stared after the younger man. He groaned, turned his horse away, and rode the other direction, fleeing the battlefield. Kine saw the trench in his backside, noticed garments already glistening with wetness. A killing blow? Likely not, but it would drive Senit into hiding like the desert rat he was. He'd bide his time for a day when he'd inevitably stab Kine in the back.

More demons to face. But this morning, Kine would settle for one.

He turned to Dormun.

* * *

SHARLA SAW SENIT TURN AND RIDE TOWARD THE HILLS. Beside her, Senkha watched the retreat of his older brother. She watched his lips curl in disgust, and his expression darken with anger. When he turned to her, a question clouded his gaze, one she instantly understood.

"Go," she said. "Finish it."

He nodded and bolted after him. As Senit made his way through the press, Senkha followed the higher terrain, apparently determined to sweep the battlefield and catch Senit before he escaped. He'd left her to fight Dormun—but then, she still had Renn.

Speaking of Renn, the man stared at her with his mouth hanging open, and his incredulous expression didn't leave when she cut his bindings with her axe.

"Sharla?" he asked. "What are you doing here?"

"It's called a rescue," she huffed. "Try to act lively and find yourself a weapon. We've no time for naps."

"You found yourself an army."

She frowned at the tone of his voice. "Of course. Coming here without one is foolish."

"Foolish to come at all."

Now his tone carried a hint of disappointment. It made her want to strike him with the butt of her axes, to pummel him until he curled into a ball and begged for mercy. She snorted as he stood before her, glaring into those green eyes. "You would rather I hadn't come?"

"You shouldn't have, Sharla. It must've been dangerous."

"You have no idea."

Chapter Twenty

He blinked at the venom in her words, and his eyebrows rose. His expression crinkled, softened. "I'm only thinking of you," he said. "I'm...touched that you came for me."

"I'm touched that you're touched." She offered him one of her battle axes—the bone one—and raised her eyebrow at him. "We can chat about this later, yeah? We have a chieftain to kill."

He eyed her for a moment, grabbed the battle axe. "You know how to fight?"

"Apparently."

He smiled. "I might know a few things myself."

"*You* know how to fight?"

"Well, it's Low Country."

"Try not to sound so happy about it. Your constant optimism is unnerving."

She eyed the slope above them and frowned. It was a steep thing, fraught with granite boulders and outcroppings. Claws already crouched at the top beside Dormun, raising bows and nocking arrows.

"Time to go." She ran forward and darted behind the first boulder as arrows glanced off it. Renn crouched beside her, licking his lips and rolling his shoulders, apparently eager to fight his captor.

A body tumbled beside them, and she turned to see Kine crouching in the grass, struggling for breath as he huddled behind his shield. So close. So vulnerable. Obviously exhausted and weak. He wrenched his helm off to reveal graying hair plastered to his head by sweat, and eyes wide and bright, almost feverish.

She could end it. A quick chop to the neck, and no one would know. Another casualty of war. Renn would be the only witness.

The wind picked up, and she turned to the battlefield. She couldn't see Jyrak anymore. The other mage—the chaos mage—stumbled through the battlefield as though he'd been winded. He gesticulated with wild motions that drew erratic gusts, but even as she watched, the elements mustered their former strength, shrieking over the landscape to draw cries of fear from both Claws and Watchmen.

"Someone has to take him out." She turned to Kine. "Can you manage that?"

He growled and hefted his mace. "Don't kill Dormun without me."

He lumbered off, crouching underneath Lion's Head as he skirted the bound captives from Opek. The rest of them still lay there, as Sharla had only freed Renn. In hindsight, that probably wasn't the smartest move, but she knew they had to to press the attack, to catch Dormun as quickly as possible. Besides, none of the other Opekians looked particularly useful in a fight, so it seemed preferable to have the one man beside her who'd probably experienced combat.

She locked gazes with him and nodded. "Let's finish it."

She turned to run for the next outcropping directly above the first, darting sideways the moment she recognized drawn arrows. She tried to dodge and weave, but ended up slipping in the grass and tumbling as arrows hissed around her. It took the Claws just as much time as Low Countrymen to redraw their bows, so she had enough of a breather to scramble upright and hurry to the next outcropping before they nocked again.

Renn crouched behind her in the next instant, breathing heavily. His expression looked worn, as exhausted as Kine had been. She felt a twinge of sympathy for him and the other captives—they probably hadn't received adequate sleep or rations—but his eyes gleamed just as bright when they caught the rising sun. She shivered at their brilliant, vibrant green.

Movement below them—she looked to see Ovis and the other Claws charging up the embankment. Confusion spread as Dormun's Claws followed and skirmishes spilled across the hillside. She deemed it unwise to count on Ovis's aid, and she shrugged at Renn.

"Looks like it's up to us."

She turned and darted around the outcropping, sprinting for the next one. The Claws were ready this time, and she saw their bows an instant before she threw herself forward. She collided with hard earth under the prairie grass, feeling it throttle her already bruised skin, as arrows hissed past her ears. She heard Renn grunt and stumble as other

Chapter Twenty

steps thrashed through the grass: bodies moving too close, too quickly. She stood to meet a Claw who barreled toward her.

She gasped, tried to sidestep, and barely succeeded in twisting around his spear as he thrusted. She found herself sideways, off balance, swinging haphazardly as she floundered like a drunkard. Fighting on hillsides helps no one a great deal, and he proved similarly unbalanced. For an agonizing stretch of time, they struggled to correct their momentum, but then his head exploded in a spray of blood, crunched bone, splattered brains. He fell under Renn's brutal stroke, and as the cowboy blinked through the spray, she tackled him and pushed him under more arrows. They tumbled through the grass and crashed against the rocks, finding their limbs dangling over a sudden precipice as they nearly rolled over the edge to land on the Opekians.

She crawled from the ledge, offering her hand to him, but he kicked it aside in time to avoid another blade that chipped the rock beside her. The Claws were on them now, with dire footing and blinding light to their advantage. The sun seared Sharla's vision, splitting the horizon in a massive spectacle, and it darkened all combatants by contrast.

Easier to tell who the enemies were when they lunged for her. She found herself on the ground, but this was nothing new. Thanks to Kine's old training, she'd fought from the ground once or twice. She rolled from the first strike and planted her boots on the blade to push herself backward, rolling to her feet. The easy motion was scrambled when multiple Claws ran for her, pressing her toward the precipice. She stepped across its edge and crouched. The Claws hesitated and she darted into their midst, ducking low to cleave the knees from the first, stepping inside the strike of the other to gash his side.

They hadn't expected this: a small woman who could fight. With her shorter stature and leaner frame, Kine's training had lent her an advantage. Thanks to him, she might survive this. The thought sparked her familiar anger, and suddenly she was the raging storm from Opek, whirling in their midst and stabbing with vicious cuts. The Claws leaped around her, struggled to defend themselves. She moved from one to the next, desperate to press the attack, to finish this before Dormun could get away.

She tangled with one Claw near the edge, but he'd watched her long enough to understand her technique. He stepped to meet her attack and her battle axe glanced from his. He enfolded her in a massive bear hug, pinning her arms as he pivoted to hurl her over the edge. She flailed as he released, grabbing his wrist with her free hand and using him as a counterweight to pull herself toward steady ground. He howled and lurched forward as she slammed against the rock ledge, shoving her battle axe clear as she scrambled on the rocks and kicked her legs in open space, searching for something to push from.

The Claw she'd swung around stumbled over the edge with a shriek, and she heard the crack of his skull against rocks. Shouts from the surrounding Opekians indicated they'd probably been caught in the spray as Sharla's fingers scraped the rocks, tangled with the fissures, cut and bruised themselves as she finally found a handhold to pull on.

Two Claws ran toward her, and she closed her eyes, waited for the inevitable blades across her wrists to send her falling to meet the same fate as the Claw she'd killed. But Renn plowed into them while dragging two Claws behind, sending everyone to the ground in a wild heap. The men roared and thrashed, heaving as each struggled to wrestle atop the others, to claim the summit of their dogpile. Meanwhile, Sharla finally pulled herself upright and rolled to safety, gasping for breath—a momentary respite while she watched the golden grass and the blushing, vibrant clouds.

A beautiful day for bloodshed.

She grabbed her battle axe and some sort of bone club as she charged again, trusting Renn to take care of the rest. One of them had already toppled over the edge, and the others appeared wounded by the ferocity of Renn's attack. He didn't even have weapons anymore; only his bare fists, and he fought with a brutality to rival Ovis.

Sharla passed the last outcroppings, determined to press the attack and end Dormun before he could escape, before things continued to spiral out of control.

Chapter Twenty

The chieftain waited for her, apparently having sent all his men to fight Renn and herself. He was a massive brute, one whose build rivaled Ovis and Jyrak. The warpaint across his dhorak skull burned a hellish red in the sunlight, and his eyes glittered in the skull's eye sockets. The heat of his gaze struck her like a fist, and she slowed her approach, crouching and raising her weapons.

The two stared at each other, a calm broken only by the distant howl of battle, the screaming of the wounded. Almost lazily, he waved his hand over the battlefield.

"I expected Kine," he said, a gruff voice that reminded her of crunching gravel. "You his heir?"

She bristled, stepping forward. "Heir to what?"

"Low Country."

She spat. "Kine's no lord of our land."

"No? Its general, then."

"Not that, either."

"Its warrior?" Dormun folded his arms across his chest. "Which makes you the…princess? Queen?"

Sharla shook her head. "I'm just a girl from Opek."

She already despaired of her odds here. She should've freed Renn before running to meet Dormun, but now the opportunity had passed. Dormun held the advantage in height, reach, and probably in speed. No amount of training with Kine could've prepared her for an opponent like this: she already recognized it from the ease of Dormun's motions, the rolling of his shoulders and the hefty muscles underneath his hide armor, the veins that bulged from his arms. This man possessed the strength of a lion and the speed of a gazelle, she was certain of it. Her plan to run away and start something new might end here.

She flinched at the thought, temporarily floundering in her approach, and Dormun looked past her shoulder. "Little girl," he rumbled. "Your friend needs you."

She hesitated, but when he made no motion, she darted a quick glance over her shoulder. It appeared Renn had been subdued, and the three remaining Claws pinned his arms to his sides while another held a battle axe to his neck. He watched her, calm and still, and she froze at the sight.

For a moment, it seemed that no one breathed. Calm stilled the hill, while below them, the battle raged as fiercely as ever. She struggled to discern the emotions in Renn's gaze, but the sunlight caught his eyes and they gleamed as fiercely as before. Impossible to tell what lurked there, but his expression had tightened, and he quivered with anger.

She stiffened at the thought, wondering what he might think of her should she turn herself in. Perhaps he'd only worried about her, as he'd said. Perhaps he'd thought her incapable, as she'd feared. Perhaps he expected nothing more from her, waiting for her to lay down her weapons and join him.

Maybe Dormun would take her as a captive, use her as a hostage to dissuade Kine. Maybe it would work, and maybe it wouldn't. Sharla didn't know; she didn't put anything past Kine anymore.

She felt nothing but the anger, consuming her from the inside out, because yet again, she found herself powerless. Bartered and exchanged and tossed around like luggage, the same luggage Hari abandoned when she'd left Sharla with Kine and the rest of his money.

Perhaps that was what Sharla wanted more than anything: to know she wasn't mere baggage. She wasn't the afterthought of a cowardly mother, the bane of an ambitious grandfather. That she wasn't another blemish on a grand heritage, the stain on what could've been a glorious family legacy. She was her own woman, free to make the choices she'd always wanted, free to find what she'd always desired, to stop running from everyone merely because they expected little else.

She was free to accept Senkha's words: that sometimes, finding peace meant letting go. Relinquishing control, stopping the race. Walking, for the first time in her life, and enjoying the simple moments: the times with Renn when they'd lain together and described their future.

But also, there were those times with Senkha, when they'd sat through the moonlit nights and discussed their lives, their futures in Low Country. When they'd dared to imagine that finding something

Chapter Twenty

better didn't mean leaving Low Country at all. Perhaps, finding something better meant accepting what they'd been given, releasing their ambitions to cherish the company they'd obtained. She'd never known a truer family than the crew she'd ridden with for only a few days. Not even Renn gave her that. He'd given her the promise of another lie: that in running with him, in fleeing Low Country, she could escape the demons that hounded her.

No, Senkha had been right. Sharla Tarroful couldn't run anymore. She was her grandfather's daughter, and a Tarroful didn't run. They stood their ground, fought the battles that mattered.

It was time to let go and confront herself.

"I'm sorry," she told Renn.

Before Dormun could react, before the Claws could move, she turned and charged the chieftain.

* * *

THE WIND AND DUST BLEW AGAIN, GUSTS THAT TUMBLED horses and men. Riderless mounts surged about the tangle, frantic to escape, kicking Watchmen and Claws with flailing hooves as they scrambled through the elements. Helmless Watchmen howled with blood streaming down their faces, clutching facial wounds or moaning in confusion as more debris knocked them around.

Kine watched it all with a grimace, turning back to his target. He'd crept around the back of the northern hills, the route of Senit's passage. Now that same hillside was strewn with slain bandits, twisted corpses either mutilated or smashed into oblivion by debris from the storm. Many of them had never seen combat, as there were no accompanying Claws. Instead, these men had suffered the brunt of the mage's attack, offering the distraction and cover Kine's Watchmen had needed.

Kine should've celebrated the notion, for he'd accidentally freed Low Country of Senit's men. Maybe even of Senit himself. Alas, the thought only spelled disaster on the home front, because now there would be chaos while Watchmen and outlaws struggled to claim the hole in Low Country's border. More turf wars, negotiations, and contemptible truces. The work of a Watchman was never over.

But maybe one more problem could be settled.

The mage was surrounded by the same nimbus of dark cloud and dust as before. Sharla's mage was nowhere to be seen, but whatever he'd done had clearly weakened his opponent. The man stumbled about, blinking and shaking his head as though he'd been dazed.

Kine crept over the hillside and made his approach, gripping his stolen mace for a deathblow. Aye, the chaos mage tired, but so did Kine. His breath rattled in his chest like a bag of gravel, and his limbs grew heavier with every step. Ancestors above, war was a young man's game—he reckoned he'd passed his prime. Perhaps only Gashar deserved to know that much…if he'd survived the battle. Kine winced at the thought, and he told himself he'd have to thank the younger man should he ever see him again. He'd have to make things right.

Stupid of him to distract himself with other thoughts. Merely a few paces from the chaos mage, he stumbled over a corpse and went down, sprawling in the grass with a startled grunt. The chaos mage whirled, black cloud dimming his features, and Kine barely saw the expression of alarm on his face before the mage raised his hands, fingers glowing.

Kine flinched, raising his shield, but suddenly the mage fell forward, screaming as an arrow sprouted from his shoulder. He went to one knee, and as he struggled to rise, another arrow sprouted from his side. He swayed and went to both knees, then onto his hands.

Kine charged forward and swung the mace to shatter the mage's jaw, spewing teeth and blood through the grass. The man toppled sideways, where Kine landed a final blow to crush his skull into a wet mess. He hauled himself upright, lifted the mace, and blinked. Peering closer, he saw that underneath the bloody mess, the man's face was…inhuman. Oddly angular, with a long, flattened nose, stretched eyes, and what Kine assumed to be birthmarks across his face—except they were pitch black in color, as though the man had stained himself with ink.

Hoofbeats drew his attention beyond the corpse, where the woman from Sharla's crew approached on her horse, the archer with black hair. The Kathagonian still rode behind her as she shouldered her bow.

"You saved me," Kine said, surprised.

"Don't remind me," she answered. "I tried to leave, but I can't get away from Arlon for the life of me. He looks at me once, and I feel guilty all over again." She shook her head and examined the battlefield. "Both of us are growing soft."

"I reckon that can wait." Kine huffed for breath and looked to Lion's Head, where a smaller battle raged as furiously as the one before them. "We've got to end this."

"Sounds like we're not the only ones growing soft, Colonel." The woman gave Kine a nasty grin. "You sure you're up to the task?"

"Don't worry about me. Worry about your man Arlon. He ran after Senit alone, and they're over the hill somewhere."

"Figures." The woman gave him a black look, as if this were Kine's fault. Which, maybe in a way, it was. "The man's always getting himself into trouble." She kicked her horse toward the hill Kine indicated and galloped away.

Kine turned to Lion's Head, rolled his weary shoulders, and started the long trudge to the summit. Fighting wars was not for the old.

* * *

SHARLA SPRINTED TO CLEAR THE DISTANCE BETWEEN HER and the chieftain, launching herself into a dive. A sweeping cut of her battle axe nicked Dormun's calf as she tumbled past; he barely hauled himself free of the strike. She hit the ground and rolled to her feet as he drew his own weapon.

The chieftain towered over her, carrying a hide shield and what appeared to be the femur of some ridiculously large animal—perhaps a dhagonrak or a dhorak—with teeth affixed to its length in rope bindings. The things were serrated, a ludicrous extension of pointed ends that made her squirm. Dormun swung it in languid, easy circles. He said something drowned out by Renn's shouting—whether of pain or anger as he renewed his attack on the other Claws, Sharla couldn't tell—and she ran forward before she could give herself time to rethink the notion.

Dormun's weapon had all the reach, and she danced and dodged as best she could, baiting him to come closer while cringing over every sweep of his blade—if it could be called a blade—and scrambling to respond with her battle axe and club. Her parries were sloppy, awkward attempts to catch his weapon under the head of her axe and the length of her bone club.

The strategy nearly cost her the axe with Dormun's first swung; he wrenched and nearly ripped her weapon free as its blade caught on the teeth. She grew more wary after that, mostly blocking with the club while she waited for an opening with her axe. Dormun moved quickly, light on his feet and always covering his naked side with the shield. It was nothing but a skirmish, a light scuffle while the two circled the summit, sought any opening, waited for the other to make a mistake.

Was he only playing with her? Buying time for more of his friends to come help? Waiting for Low Country's savior to make her fatal mistake? But he never gloated, never taunted. He merely watched and waited, calm.

Blood and ashes, it made her furious. She'd traveled the length of Low Country for this? Hopping around while a Claw chieftain watched from the safety of his tiny shield and obnoxious spear?

She feinted with the battle axe and dove underneath his weapon, rolling to smash his boots with the bone club. He was faster than her, already moving to bring her within reach of his weapon, so she threw the battle axe at his face. He flinched, jerking his head sideways as the blade clattered from a dhorak horn, but it disrupted his attack for the moment she required to step closer and draw the knife in her belt. Pressed against his bulk, with no room for her to use the club or reach his side, she jabbed for his shield arm, catching the meat of his wrist and spurting blood down her front. Dormun howled, fumbling the shield as he grappled for her with his other arm. She ducked his grasp and found herself by his boots, scrambling to swing her bone club—but he kicked out, catching her under the ribs and tossing her with a blow that winded her, *again*.

She rolled and dove, anything to stay on his shield side, away from that terrible bone weapon. She swung the club again, as hard as she could, and caught the side of his knee with an ugly crack that wrenched

Chapter Twenty

his leg and folded it sideways. He growled and retaliated with a mighty sweep of the shield. Its rim caught her in the side—the same spot where he'd already kicked her. The blow punched pain through her chest, inflaming her lungs and making every breath an agony. It tossed her several paces backward, and from the first instant she tried to push herself up, she knew her fight was over. He must've cracked or broken several of her ribs.

She floundered for a moment, watching him turn and rear that ugly weapon as he limped forward. She saw it blot out the clouds with its terrible shaft, falling—

—into a body that slouched before her, toppling as the weapon rent and tore flesh with a gruesome squelch. Someone howled and breathed hot fumes across her face, a massive shape that pushed her to the grass. She gasped under the weight and struggled backward to see Ovis grimacing at her.

"Little lady," he groaned. "In my coat…your fancy weapon."

Blood dribbled down his chin and across her fingers as she searched the pockets of a dying man, finding a crossbow—maybe her own—that Ovis had taken from one of the horses. Already cocked.

She pushed him aside, raising it to take aim. Even that action hurt; it left her moaning and falling into the grass, upsetting her shot. She settled for Dormun's leg rather than his chest, punching her bolt through the kneecap she'd already hit. Dormun howled as his leg gave out. He went down on his other knee, which pitched him sideways. He scrambled in the grass while Sharla dropped the crossbow, groaning with pain.

"Hurts like hell, don't it?"

She turned to see Ovis staring at her, Dormun's hideous weapon still buried in his back. She swallowed at the amount of spilled blood. He was done for.

"I'm sorry." There wasn't much else to say.

"The spirits smile on us." Ovis managed a final, broken grin. "I'll see you at the Third Horizon."

"I don't know what that means," she whispered. But the Claw had already passed, his eyes glazing over as he slumped into the grass, still grinning like the wild fool he'd always been. She frowned at the unexpected lump in her throat, the burn of tears behind her eyes. She'd almost grown to enjoy the man's company.

After a moment, she reached over, clenching her jaw at the effort, and closed his eyes. "Ancestors grant you mercy on your journey," she mumbled. "Or…spirits. Whatever suits your fancy."

A growl drew her gaze to Dormun, who'd finally managed to stand. He swayed on his good leg, and he looked beyond her to the battlefield, now calming, and to the side, where the rest of Ovis's Claws fought the remainder of what must've been Dormun's personal guard. The chieftain of the Skull Tribe weighed his odds with a despairing gaze. Then, he looked to something behind Sharla. His eyes widened, and he shouted with pain as he turned and hopped south, a desperate motion that might've been funny if it didn't hurt Sharla to laugh.

It was done. With Dormun's flight, they'd finished the Skull Tribe. The rest of the Opekians could go home, and judging by the absence of wind, it seemed the mage was dead. With any luck, Senkha would finish Senit and find the peace he'd always sought.

Peace. Sharla grunted at the notion, sinking into the grass and staring at the clouds. If peace hurt this much, she didn't think she wanted it.

Footsteps through the grass, and Kine loomed overhead. "Not dead after all," he said.

"Sorry to disappoint."

"Do I look disappointed?"

"You look angry."

"No." Kine frowned, thought for a moment, and shook his head. "Well, not at you."

"At him?" Sharla waved her hand in the direction of Dormun's departure, and Kine nodded.

"We used to call ourselves brothers," Sharla's grandfather said. "Now he runs from battle like a bandit. No better than Senit or Marast or any of the rest."

"No better than you?"

Kine stiffened at the words. "You'd judge me, too?"

Chapter Twenty

"I reckon we're past that, grandfather. We both know who you are."

Kine stared at her for a long moment. "You going to die?"

"I think some ribs are cracked."

"Aye." Kine raised his gaze to the horizon. "It hurts something terrible, but you'll live."

"I guess I won't be running after all." Sharla closed her eyes and grimaced at a fresh wave of pain. "I was going to, you know. After everything was settled. Break my end of the bargain so I wouldn't have to leave with you."

"But you stayed to fight."

"I wanted to free the Opekians."

"Could've let us do that. So why?"

Sharla frowned at the notion. "I decided I was tired of running."

Kine said nothing for a long moment. Sharla only heard the distant clamor of battle, the sigh of wind through the grass. When she finally opened her eyes again, Kine was staring into space.

"So, Colonel. Are you ready to take me in?"

"Not yet." Kine exhaled. "I have to kill a friend."

* * *

DORMUN REDSKULL HOBBLED LIKE AN OLD MAN. PERHAPS HE was one, but never had it been so glaringly obvious. Never had it been so infuriatingly final. In one morning, everything had been swept away. His entire tribe, his shaman, and all his ambitions. Thoughts of a redeemed homeland? All gone, forever banished.

With the shaman dead, the dark lands of the east would never lend him their support. They'd taken a risk on him, and he'd trampled it. The spirits had warned him, the elders from the south had *all* warned him, but he'd done it anyway. He'd been too proud, perhaps. Too impatient to admit his homeland would never be reclaimed in his lifetime. Perhaps it would never be reclaimed at all.

But he'd tried. Even if all his people—the other tribes, everyone who called themselves his kin—had abandoned the effort, he never had. He'd held his dream till the end, and he regretted nothing.

He knew Kine Tarroful to be following him long before he heard the other man's footsteps. He finally ceased his hobbling and turned to meet his former friend. They hadn't traveled far—impossible for Dormun to manage much with his ruined leg—merely to the summit of the next hill.

The badlands stretched around them, flowing and beautiful: golden grass, glowing granite, and lush trees that shivered under the glorious sunrise. A beautiful territory, but nothing like the silent spaces of the northern homeland—the desert flats where the land lay so still that the spirits were said to descend, to dwell and commune with Dormun's people. Would they ever do so again?

"I walked after you," Kine said. "*Walked*. Took my time, too. All the while, you limped away like a wounded dog. Where's your pride, Dormun?"

"You say pride, but call me a dog?" Dormun pulled his skull off to snarl at Kine, matching the man's glare with his own. "What are *you*? Stealing our land. Chasing our spirits out. You northerners are rats."

Kine hesitated, perhaps because he saw Dormun's face for the first time since they'd spoken decades before. Perhaps he was shocked at how Dormun had aged. But Kine looked no better, with his face as weathered as an old hide, his eyes sunken from exhaustion, and his graying hair and beard tangled with sweat, dust, and dirt. His armor was streaked with blood, and his cape appeared permanently discolored. The Owl insignia was no longer visible.

In short, Kine Tarroful looked like a walking corpse.

"I reckon we're the future," Kine said. "My men own Low Country. We're here to stay."

"The future." Dormun curled his lips. "You look like the past."

"Maybe I am. But Low Country remains."

"Not forever. You know that."

Kine watched him for a long moment. Finally, he stepped forward. "I don't believe you. I don't think you do, either. My only question is, why? You could've kept to yourself. We could've lived the rest of our days without this. Without spoiling what we used to have."

"You took our homeland."

Chapter Twenty

"Your men took my *wife*." Kine glared at him. "You destroyed our towns and took our people."

"They took our homeland. Our birthright."

"The same nonsense your so-called spirits always said. If they wanted it for you bad enough, they would've told us so."

"They won't speak to dishonorable man like you."

"Dishonorable?" Kine hissed the word like a snake. His gaze narrowed, and he halted his advance. "The Dormun I knew never would've used that...*thing* that threw magic at us. What was he, Dormun? Do you even know?"

"An answer to prayer. Spirits sent him from the east."

"The east?" Kine wavered, recognizing which country Dormun spoke of. Maybe northerners feared the east even more than the elders. "You thought that wise?"

"Doesn't matter. It's over."

"You'd better hope so. If they get angry and send more of those monsters here, ancestors only know what will happen to our country."

"Not *our* country."

Kine wheezed with dry laughter. "You're impossible."

"The Kine I knew would never ride with murderers."

"Trouble on both sides, eh? But I'm a Colonel of the Third Regiment. I *own* Low Country's Watchmen. Tell me how this is dishonorable."

"What do you rule? A land of thieves. You think this better than the Savage Land?"

"Better?" Kine snorted. "Maybe it isn't. But it's something different. Peace for my people, peace for yours. At least, that's what it could've been, before you ruined everything with your mage and your pack of strays. Good riddance to the lot of you."

Kine spat, but now, the act lacked its prior bluster. The heat left his expression, and he appeared as drained as Dormun. The two men watched each other, and Kine finally shook his head.

"I'd hoped to avoid this," he muttered. "I'd hoped we could live the rest of our days without seeing each other again."

"Afraid?"

"Tired," Kine growled. "I'm sick of this."

"You die soon."

Kine nodded, as though he'd settled the matter. "Let's get it over with, then." He hefted his mace. "I don't have my sword, so I'm afraid this won't be quick. It's going to hurt."

"Yes," Dormun whispered. "Hurts you a lot."

He lunged forward, springing off his good leg as he swung the bone club he'd taken from the girl who'd cut him.

Chapter Twenty-One

RENN LOOKED FOR SHARLA EVERYWHERE HE COULD. HE'D survived the Claws—apparently helped by Ovis's men—and after he'd tumbled down the hillside, he'd roused himself and headed back up. Sharla, meanwhile, had hobbled west, returning to where she'd sat with Senkha earlier that morning.

From here, Lion's Head stood silhouetted against the sunrise. He did too, and she heard him shouting, even from this distance. Desperate cries, perhaps a bit afraid. The same fear she'd felt in the canyon? No—he'd never know that. From his reaction when she'd come to cut his bindings, he probably wouldn't have traveled the same distance if it were her that had been captured.

Perhaps that was a little harsh. She winced, though she didn't know whether it was because of guilt or her flaming ribs. Renn had been nothing but good to her. He'd offered her the world, and she would've taken it if she hadn't met Senkha. If she hadn't learned that all this time, she'd been trying to run from her demons rather than confronting them.

All this time, she'd been running from herself, too angry and scared to face her true colors. Now that she'd seen them, she felt…better. Not quite peaceful, as Senkha described. It certainly wasn't gratifying to feel like your chest was splitting apart. But at least she felt as though she'd taken her stand. She'd fought a chieftain, and she'd…won? At the very least, she'd wounded him. And she'd done it without Renn. She'd done it by herself, the disgraced granddaughter of a colonel, the unwanted child of a runaway coward. She'd proved she could move past her family's mistakes.

Well, it depended on what Kine chose to do with her. She curled her lip at the thought and watched his approach. She knew he'd find her; she hadn't exactly been sneaky when she'd departed Lion's Head. Hard to do that when you're holding your side and blundering about, but at least it got her away from Renn, because now she understood she couldn't outrun her mistakes with him. Instead, she'd only postpone them until they caught her again. Drinking and sleeping until the excitement wore off, the cowboy returned to earth, and they found themselves in the same bodies they'd always inhabited. Feeding on each other to outlast the storm, but the storm never ceased. You only passed through the eye of it, at least for a time.

Staying in Low Country would bring Sharla another storm, that was certain. But at least now she knew she could endure it. She knew she'd survive.

"You look terrible." Sharla jumped and turned to see Keryn, who'd snuck up on her with her horse and Hesher in tow. The woman eyed her with an amused smirk, somehow not scratched or bruised in the *slightest*.

Sharla scowled and turned away. "You look like a whore."

"I feel like one after you promised me so much gold."

"I could've been lying," Sharla muttered.

"Then I'll find you and cut your throat while you sleep."

"I'm glad to have met you too."

"That makes one of us." The two women stood for a time, watching Kine's trudging figure and Renn's stumbling one.

"You're not going to run?" Keryn finally asked.

"Do I look like I could?"

"Maybe not." Keryn gestured. "You could at least go to your man over there. After all, he's why you came, isn't he?"

Sharla frowned at the thought. It might've stirred guilt hadn't her ribs hurt too much for her to dwell on the notion. "He isn't my man. Not anymore."

"Arlon, then."

Chapter Twenty-One

Sharla turned to Keryn and opened her mouth to correct the notion, but she remembered that Keryn didn't know the truth. Senkha said no one knew the truth but Jyrak, meaning that the rest of Senkha's crew were oblivious.

"I saw you climbing over each other like humping dogs," Keryn scoffed, apparently misreading Sharla's facial expression. "No need to hide it. I'm sure he's convincing when he wants to be."

"I'm my own woman," Sharla finally said.

"Of course." Keryn shrugged. "But he's over that hill when you change your mind. I think he's coming this way."

Sharla's heart fluttered in her chest like a tumbling wren, and it was all she could do to stop herself from looking in Senkha's direction. "Thanks for the heads-up."

"It's the last one you'll get." Keryn hoisted herself onto the horse, where Hesher already waited. She turned northward, toward Low Country. "I'm riding out of here if no one else will. I'm not going into a Watchman prison with the rest of you." She watched Sharla for a moment, as if awaiting a response. When Sharla said nothing, she finally turned and spurred her horse forward.

"Thank you," Sharla called after her. "Thank you for helping."

Keryn turned to her. "You're strong, girl," she said. "You can make it in Low Country if you keep a level head. Don't throw everything away with men like Arlon or Renn."

Sharla sighed, wincing at the pain. "I know what I'm doing." She looked to Hesher. "I'm sorry about Nithan."

Hesher grunted. "He always snored something terrible."

With that, the two riders departed. They turned and said something to someone on the other side of the hill, and, after a moment's conversation, continued forward. Senkha finally paced into view, leading a horse that must've been Senit's. Sharla felt herself smile, but she turned away before he saw her staring like an idiot.

In the clearing below Lion's Head, Kine had reached the battlefield and was attempting to organize the survivors. She saw Renn in their midst, helping free the Opekians while he continued to look around. She stepped backward, pulling herself out of sight until other footsteps drew her attention to where Jyrak stumbled over the rise. The mage looked as though something had struck his face, with its left side puffy and the eye swollen shut.

"He hit me with a wind gust," Jyrak grumbled when he saw Sharla staring. "Could've broken my neck. Man doesn't fight fair."

"At least you killed him."

"Not me." Jyrak shook his head. "I played dead, and it must've worked. I crawled clear after he hit me. I was going to try again, but I think it was your grandfather who killed him."

"Oh." The thought of Kine saving the day—both because he killed the chaos mage *and* Dormun—somewhat upset the moment.

Jyrak frowned at her expression, a gesture that made his own turn more gruesome. "Sorry," he said. "Don't mean to be the bearer of bad news."

"I'm just glad you're alive," she said. "Ovis...didn't make it."

Jyrak closed his eyes and said nothing. For a moment, Sharla worried she'd sent him into another somber spell, like when his bloodkin died, but she finally heard him muttering under his breath. Something that sounded like, "That bloody idiot."

He cleared his throat and opened his eyes. "I see Keryn and Hesher did make it." Jyrak nodded to the hillside behind her. "Arlon, too."

"Senkha, you mean."

Jyrak blinked at her.

"I know who he is," Sharla said. "He told me."

"Ancestors above. You sleep together or something?"

"No." Sharla shook her head, knowing that now Senkha's lean, muscled physique would occupy *all* her thoughts. "He just...told me."

"Huh." Jyrak thought for a moment. "What a moron."

"Maybe."

"Who's the moron?" Senkha asked, stepping up beside Sharla with the horse.

Chapter Twenty-One

"I am," Sharla said. She turned to him and caught herself looking for injuries, relieved to see he'd suffered nothing seriuos. "I'm a moron for letting you kiss me."

"You kissed *me*," Senkha said. "I never asked for that."

"You're impossible."

"Anything but." Senkha turned to Jyrak and frowned. "Fire smite me, you look terrible."

"At least the chaos mage is dead."

"Aye." Senkha nodded. "Senit's dead, too."

"You killed him?"

Senkha nodded. "He won't hurt anyone anymore."

"Did it bring you peace?"

He locked gazes with her for a long moment. "I don't know yet."

"I know the feeling."

"Do you?" He looked her up and down. "Or are you just in pain?"

"There's that."

"Can you still ride?"

"I don't know."

"How's she to ride without a horse?" The three of them turned at the sound of Kine's voice, who'd crested the rise with the reins of two horses. He watched each of them in turn before his gaze settled on Sharla. "Luckily for her, I have a horse right here."

Senkha stepped to the side, drawing his stiletto. "Jyrak."

Kine raised his hands. "Peace. I don't wish to fight."

"We won't let you take her."

"Who said anything about taking her?" Kine shook his head. "She's free to go."

Sharla's mouth dropped open. "I'm sorry?"

Kine hesitated. "You still want out of Low Country? Then go. None of us will know what happened. I couldn't find you with the rest of the Opekians, and I guess you either ran away or the Claws carried you off."

"I..." Sharla caught herself looking at Senkha, as though he could tell her what to do. She cleared her throat and swallowed. "I'm staying here."

"Staying?" Kine grunted as though the word hurt him. "I'd recommend against it. The law of the Watchmen rules here, and it recognizes you as a criminal who's stolen Watchmen gold. You'd be a stranger anywhere else, someone nobody would recognize."

"I'm not leaving Low Country." Sharla shook her head. "Not anymore."

"Why?" Kine demanded. "Just because you're tired of running?"

Yes, but more besides. It felt as though Sharla had learned enough for a lifetime, all from a crew she'd only known for a few days. She reckoned you couldn't choose the family you were given, but you could choose whether to love them or not, and she didn't consider Kine to be her family—not truly. Instead, she reckoned she'd found family in the men beside her. Perhaps, she'd even found peace.

"I won't run anymore," she finally said. "Low Country is my home. I want to stay."

Kine's expression seemed to soften, as though he stared at something behind her. "I can give you a year," he said. "A year to go free."

"And then what?" she snorted. "You'll send your dogs after me?"

"We're not dogs." He gave her a tired smile. "Sometimes it seems we're little more than murderers and thieves, I'll grant you. But I want this all to mean something, Sharla. I reckon maybe…you've taught me a thing or two. I want it to mean something to you, too." He shrugged, barking a humorless laugh. "Call it a grandfather's legacy if you want. Make of it what you will. But maybe after a year…consider joining my regiment."

She frowned at him, unable to fathom his true intentions. He appeared to be serious. But why? All this for the sake of legacy, for a family name everyone feared and hated? A family name she'd avoided for as long as she'd been on the road? Then she looked harder at him and saw the exhaustion in his eyes. He appeared to have aged in the battle, to have weathered another decade in the span of a morning. In that moment, he didn't appear the proud, noble colonel at all, but a weary man who yearned for relief. Maybe he wanted to know he'd accomplished something of value, and she could sympathize with that.

Chapter Twenty-One

After a moment's hesitation, she reached out and took the reins he offered. "I won't call myself a Tarroful," she told him.

He nodded. "Rest up. Heal well. Don't come looking for me, and don't give me an excuse to come looking for you."

She nodded back, biting her lip at an unexpected swell of emotion. It burned through her chest, and she couldn't tell whether it was joy, gladness, or sadness. It just felt warm, beautifully so.

He cleared his throat and stepped backward, turned to Senkha. "That looks like Senit's horse."

"It is," Senkha said. "He's dead."

"Dead." Kine frowned at the notion. "Don't know whether that's better."

"Low Country will be in chaos until someone claims his territory."

"You knew this would happen." Kine stared at him for a long moment. "You expected it."

"Maybe I wanted it."

Something flickered in Kine's gaze and understanding passed between the men. The colonel inclined his head, his eyes narrowing. "You almost look like him."

"You flatter me."

Kine grunted and clambered atop his horse with a weary grunt. "You're Senkha."

Senkha said nothing.

Kine nodded, turning his horse toward the clearing. "Should I expect a visit from you?"

"I reckon I'm going the same way as Sharla," Senkha said. "I'm done with this business. You and Marast decide what's next."

"I'm sure that will be fun." Kine hesitated. "Technically, this makes you an outlaw for your past crimes. No longer pardonable under the terms of the peace for holding the border."

"I don't come looking for you. I don't give you an excuse to come looking for me."

"That's the spirit." Kine looked to Sharla. "There's a man down there asking if anyone's seen you. Says his name is Renn. What do you want me to tell him?"

Sharla's heart lurched into her throat. "Don't tell him anything."

"He'll want to know where my second horse went."

Sharla hesitated. She wondered why she'd ever cared enough to hide everything from Renn. "Tell him the truth about who I am and what I've done. Tell him you've granted me temporary amnesty for helping to free the Opekians, but I remain a wanted criminal."

Kine grunted. "He won't follow you after that?"

"He won't," Sharla whispered. "He's a good man."

Kine nodded. "Those are hard to find. It's a low country, after all." He turned to Jyrak. "Runemaster." A nod to Sharla. "Granddaughter." A final stare at Senkha. "Senkha."

"Colonel." Senkha nodded, and after a moment, Kine turned and headed down the slope.

Jyrak puffed his cheeks and stepped toward Senkha. "Well. That went better than expected."

"Truly," Senkha agreed.

But he still didn't look at Sharla. She'd known something was different ever since he'd stood beside her, barely meeting her gaze and guarding his expression. She hesitated, recognizing the world hadn't stopped changing, that the morning remained young. Something was about to be spilled, something to change their future.

"You're leaving," she said quietly.

He only hesitated for a moment. "We're all leaving."

"You're leaving *me*."

He eyed Jyrak before looking to her again. "You're a wanted criminal. So am I. I killed the last of the Blackhairs and brought Low Country to ruin. Marast will want my head, and I'll be running. So will you."

She only saw his eyes, like before, and barely noticed that he'd stepped closer until his proximity was just as unbearable as the prior

Chapter Twenty-One

night. He reached for her cheek, brushed hair from her face. "We wanted to stop running, remember?" he asked.

"I remember," she whispered. Her chest had squeezed painfully tight, as though her heart pressed her ribs. The moment stretched into an agonizing breath, a silent torment while the best of her world slipped away, escaping alongside everything she'd stood for.

"This isn't fair," she heard herself say.

"It isn't." He shook his head. "In any other time, any other place, we might've worked. But you want peace, and so do I. I can't give it to you, not after I killed Senit. I put a price on my head for Marast and anyone else who thinks I'll come back. They'll all want me dead, and I can't bring you into that. Not when you've just found your own peace."

"I don't know what I found," she said. "It isn't peace."

"But it isn't fear." He watched her for a long moment. "You're not afraid anymore, Sharla. I see that. I want you to keep that, and riding with me could cost you."

"You don't scare me. Marast doesn't scare me."

"No. But I reckon only a fool tests their strength by fighting the whole world."

"That makes you the fool for trying."

"Yes," Senkha breathed. He leaned toward her, close enough for them to kiss. "I was a fool for choosing this life. I was a fool for taking Henit's territory, for living the life of empire. It was nothing I wanted, and it's nothing you deserve. I don't think I'd felt anything in years...not until you showed up."

"Hah. So it's all my fault."

"It's mine." He cupped her hands and held them before his lips. "Let me fix this, if I can. Let me spare you."

"By running away?"

He blinked at her. Said nothing.

"You're running away, just like I did," she said. "Hiding is how we fix this? How do we move forward?"

"You keep saying 'we' as though there's a future for us."

"Maybe I want there to be. And I *know* you want there to be one just as much as I do." She shook her head. "Don't play the hero by riding away. I already traveled Low Country for one man. I don't need another to sacrifice for me."

He remained silent for a moment. "I suppose I fix it by killing Marast."

"Then there would only be Kine to worry about."

"And I already said I wouldn't see him again."

She nodded. "Then we kill Marast."

"No." He gave her a weary smile. "You need to rest. Your fighting days are over, at least for a while."

"Just you and Jyrak, then?" Sharla regarded the runemaster with his puffy, bruised face. "You're all there is?"

"We're all there's ever been. No one knows Low Country better."

"If you go after Marast, you'll let Keryn have the gold."

"She can have it. Always complained that we stiffed her, anyway."

"If I let you go, you'll never come back." Sharla snorted at the thought, or maybe the gesture was just an excuse to swallow whichever emotions clenched her throat, to blink the tears from her eyes. "We're too used to running."

"It will just take time."

Then there was nothing else. Nothing but to let go, as he'd originally told her. To relinquish control so she could finally, *maybe*, approach the peace he'd spoken of. The peace you couldn't grab, control, or wrestle under your dominion. There was nothing but to enjoy the blessing of the present moment, to cherish the times she'd had. To leave the past behind, with all its weights and hindrances. To move toward the future.

She told herself she felt peace when she drew him in for a kiss, that it was peace squeezing her lungs and chest in that horrid vise.

But in truth, she only felt her aching ribs.

"Ride hard, Senkha Blackhair," she whispered into his ear.

She pulled away from him and they watched each other for a moment. Then, Senkha cleared his throat, beckoned Jyrak over, and climbed atop his horse. The two of them looked ridiculous when squashed onto the saddle together, but Senkha always had a peculiar air. She'd recognized it from the first moment she'd seen him in Mela, when he'd sat in the corner with that ridiculous hat and wry grin that never communicated whether he laughed at her or the rest of the world.

In the end, she supposed it didn't matter. Not when he gave her that grin again, here on the hill outside Lion's Head, where they'd both glimpsed the future they could share. The future that might still be theirs should he ever stop running and release his burdens.

Runemaster and outlaw settled themselves. Jyrak appeared as though he could topple at any moment. He frowned as he hugged Senkha about the waist, squeezing his coat.

"Too tight, old man," Senkha muttered. "You trying to kill me?"

"Only if you don't kill me first." Jyrak swore under his breath, turning to Sharla and inclining his head. "It was a pleasure to ride with you, Sharla. I hope to see you again someday."

"And I you."

Senkha turned to Sharla, offering her a final grin. "Keryn had the right of it all along. I *was* just trying to impress you when we fought my men in Mela."

"Consider me impressed."

Senkha laughed, turned his horse, and kicked it forward. "Goodbye, Sharla."

"Goodbye, Senkha."

She stood there long after, watching Renn and Senkha depart from opposite sides of the hill. The two men of her past, like two sides of a flipping coin. As though the ancestors tossed them in a game of chance, wondering which man would find her again. Renn wouldn't run, but Senkha would, and by now Sharla knew how to play the game. She could run too, if need be. She could run to find Senkha again.

But for now, she could wait and enjoy this momentary calm, what might've been peace. She still wasn't sure she'd call it such, but it was closer than anything she'd felt before. It wasn't fear, and it didn't feel like wreckage.

Not anymore.

She smiled at the thought and watched as Senkha and Jyrak dwindled across the badlands.

* * *

RENN'S FACE HAD CRUMPLED WHEN KINE DELIVERED THE news about Sharla, and the younger man mumbled to himself many times after. Unfortunately, Kine was close enough to hear his ramblings, and many of them carried the same regret Kine had hoped to outdistance.

"It could've been different. I should've welcomed her, been more excited to see her, but I was just so worried. I didn't know she could fight, didn't even know who she was. How was I supposed to know she'd travel here by herself?"

Perhaps the lad simply hadn't spoken to anyone in a while and he just needed to vent. Kine supposed he understood the notion, but as the Watchmen headed north with the reclaimed Opekians, minus both Senit and his crew, Kine found sudden exhaustion overtaking him in leaden waves, and Renn's mumbling grew more and more irritating. Aye, fighting wasn't what it used to be, and Kine's stamina was sorely lacking. He was in a rough way, make no mistake, and he had no idea how long it would take to recover.

At the end, Dormun's club had nearly taken his head off. Perhaps what followed was pitiful: a scuffle of old men through the grass, stumbling around as they wrestled for control of their club and mace. Inevitably, a blow to Dormun's leg had sent the Claw into the grass again, and Kine had pounded his head in before the man could say anything.

He *had* been trying to say something—whether it was more taunting, another regret, or perhaps an apology. But Kine had tired of all that; he'd just wanted quiet.

Even when he'd reunited with Gashar—who, thank the ancestors, was still alive—he lacked the energy or wisdom to know what needed saying. There were so many things he'd wanted to explain, to thank the younger man for, but in the end, he'd simply nodded. Gashar nodded back—his shoulder in a makeshift bandage—and grimaced with the

Chapter Twenty-One

effort. He looked as bad as Kine suspected himself to look: Owl plating streaked with dirt and blood, face colored brown by all the dust from the mage's sandstorm, and his hair in disarray. With the two riding once again side by side, Kine reckoned they made for a ludicrous victory party.

Finally, Gashar leaned closer to speak out of earshot of Renn. "You didn't hold Sharla to her word?"

Kine pondered this for a long moment. "A man once told me to think about my legacy. Ancestors know I can't fix my family, not anymore. But maybe this is a start."

The ghost of a smile touched Gashar's lips. "Aye. It's in the ancestors' hands now."

Kine dipped his head. "Thank you." He shrugged, helpless. "For...everything."

"Of course, Colonel."

They lapsed into silence, and Kine found himself wondering—again—if what Gashar had said over the canyon was true. Had he really learned something from the Colonel of the Third Regiment? Kine Tarroful, the notorious drunkard of Keth, had impacted another Watchman in a meaningful way?

Enough. Let's just enjoy this. If we can.

Dormun was finished. The war with Claws was over. There was Low Country's own war to think about: it would begin in Senit's absence, and now Senkha was out of the game. Two cartels needed replacing, or else Kine would have a war with Marast on his hands.

Blood and ashes. Those were bright thoughts.

Kine frowned and struggled to think of something else, which inevitably led him back to Sharla. He reckoned legacies had to start somewhere, and he hoped his offer of temporary amnesty wouldn't bring trouble from her. If she knew what was best, she'd stay out of his way. Maybe she'd even consider joining the Watchmen.

Kine snorted. No, there'd never be that.

"I suppose I'll never see her again." Kine blinked back into the present and turned to Renn, who still stared at the ground. The man wore a grim expression, the kind men wear when they've prepared themselves for the worst. *Aye, young love.*

Kine frowned at the thought and turned west, where he assumed Sharla would've ridden. For a moment, he glimpsed a horse several hills away, and his breath hitched before he recognized the horse bore two riders. The mage and Senkha, then—which meant Sharla remained some distance behind them. Waiting for her chance to escape? To leave Low Country for good?

Kine shook his head. No, he'd seen it in her eyes. She'd claimed this land as surely as he. Neither of them could leave—it wasn't in a Tarroful's blood. Even though his daughter Hari had run away, she'd already married herself to a lesser man, irreversibly tainting herself—or so Kine would've explained it. It was a complicated matter.

But Sharla was different. She'd accomplished more than Kine could've imagined. She'd gathered a crew for herself—Senkha among them—evaded an army of Watchmen and outlaws all the way through Low Country, fought Dormun herself, and emerged with only a few cracked ribs to show for it. So long as she took her slow, sweet time to return home, following the Watchmen from a safer distance to keep her cover, she could start over in Low Country. He had no idea what she'd do, and again, he wondered if he'd regret the mercy he'd shown her. One day, she might stab him in the back.

At the same time, Gashar's words on legacy stirred Kine. He allowed himself to wonder—maybe even to hope—that Sharla could accomplish something he hadn't. Maybe she'd bring better to Low Country than he had—somewhere, somehow.

And that thought made it all…worthwhile.

"Sharla will come around." Kine grinned, what felt like his first genuine smile in ages. "You'll see her again. I'm sure of it."

Chapter Twenty-One

You made it! Thank you for helping bring Azdhagon to life!

If you enjoyed the adventure, I encourage you to leave a review on Amazon or Goodreads…or both! Even if you only leave a rating, it helps this book rank better in search results, and that means more readers can find it!

I've got more books coming, and I'd love to continue the journey with you. You'll find all my work with a FREE novella exclusively found on my website at the "free book" link at www.shankbooks.com

Or, find me @shankbooks on Facebook, Instagram, or Twitter. Feel free to reach out with questions, comments, or suggestions! I always look forward to hearing from readers.

About The Author

In middle school, Morgan finally broke away from incoherent clumps of algebra to fill a composition notebook with his first handwritten novel. Since then, he's imagined his own Skyrim rather than fumble through objective studies.

For reasons unknown to anyone, he somehow found his way into a trucking gig, and he now enjoys a day job hauling freight. When he's not trucking or writing, Morgan spends his time dabbling in landscape photography, running Spartan Races, and staring at the mountains that surround his hometown of Harrisonburg, VA, which provide ample inspiration for his fantasy novels.

Printed in Great Britain
by Amazon